DEVOURED WORLD

VOLUME ONE

RICKY FLEET

Brick, New Jersey
2018

Devoured World Volume One

Copyright © 2018 by Ricky Fleet.

All rights reserved. Printed in the United States of America. No part of this book may be used or reproduced in any manner whatsoever without written permission except in the case of brief quotations embodied in critical articles or reviews.

This book is a work of fiction. Names, characters, businesses, organizations, places, events and incidents either are the product of the author's imagination or are used fictitiously. Any resemblance to actual persons, living or dead, events, or locales is entirely coincidental.

For information contact:

Optimus Maximus Publishing, LLC

www.optimusmaximuspublishing.com

Edited by Christina Smith

Cover design by Jeffrey Kosh Graphics

ISBN 13: 978-944732-37-0

ISNB 10: 1-944732-37-3

First Edition: October 2018

DEDICATION

To my amazing beta reading team, thank you.

CHAPTER ONE

June 14th, 2038
Heathrow Airport.
London, England.

"What time's their flight due to land?"

"According to the announcer, twenty minutes ago."

Lance frowned at the arrivals board which hadn't updated for over an hour. Turning to Helen, he shrugged and returned to the newspaper. Allowing himself a sneaky rub on the crumpled pages, Lance smiled. He'd always preferred the real thing to the electronic devices favoured by the kids. There was something in the rustle of a broadsheet, the struggle to manhandle it into submission so you could read.

"I do hope they're ok," fretted Helen.

Grunting, Lance didn't look up from the story. Eastern Europe was suffering from a massive refugee crisis whose origins lay in the country once called Russia. Fanciful tales of cannibalism and murder without cause littered the news cycles.

"It's what those brutes have always done," he muttered. Bloody commies. They were either killing themselves or some other poor population who happened to upset them.

"They helped us defeat the United States of Europe though," said Helen, reading the headline over his shoulder. She was used to his rants by now, but history couldn't be changed to suit her husband's biases.

"We'd have beaten them in the end anyway," he huffed.

"Ok," she sighed. It was pointless to argue.

Glancing at him, Helen felt a wave of disgust and hid her grimace by looking out through the airport windows. It was becoming more and more difficult to put up with his attitude as time went on. The tick-tock of her life wasting away was an ever-present accompaniment to their day to day existence. If it hadn't been for their poor daughter she would've already left him. *We'd have beaten them? Ha, as if,* she thought. He was a coward of the worst kind. One that was only too happy to snipe and moan and tell the real men what they were doing wrong. Helen could still remember the day the draft letter dropped through the letter box. Lance had quickly retrieved it, thinking he was unobserved when in fact she was watching from the kitchen doorway. The first went straight in the furnace. Her respect for him died as surely as the paper that burned and fluttered as ash up the chimney. She made sure to be ready when the final summons arrived. Lance was furious, and for the first time, Helen feared he would actually hit her.

She could picture it as if it was yesterday.

"How dare you open my post!" Lance sneered, fear tinged with anger.

"It's your final warning for the draft. You're to report to the local barracks by Thursday. We should start packing," Helen explained, holding the paper out of reach.

"I'll do no such thing! Bloody fools and their bloody war! I told you no good would come of those experiments!"

"Still, you don't want to get locked up. I'll fetch the suitcase from the attic."

"Don't you dare!" Lance almost shrieked, his voice rising into previously unmanageable octaves.

"Well what do you plan to do? Hide?"

"Of course not. I'll just explain that I've got no interest in going to fight for a leader who has to use threats to recruit."

"But you have to," Helen insisted. "If the European army makes it much further through the rebel lines they could be invading Spain next. Our daughter could be hurt or even killed!"

"She was killed the moment she took that stupid pill."

The comment hit her like a physical blow. "You bastard!"

"I didn't force her to take it. I explicitly forbade it, but you had to insist, didn't you? Always doing what the 'experts' tell you is best. Now you have to live with it."

Helen fell silent. As much as she detested his accusations, Lance was right. Corinne's ailment was entirely her fault.

"I thought it would help," she said weakly. "It was meant to save mankind."

"Well it didn't. Now give me that bloody letter!"

Snatching it from her, Lance stormed into the back garden, disappearing through the bushes towards his vegetable patch. Helen sat at the kitchen table, sobbing quietly at the future she had stolen from her only child.

A shrill cry broke into her thoughts and Helen rushed from the house. Cradling his foot, Lance was writhing on the muddy ground between the cabbages. An errant jab with the garden fork, which had stabbed through his boot, severing two tendons and shattering the metatarsals. An 'accident' he'd called it. Conveniently, it ended his ability to be drafted into the rebel forces to help in the civil war. Snivelling coward.

"What was that?" Lance muttered, not taking his eyes from the paper.

"Nothing," Helen replied.

A commotion was breaking out around the arrivals board. Helen stood to get a better view and her heart sank as every inbound flight was changing to a red 'cancelled' notice.

"What on earth's going on?"

"Well that's just bloody marvellous! What a waste of a day."

"How is picking up your daughter and her husband a waste of a day?" Helen demanded.

Lance scowled at the vehemence of the question. "Is she landing? No. That's a day wasted. Let's go."

"I'm going to wait and see what's happening."

"It'll be a strike or something. You know how they love to moan and mess everything up as soon as they're expected to do some work."

"What the hell are you blabbering about? There hasn't been a strike since before the war."

"They're still lazy. I'm going back home, are you coming?"

"I told you, I'm going to see what's happening. I need to speak to Corinne."

"Fine, I won't be coming back to pick you up."

"I don't want you to. I think I'm going to spend a few days with my sister."

"What?" Lance was taken aback. They had never spent a day apart in twenty-eight years of marriage.

"Just go."

"I don't understand."

"Clear the way! Move, move, move!" Ten heavily armed security officers barrelled through the onlookers. More were coming, parting the crowds like Moses and the Red Sea.

A fraught voice came over the Tannoy system. "Ladies and Gentlemen, we're sorry for the inconvenience, but we must ask all members of the public to vacate the airport. The government has grounded all air traffic in light of a potential biological infection which is threatening to spread out of control. A curfew will take effect in two hours. More announcements will follow on the Divinity Alliance emergency broadcast channel."

"Oh God, I knew those reports were true. We need to get in touch with Corinne right now and find another way of getting her home. See if you can reach her on the phone."

"She won't have it turned on."

"Can you just try?"

"What's the point? It's not allowed."

Helen rounded on him. "Just phone her, you pathetic bastard!" she screamed, flecks of spittle hitting him in the face.

Onlookers stared on, some shocked, others smiling to themselves as Lance's cheeks turned a deep scarlet.

"How dare…"

"I said *now*!" Helen yelled, pushing him in the chest.

"I…" Lance gulped, eyes scanning the laughing spectators. A look of confusion came over as he ferreted inside a coat pocket. Taking out the phone, he looked at it as if seeing it for the first time.

"It's Corinne," Helen gasped, snatching the vibrating handset and pressing answer.

"Mum? Is that you?" asked their daughter, the picture shaky.

"Hi, sweetheart. Where are you?"

"The pilot said we're returning to Madrid. We're directly over the airport, but we've been denied permission to land. What's going on?"

"I think the people getting sick are carrying something they don't want spreading. Don't worry, though. We'll get you on a ferry out of Santander or somewhere as soon as possible. You'll be home in a few days."

"Mum," Corinne said, voice filled with dread. "There are sick people on the plane. A doctor who was travelling to London with us is trying to help one who collapsed."

A scream from onboard shrilled through the handset.

"Corinne? What was that?"

The picture became even more chaotic as she tried to shift and see what was occurring further down the plane. "I don't know, mum."

More yells burst from the speaker and Helen nearly dropped the phone in shock. Unimaginable agony was evident from the tortured cries.

"Corinne, lock yourselves in the toilet and don't come out until they land, do you hear me?"

The picture flashed with the movement of her arms, faces appeared and disappeared in an instant. Even in those brief snapshots, Helen could see the terror written plainly on each person's face, the deep lines and fevered eyes. A clash of metal on metal preceded the snick of a lock being engaged.

"We're in there, mum."

"Did you see what was going on?"

"I… I don't know. I thought I saw the doctor, but he was covered in so much blood. I think he had a wound on his neck."

Lance was ashen, listening in to the conversation but paralysed by indecision.

"You need to get help! Go and tell the guards that the planes need to land, right now!"

He just gaped at her, mouth bobbing. Bringing a hand back, Helen slapped him as hard as she could. The blow rocked his head and the stinging pain brought him back.

"Go! Now!"

"Mum… Love… Going… I…"

The garbled message was drowned out by a whining drone that grew in intensity before being cut off completely.

"Everybody! Get away from the windows!" screamed one of the guards, urgently pushing at the uncooperative public.

The missing whine returned, but not from the phone. Looking through the glass towards the landing pads, Helen's mind couldn't process what was happening. The vertical take-off and landing jet emblazoned with Air España plummeted from the sky like a rock. Crashing directly onto a twin craft from the German Federation, they erupted in a massive fireball. The displaced dust from the concussive wave raced towards the airport lounge, blowing the windows apart with a deafening roar. Adding itself to the din were the injured laying stricken on the polished floor. Helen probed gently at her face, feeling the trickling blood from multiple lacerations. Lance was nowhere to be seen. With the chaos of people fleeing and falling over each other, he could've been trapped beneath the crush of bodies. Helen realised that she didn't care, and it wasn't just from the shock.

"Corinne?"

Whispering her name, the heated air stole the word away. One of the engine blades still spun lazily from the rear wing which had torn free upon impact and buried itself in the lounge wall. The raging inferno was being hosed down with foam by the automated fire suppression systems of the landing bay. Emergency vehicles careened around the corner of the complex before pulling up to assist the machines with their own hoses.

"Corinne?" Helen sobbed, dropping to her knees. Such was the emotional rending, she didn't even feel the fragments tear into her flesh. Her baby was gone. Life was over.

Nothing could possibly have survived the impact, much less the fire which tore through the aircraft. The white extinguishing foam flowed from the smouldering wreckage, draining into the steel grates below. *Wait! Things were moving within the fire-retardant coating! Were there survivors?* Helen's heart soared with hope. Maybe the reaction of the automated hydrants had been quick enough. Maybe the craft was sturdier in certain areas. Maybe Corinne had been lucky.

"I'm coming, sweetheart!" Helen yelled over the bedlam.

Racing for the closest disembarkation point, Helen heard her name being called weakly. Coming to a halt, she looked around at the prone figures on the ground and discovered Lance. He was clutching at his throat, blood pumping through clamped fingers. One hand reached out imploringly towards his wife.

"Help me," Lance gurgled, crimson running from his open mouth.

"No."

And with that, Helen moved through the tunnel and jumped down the steps two at a time. Landing awkwardly at the bottom, an ankle gave way and she fell to the concrete. The adrenaline was numbing most of the pain, but she screamed as the shards were driven deeper into her kneecaps. Clutching at a nearby rail, Helen stood up and stumbled towards the crash. Wincing as the foam-soaked figures dropped the remaining ten feet to the ground, her elation grew when they stood up, uninjured. Ambulance crews ran in without hesitation, ignoring the occasional flare of igniting fuel. Grabbing survivors, they tried to pull them away from the danger. Instead of complying, the injured passengers wrestled the paramedics to the ground. It must be the shock, Helen thought, leaving droplets of blood as she hobbled onwards. The jets of scarlet which sprayed from torn arteries ended that thought. White turned to pink as the different liquids mingled on the landing pad.

"Get out of the way!"

The angered shout caused Helen to flinch as the security team ran towards the scene of growing carnage. Water hoses washed the froth from the survivors, and she could finally see they weren't survivors at all. Moving amongst the emergency workers, their charred flesh split open, leaking yellow and red fluids.

"We have contact with the infected! Open fire!" yelled the commander.

Automatic gunfire tore through the assailants. Hit multiple times, some of the blackened creatures still came on, heedless of the threat. Thrashing on the ground, partly eaten first responders suddenly stood up on unsteady legs. Seeing the black clad security team, they shrieked. Surging forward, they were stronger than the scorched husks which had fallen from the jet. In seconds the men were overwhelmed, going down in a tangled heap, fingers still pulling the triggers. Bullets ricocheted around the enclosure, stray rounds whining as they passed dangerously close to Helen. A dripping monster approached.

"Corinne?"

The horrifically burned figure was no longer recognisable as a man or a woman. It lumbered forward, cracking lips peeling back to reveal white teeth. It fell upon her.

As Helen was devoured, she watched the unfolding horror from a numbed mind. The base of the air traffic control structure was hit by another craft. Lack of fire indicated the pilot had jettisoned as much fuel as they could before impact. Unable to hold the weight of the circular viewing tower any longer, a support column imploded and started to topple. Doomed people leapt from shattered windows, hitting the ground with a sickly squelch a second before thousands of tonnes of steel and rubble joined them. Across the airport, more planes dropped from the sky, some trying to land, others out of control.

Running between the buildings and landing pads were a growing crowd of crazed humans. Anyone they caught were instantly ravaged by teeth and clawed fingers. As flesh and organs were strewn far and wide, Helen wondered, *is that what I look like?* Before Helen could turn her head, another jet crashed to earth, ending her life and that of her attacker in a mushroom cloud of searing fuel. The infected swarmed from all corners of the sprawling airport, tearing through the meagre security or leaping the razor wire topped fences, spreading their contagion.

In less than eighteen hours, London was lost.

CHAPTER TWO

Present Day
Quadrant PR-12

Hazy visions. A winter's morning. Ice crystals formed on glass. Warmth. Comfort. Fire. Children's joyous cheers. Tearing paper. Excitement. A woman, smiling adoringly. Turkey. Feasting. Yuletide songs. Happiness. Contentment. Fading. Foreboding. An offering from the stars. Uncertainty. No longer alone. Friend or foe? Miracle. Cancer beaten. Disease eradicated. Celebration. Cooperation. Doubt. Mistrust. Rejection of the gift. Anger. War. Man killing man. Genocide. Revelation. Terror. Infection. Mutant War. Humanity against the risen. Teeth. Claws. Pain. Nuclear Armageddon. Eternal darkness. Blossoming light. Uncomfortable. Trapped! DROWNING! CAN'T BREATHE!

"Whoa, calm down. You're going to hurt yourself!"

"Turn him on his side or he'll go into cardiac arrest!"

Firm hands grasped the flailing figure, twisting him over to allow the yellow substance to drain from the new-born lungs.

"That's it, let it all out."

Hacking coughs sprayed a mixture of bile and phlegm across the polymer casing. From around the room came sounds of similar struggles as the woken took their first breath of real oxygen. A high-pitched whine rose above the tumult. Three rapid beeps and a dull thud silenced the infernal noise for a moment, but the insistent wail resumed.

"Again!"

Three more chirps and the thud sounded again. This time, the electronic squalling did not return.

"Take him to intensive care until we can run a full neurological diagnostic."

"Yes, Doctor."

The trembling figure had expelled the last traces of liquid and lay exhausted in the clear tube. A hinged door to his vessel dripped with remnants of the mucus-like substance.

"Take your time, there's no rush. You're ok now," said the owner of the hands. His voice had lowered by several octaves and cooed like a father addressing a fearful child.

A gloved hand wiped at his neck before pressing a cold, metallic probe against the untainted skin.

"Heart rate thirty-five beats per minute, blood pressure is one ten over seventy."

"Impressive. It's been a while since we've seen one that strong right out of the gate."

"He'll make a good asset, that's for sure."

His short brown hair was slick from the gelid coating. The man's eyelids fluttered open, revealing pale blue irises with slivers of grey. Glancing around, they started to widen in fear.

"You're not blind, don't panic. Your eyesight will return in the next few minutes."

"I…" croaked the figure.

"Just lay still and conserve your strength. Everything will be explained in time."

Closing his eyes, the man visibly relaxed. All tension left the thick, bunched muscles and his harried breathing slowed.

"That's good. We're going to help you out of there and into a chair. Your legs are going to feel weak to start with, so hold onto us tightly until we get you sat down."

The nurses clasped the man firmly beneath each arm and hoisted him over the lip of the gestation tube. Legs flopping, he allowed himself to be manhandled, providing as much assistance as the unsteady limbs would allow. A strap was pulled tightly across his chest and the buckle secured with a snap.

"Good job. We need to get you moving to check for any impulse weakness."

He nodded.

"Firstly, I want you to curl your toes."

The man complied. Taking it a step further, he rotated an ankle then stretched out the lower leg. Flexing his thigh, mounds of glistening quadriceps stood proudly.

"Slow down, speed racer. Now I want you to squeeze my hand."

Taking the offered palm, he applied pressure until the nurse hissed in pain.

"Ok, that's enough!"

"Pussy! He's a spawnling."

"Let him crush your hand if you're so tough."

"Sorry," croaked the seated figure.

Uttering the apology triggered a coughing fit and more of the gelatinous goo flecked the pristine white trousers of the nurse.

"Don't sweat it. It's an honour to be helping you, Andrew."

"Andrew?" he asked, confusion fogging his mind.

"The commander will explain everything once we've got you cleaned up and into the recovery suite."

"Where am I?"

"She'll explain that too, don't worry."

Blurred lines and obscure, blended colours firmed in Andrew's vision. The room was dazzlingly white, with every surface reflecting the fluorescent ceiling lights in the glossy finish. Squinting, he tried to ascertain the length of the bizarre suite, but the haziness thwarted his attempts.

"I still can't see properly."

"Full depth of vision will return in a while, Andrew. For now, just enjoy the ride," replied his nurse, twisting the wheelchair and moving away from the pod.

"Call me Andy," he croaked.

"Do you prefer that?"

Frowning, he tried to concentrate on the fragment of memory that danced on the edge of his mind. "I think so, yes. It seems… familiar."

The second nurse cast an astonished glance at his partner. "First stages of memory restoration after four minutes. That's got to be some kind of record?"

"I've never heard anyone come close to that," he confirmed. "I'm Tom."

Offering a hand, Andy shook it and winced when he saw the gelatinous residue left on Tom's palm.

"And I'm Eric," added the other, choosing to remain clean and keeping his own limb well out of reach.

Hundreds of medical staff working in pairs were bustling industriously around rows of clear, identical cylinders. Faces set, they focused on the task of safely extracting their charge from the incubators. All along the left side of the room were men being assisted into stainless steel wheelchairs. The only obvious trait shared between them was the high level of physical strength, with well-defined muscles untouched by an ounce of bodyfat. Glancing to the right, it was a similar scene except they were all female. Lacking the same muscle mass, still their bodies were wiry and athletic. Every ethnicity was represented in their number; African, Chinese, Middle-Eastern, European. Andy could see the same feeling of confusion etched on their faces as he passed.

"Great work, everybody. Get them cleaned and clothed while I inform the commander the spawning's nearing the end of phase one."

"Yes, ma'am," said Tom as they passed the senior physician.

"Spawning?"

"All your questions will be answered shortly, Andy. In the meantime, let's get you in the shower."

Falling silent, Andy joined the long procession of sterile wheelchairs as they moved towards the pneumatic exit doors. With a chirp from the overhead sensor, they glided open revealing a small chamber beyond. Lining up alongside eight others, the door closed, and a red light blazed to life turning everything a dark crimson.

"Hold your breath," said one of the other nurses. "It smells like a mixture of lavender and shit."

Andy glanced back at Eric who nodded and wafted a hand in front of his face. With a hiss, jets of mist covered them from every angle. Curiosity got the better of him and he took a tiny whiff of the decontamination gas. Regret quickly replaced the inquisitiveness as Andy bent double, dry heaving from the stench.

"She did warn you," teased Tom light-heartedly, rubbing his back.

"You're lucky your stomach's empty or we'd have to go through it again after you were hosed down," chuckled Eric.

"To hell with that," Andy offered weakly.

The red light was replaced by a green signal and the second set of doors opened silently.

"Time for that wash," said Tom, wheeling him through.

After donning waterproof suits, the nurses positioned Andy beneath the shower.

"I'd like to stand if that's ok?"

Tom looked at Eric and shrugged. "Ok, buddy. But I'll leave the chair close just in case."

Unsnapping the plastic restraint, the two men helped Andy to rise gingerly from the seat. After a brief wobble, he managed to maintain balance.

"Thank you."

"Our pleasure. Now hold still while we wash the amniotic fluid off."

Andy considered asking what he meant, but their repeated claims of forthcoming answers silenced him. A shudder of intense pleasure coursed through his body as the warm water sprayed down from above. It was as if he'd never experienced the sensation of the balmy liquid before. The way it ran down his face, cleansing the sticky gel. The tickle as it traced its way down his firm body, running between the cleft of his buttocks. Turning around, the water trickled from his penis, triggering an awkward growth.

"Oh shit, I'm sorry," he groaned, cupping himself.

"It's normal, don't worry about it," Tom said matter-of-factly. Neither of the men, or any of the other nurses in the vast shower block, were the least bit perturbed by the dozens of bobbing erections and the embarrassed looks of their owners.

"You do this often?" Andy asked.

"More than we'd like," sighed Eric.

A thought struck Andy as he stood there in the luxurious downpour. Dozens of his fellow 'spawnlings' as he'd heard themselves named were all buck naked, yet he felt no desire towards any of the women being washed. In the back of his mind he knew they were all remarkably attractive, even stunning, but there were none of the usual human impulses. Maybe it was the effects of their treatment wearing off? Obviously, they'd been kept in the strange vessels because of injury or other cause which would be explained later. Whatever medicine had been administered would likely account for their hazy memory as well.

"All done."

Allowing himself to be seated, Andy tried to penetrate the frustrating fog hiding his past. The vivid flashbacks which preceded his abrupt awakening were fading in and out of focus. Where were the people in his dream? Who were they? Each time he tried to draw them into the light of understanding, a pang of discomfort shot through his brain until he finally gave up.

"Are you ok?" Eric asked with evident concern.

"Just a headache," Andy replied.

"I'll get you a shot of painkillers while you relax in recovery."

"Thanks, Tom."

As they exited the steamy shower facility, the next batch of patients were being brought in. Andy scanned the faces of the crowd and scowled. A feeling of déjà vu accompanied a vague impression that he knew these people. Some of the dazed looking men and women looked so familiar. Probing at the frustratingly unobtainable truth, a fresh wave of pain radiated through his skull.

"Don't force it," Eric remarked, knowingly. "They'll come back in time."

"Truth be told, you may wish they hadn't," Tom finished.

Rows of seats were lined up facing a huge projector screen set in the wall. Moving to their designated space in silence, the room quickly filled with spawnlings. Hovering at the periphery were the medical staff, all watching their patient for any unforeseen ailments. Andy had been informed that the monitoring would continue for another twenty-four hours until they were finally released. Nervous coughs and restless shuffling were the only sounds in the auditorium. A door opened, and a stern looking soldier walked briskly to the podium below the display. The uniform was immaculately pressed, and rows of medals stood proudly on her chest. A cluster of gold arrows adorned each shoulder. Her blond hair was pulled back and secured in a tight bun. Staring at the expectant faces, her steely gaze softened slightly, and she smiled.

"Welcome, everybody. I'm General Ashdown and I lead the Sovereign Guard armies of the Divinity Alliance. I'll explain more about myself in the coming days, but for the time being, please direct your attention to the display overhead."

Moving to one side, she too craned her neck upwards as the white background was replaced by a live stream. Seated at a carved onyx desk was a middle-aged woman wearing a red silken gown. Frizzy blonde hair giving way to grey at the temples sat atop her head and Andy couldn't help but liken her to a female Einstein. Intertwining her fingers on the desk, she leaned towards the camera.

"Good morning, my children. I call you that because to me you're all my children, in thought if not in blood. What I'm about to tell you will come as a shock, but please bear with me until the end. Any questions you may have can be directed to General Ashdown, your nurses, or your area coordinator."

She paused for a few seconds, choosing her approach. It didn't matter that this was an address she'd made a thousand times before, it still filled her with trepidation.

Taking a deep breath, she began. "The year is 2182 and the world you once knew is gone."

Shouts of disbelief burst forth around the room.

"That's impossible!"

"What is this bullshit?"

General Ashdown raised a hand to hush the questions and turned back to the screen.

"My name is Empress Verena and I'm the elected Ruler of Planet Earth. Or what's left of it. To understand what's happening and your role in the struggle, I need to take you back one and a half centuries. Our world was tearing itself apart with conflict. Across the globe, governments were trying to further their own ends at the expense of their fellow man. Peaceful cooperation for the betterment of humanity was as far away as it had ever been. A fascistic New World Order arose in the early part of the twenty-first century and was swiftly crushed by the people who disliked being enslaved for corporate profit. Their victory didn't come without great loss of life, however. After the horror of the civil war, nation states had returned, and an uneasy peace took hold. It was at this time that a miracle happened. Or so it seemed."

A couple of the audience members gasped as hidden memories revealed themselves.

"Small meteors impacted every corner of the earth on that warm July day in 2036. The rocks were quickly discovered to be nothing of the sort and were, in fact, extra-terrestrial pods from an unknown source in the universe. Contained within them was knowledge, far in advance of our own. The most incredible material was a complete mapping of the human genome on a far deeper level than our own scientists had achieved. On top of this was the technology which would allow us to eradicate every illness and disease known to man by making slight changes to the DNA of the subject. After much speculation, trials were carried out in a limited global capacity and for the first time in a long time, we were working as one. The tests proved conclusive; people with life shortening diseases such as Alzheimer's, cancer, HIV, all recovered completely. What's more, it seemed their biology had been altered to such a degree that the aging process was slowed down by a factor of three. It was a miracle!"

More of the patients had started to recall brief snatches of the events of the time. Eyes narrowing, they knew it was anything but a miracle.

"Within twelve months, a single dose capsule had been created that worked on a cellular level to achieve the same result. Billions of people took the pill willingly, but a resolute minority held out against the promises of longevity. It eventually transpired that several doubting nations had even destroyed the tablets, providing their populace with a placebo in its place. The same powers that brought into being the first One World Government in Europe had resurfaced and pushed their puppet leaders to force the treatment on the unwilling. War broke out again, but it was short lived. The first reports were coming in about a spike in stillbirths. Within a month the minor spike had reached one hundred percent of all pregnancies in the women who'd taken the drug. Mass testing was undertaken, and the results were beyond comprehension. The DNA changes had continued after the initial chromosomal improvements, resulting in every single man and woman who had undergone treatment becoming sterile. With the advances in our own technology, it was discovered our benefactors had boobytrapped their gift. Without thinking, we'd fallen for their promises and doomed ninety percent of the population to a long, childless life. If it hadn't been for the caution of the United States, United Kingdom, and a few other nations, humanity would've ceased to exist in under three hundred years."

More than a quarter of those watching had regained their memory of what came next and shuddered.

"We think the plan had always been to trick us into wiping ourselves out. Once humanity was gone, the aliens would swoop in and either settle our planet or take whatever it was they wanted. It turns out that even the plans of a highly advanced extra-terrestrial species can go awry. The first infections started to manifest around a year later, and at first no one knew what was happening. Our chief scientists discovered the treatment had gone rogue, mutating into something far worse than the inability to conceive. Changes were occurring on a molecular level, altering the host in horrific ways. A week after isolation, the brain of the victim had lost all but the most basic functions, while the body became incredibly powerful to compensate. Attempts to combat the infection were fruitless, and within a few hellish days, the world was overrun by what can only be described as mutants. Mindless hunters of flesh, with no emotions or empathy. A single bite or scratch was enough to doom the victim. Some turned in seconds, some in an hour, but they all turned. Mankind was on the brink of being destroyed, so the remaining governments launched their entire nuclear arsenal to try and hold back the tide of infected. It worked, but not without inflicting a heavy toll on the survivors. Radiation sickness took millions of lives, but their sacrifice wasn't in vain. Given a window of respite from the risen, we hid from the fallout. When we surfaced, the infected were licking their wounds too, and we were able to construct fortress cities from the ruins in which to survive. I'm speaking to you from one such place; Tempest City, once called New York City. A sprawling metropolis covering nearly one thousand square miles. Dozens of similar bastions of humanity exist, with thousands of outposts servicing the requirements of our remaining population."

To her rear, a floor to ceiling mirror morphed into clear glass, revealing a grey, forbidding landscape of towering buildings and dark clouds, fitful lightning tearing across the sky. Flames burst sporadically from large vent stacks, adding to the overall bleakness. Thick pipes belched steam into the night air, expelled by a subterranean power station.

"This is what we have to live with now," she said, sadly. "Miles below my feet, water gets diverted from a tapped aquifer into magma coils. The huge energy produced by the turbines enables the processing of two of our most valuable commodities from our mines; Catyminum and Jajovium. We discovered them during the earliest days of our supposed golden age before the full nature of the impending apocalypse revealed itself. They now form an integral part of our defences, keeping the last traces of humanity from ultimate destruction. Tiny quantities of the former, when broken down, can be vaporised in weapons to produce plasma discharge. The turrets of our perimeter defences use it to great effect. The latter gave us a metal both lighter than aluminum, and stronger than titanium. Our explorations moved deeper and deeper in an effort to discover even rarer elements and the qualities which could be utilised in this never-ending war. Whether it'll be enough when *they* finally arrive? Only time will tell, I'm afraid."

Leaning even further forward, Empress Verena stared down from the screen with gratitude.

"You are the bulwark against Armageddon. Your bravery and sacrifice ensure our survival against the creatures of the darkened wastelands beyond our walls. We owe you a debt that can never be repaid. Thank you."

The huge face was replaced by the logo of the Divinity Alliance and General Ashdown marched back to the podium. Once again holding a hand up to end the barked questions, the room fell silent.

"I know you all have questions, so I'll take a few now and then meet with you all when you've been assigned a squad."

Looking around the room, she pointed to a woman.

"Is this really 2182?"

"I'm afraid so."

"But where've we been?" she called out. "You can't expect us to believe we've been asleep for all those years. What's happened to our families?"

"No, you haven't been asleep. As for your families, that's a question I'll answer in due course, but not right now."

Pointing out an Asian looking man, he nodded and stood up.

"Are we infected?"

"No, you're completely healthy. In fact, you've been provided with attributes far in excess of normal people."

Perplexed by the second part of the answer, he was still satisfied that the infection was not an issue and sat down. Andy raised his hand and the General's blue eyes settled on him. Indicating he should proceed, he asked, "What did Empress Verena mean by assigned a squad?"

"I'm glad you asked. On your seat you'll find a coloured access card.

Once you leave this hall you'll follow the designated colour coded walkway to your assigned bunkhouse. From there you'll be debriefed further and then your training will begin in earnest. I'm sure by now some of you will have realised you're all ex-military with impeccable records and unflinching honour. It's for this reason you were selected for the program."

Andy watched as several faces contorted, the flashbacks bursting into their minds.

"I'll answer more questions later. For now, dismissed!"

Picking up the green card, he looked for Eric and Tom who beckoned him over.

"Follow us, we know the way," offered Eric.

"Did you know I was in the military? I can't remember it…"

"We knew. It's what makes us so proud to be doing this job," Tom replied.

Rubbing a hand over his face, Andy paused before the door and leaned against the wall. The nurses immediately rushed to his aid until he pushed them away.

"Sorry, guys. I'm not ill, just mindfucked. I keep thinking I've been here before, but how's that possible? I think a good meal and rest will work wonders."

"The one thing I can guarantee is a hearty meal. Once you've eaten we're able to fill a few more of the blanks in for you."

"I'd like that," Andy sighed. "At the moment this all feels like a nightmare."

"It is," replied Eric.

"One that you can't wake from, unfortunately."

"Well that's great! Any chance you can put me back on ice?"

"I'm afraid not," commiserated Tom, leading him out into the corridor with the rest of the spawnlings.

CHAPTER THREE

Seating himself at the long dining table, Andy looked around at his fellow green card carrying spawnlings. Blue, red, and black were heavily represented in their own areas. Andy guessed the total number to be in the region of about four hundred souls. Considering the dire news delivered only minutes ago, he expected to see despondency, even fear. The faces that stared back at him bore none of those traits, only a grim determination. One of each pair of the medical team queued at the mess hall serving counter, while the other hovered like a concerned parent to their rear. Tom was a veteran of the food hall and had quickly positioned himself at the front of the long procession.

"I'm Gillian Dowling, but my friends call me Zip."

"Andy Burton," he replied, reaching out to shake her hand. "I'm not even sure if I've got a cool sounding nickname. Do you mind if I ask how you got yours?"

"It's one of the only things I can remember at the moment if you can believe that. Whenever we would go out on patrol I'd raise then lower each zip on my uniform three times for luck."

"Sounds a bit like OCD."

"It might be, who knows. All I remember is it seemed to work, and the rest of my squad would get all antsy if I pretended to forget."

"I'm Tengfei Bojing, but you can all call me Teng," offered another man of Asian descent.

"It rolls off the tongue a little easier," teased Zip while they all nodded in greeting.

"How about the rest of you?" Andy posed to the other diners at their table.

"Mohammed Mokrani, also known as Mo."

"Good to meet you, Mo," Andy replied to the fierce looking Arabian.

"Suzanne Cambridge-Green," said a young woman to Andy's right.

"Nice to meet you, Suzanne," Zip grinned.

"I keep remembering people called me… Loco," she replied, cocking her head and frowning as if trying to hear something echoing in the recesses of her mind. "Maybe I was into trains before joining the military?"

"Could be," agreed Andy.

"Zip 'n Loco!" Gillian grinned. "That's a winning combination if ever I've heard one."

"I like that!" Loco beamed.

"I'm Rocco Fletcher," said a stocky bald man from the head of the table.

Zip clicked her fingers. "Let me guess, your nickname's Rock?"

"Nope, Bob."

"Huh? Why Bob?"

"Fuck knows, but it's definitely Bob."

"Ok, Bob it is. What about you, friend?" Zip asked the final person on their table.

The man seemed oblivious to the goings on around him. His dark brown eyes stared vacantly ahead, seeing nothing.

"Is he ok?" Andy asked the man's nurse.

"He was fine when we brought him in," he replied, rushing forward. "Paul, can you hear me? Paul!"

Seeing the commotion, the second medic left the queue and came running over.

"What's going on?"

"He's gone into catatonic shock. Get a chair!"

Wasting no time, he raced out of the room.

"Is there anything we can do to help?" begged Loco.

"No, but I appreciate the offer. We need to get him to intensive care immediately."

Doors crashing open, rubber tyres squealed on the tiles as the nurse navigated the rows of startled people. Hoisting him aloft without ceremony, they placed Paul down and secured the harness across his chest. Shouting at people to get out of the way, they charged through the hall and were gone from sight.

"What the hell was that?" Andy demanded, turning to Eric.

"It happens sometimes. When we pull you out everything can seem fine, but then it's like the brain just short circuits."

"Will he be ok?"

"There's a slim chance he'll recover."

"How slim?"

"Very slim. Less than one percent."

"Fuck!"

Loco pressed anxiously at her scalp. "Will it happen to us?"

"It's unlikely. His is the first case I've seen in months. The geneticists have made massive strides in eradicating the problems that used to occur."

"I think we need some answers, don't you?" stated Andy in a tone that brooked no argument.

Eric looked at his fellow nurses for permission to divulge the truth and they consented. Seating himself in the now empty space, he looked at the expectant soldiers. "I'd have preferred to wait until after you've eaten, but I can see how worried you are. This may be hard to take in, but you've all been... grown. That's why we name you spawnlings."

"Grown? What the hell does that mean?"

"It means exactly what I said. The tubes that we pulled you from are birthing pods, highly advanced cloning technology developed in the years following the mutant outbreak."

Bob grabbed Eric's forearm and pulled him close. "Did you say cloning? As in, *we're* clones?"

"Yes, each and every one of you are exact genetic copies of your original self," he replied, prising the painful grip away. "Well, almost exact."

"This has to be some kind of nightmare," groaned Mo.

"It's not, I can assure you. Let me explain. When it was discovered what the aliens had sent us, every person on the planet had their DNA taken before being treated. For what reason I can't say, but it was one of the decisions that's allowed us to survive this apocalypse. After the devastation of the nuclear war, we fell into despair for a long while. It was only thanks to the vision of Empress Verena, Doctor Callaghan, and the Genesis Initiative that we found a solution. Rapid advances in somatic cell nuclear transfer were achieved following the genetic resequencing technology we'd been given. Instead of using a surrogate womb and waiting nine months for a baby, then a further twenty years for maturity, we use the incubation pods. With subatomic cell acceleration, we can have a fully-grown adult in only four months."

"You're shitting me," Andy blurted.

"Not at all, my job is to help you adjust to the situation you face yourselves in. I'll tell you no lies, I promise."

"How many times have we been cloned?" Bob asked, cautiously. He seemed to be accepting the unbelievable story faster than most.

"Some of you, once or twice, some of you, dozens of times."

"You're saying there are more than one of us out there?"

"No..." Eric said, then paused.

"What is it? What aren't you telling us?" Teng pressed.

"You're only cloned when you fall in battle."

Loco gaped at him incredulously. "So, you're telling us that we've died before?"

"I'm afraid so."

"This is blasphemy," muttered Mo.

"It may seem like that, but the alternative is the end of mankind."

"Wait a minute," Andy said. "If we're clones of our dead selves, how come I recognise some of the people in this room? I can't possibly have known them all before."

"With each new version of yourself, a small sample of your improved DNA is spliced into the original strain. For what it's worth, it means you get stronger and stronger."

"When is the sample taken?"

"Before you're removed from the tube."

"But that doesn't make sense. How can I have memories of people that I haven't technically even met before. I'd only be aware of them after being woken up."

"The greatest minds of the Genesis Initiative have been looking into this anomaly for decades."

"And?"

"They don't know."

"They don't sound that great then," scoffed Zip.

"My own opinion, and it's worth exactly nothing, is that it may be a fragment of your spirit, or consciousness, something like that."

Mo's brow furrowed contemplatively. "Considering that we know no more about the soul than we did a thousand years ago, it's as good an explanation as any."

"Dinner is served," remarked Tom, breaking into the conversation.

Placing a bowl of green paste in front of Andy, he chuckled at the grimace of disgust.

"Your stomachs have never eaten food before. This is a balanced nutritional supplement with all the needed proteins, vitamins, fats, and amino acids you'll need."

"It looks like baby food."

Zip groaned as her own portion reached the table. "It looks like baby sick."

"I want a steak, rare," sighed Bob, pushing the awful concoction around the bowl.

"Meat no longer exists as a food source."

"You better be putting me on!" Bob spluttered.

"I wish I was. It wasn't just human flesh the infected craved. Most of the animal species on the planet have been wiped out… or changed."

"Fuck! I can remember the taste of the juices."

Andy was close to spooning a dollop into his reluctant mouth. Mind reeling, he paused the utensil at his lips. "Did you say the infection was transferred to animals?"

"Yes. The human infected are far from the worst threat we face out there in the ruins of civilisation."

"Holy shit," he groaned.

Placing the unappetising cuisine into his mouth, Andy couldn't taste a thing. Whether it was the repeated hammer blows of the revelations or the normal flavour of the food, he couldn't tell. As the others withdrew into their own thoughts, he tried to conjure the image of his late family. Chaotic images of Christmas and death fought for supremacy until he finally gave up.

Energised by the tasteless fare, the soldiers followed their handlers out from the mess into a drab, grey courtyard.

"It's time to meet the team who'll get you combat ready," Eric explained, pointing out the row of waiting officers.

"Squad, fall in!"

Instinct took hold and they ran across the concrete, forming two rows before spacing themselves with an extended arm. The memories of basic training burned brightly in the psyche and all felt the rush which separated them from the civilian world. Honour, loyalty, integrity, selflessness, bravery; all were as much a part of their being as the blood which surged through their veins.

Offering a crisp salute, the senior officer looked on them with pride. Five feet ten, stocky and powerful, with closely buzzed hair and scars marring his face from previous battles, he was an impressive figure. "At ease! Good afternoon, everyone. My name's Master Sergeant Tony Hardie and my team and I are here to begin the task of ascertaining your individual capabilities. After you've been shown to your bunkhouse, you'll be put through some basic physical examinations; eyesight, hearing, reactions, the works. Tomorrow, your fitness and strength level will be determined. This initial analysis will be the first step in determining your role in the Sovereign Guard. Do you have any questions before you're dismissed?"

Zip raised her hand.

"Go ahead, soldier."

"Yes, Sergeant. We keep hearing about the different roles and squads, can you explain what that means?"

"Certainly," he replied, beginning to pace the line. "As I'm sure you'll appreciate, the traditional combat roles have gone out the window. In the mutant war, you'll fall into a class of specialist operators. V-Class, or Vanquishers, are the bedrock of our forces. They're well versed in light weaponry and are the shock troops of our army. Capable of quick strikes into the wastelands, they're a vital pacification tool. D-Class, or Devastators, are our heavy weapon and close quarter combat specialists. You'll see them manning the walls of our cities and outposts, repelling the waves of mutants with guns, plasma launchers, or Jajovium swords if the need arises. Backing them up are the M and T-Class operatives. The M in this case stands for Mechs, the massive armoured sentries that can hold the line when everything else falls. They can also be transported via Magjet, Dreadhulk to reinforce a cut off squad. I can promise you when those things fall from the sky, you'll give thanks to whatever God sits watching us. These air assets are piloted by the T-Class operatives, or Tempest, so named after our capital city. Generally, they'll be selected from their previous air force experience. Master Sergeant Steven Smith will now explain the covert operations divisions."

Stepping forward, the tall, dangerous looking trainer eyed them all. "Those of you that're unfortunate enough to end up with me will be fighting in the shadows. If Master Sergeant Hardie's troops are the hammer, we're the nail. You'll either join the S-Class, our Shadow operatives, or the A-Class, the Annihilators. Annihilators have enhanced night vision, which brings us back to the tests you'll be undertaking. You don't fight face to face, but with hit and run tactics, futuristic guerrilla warfare, if you will. The mutants will only know you've attacked when they find the tattered bodies of their ungodly brethren. Shadow operators have similar optical gifts. Their role is to scout the wastelands and identify targets for our soldiers, divinity missile batteries, or seismic cleanses. I'm sure you'll all understand the hazards of this posting, so you won't be ill thought of if you decline."

"Thank you, Master Sergeant. Does anyone else have a question?"

Nobody raised a hand.

"Very well. I'm sure you all have a great deal to process, so you've got a few hours of R and R to acclimatize and get acquainted with the rest of Green Company. You'll be woken at 0530 for the start of your physical testing. Dismissed!"

Eric and Tom followed closely behind Andy as he entered the bunkhouse. Nameplates were secured to the wall above each bed. A locker and chest stood open, revealing combat and training uniforms and recreational clothes.

"You know the drill," said Eric as they found his personal bunk. "Keep everything spotless and you won't get beasted."

"I haven't been beasted since basic. I'm sure I can keep my stuff ironed and stowed properly."

"Is there anything else we can get you before we go?"

"You're leaving me?"

"We need to fill in our reports for the spawning, but if you need us for any reason, just push that button," Tom explained. "We're only in the next building."

"And we do mean anything," Eric continued. "If you're feeling unwell, call us. If you start to feel confused, call us. If you just want to chat…"

"Call you?" Andy finished.

"Exactly."

"I was hoping you could fill me in about my previous life. Clear up some of the flashbacks and memories I'm getting."

The medics looked at each other. "It can be counterproductive. The trauma that can occur with the rapid recollection of past life events has been known to induce the same kind of catatonia that poor Paul suffered from in the mess hall. The higher ups generally like the subjects to slowly reveal their memories over the course of a few days."

"Look, guys, I'm strong enough to handle it. It's the not knowing that is causing me the most stress."

Eric and Tom exchanged another look of uncertainty.

"Please?"

"I can take care of the report," Tom offered with a sigh. "Stay with him a while."

"Are you sure?"

"Yeah, but you're completing the next one."

"Done."

As Tom bade them farewell, Andy and Eric sat down. The mattress was pliant and springy, nothing like the cheap, hard beds he could vaguely remember from his previous military career. The majority of his fellow troops had waved off their team and lay sprawled on top of the soft duvet, staring at the ceiling in quiet contemplation. Zip glanced over and smiled warmly. It was a look that said; 'We're in this together'.

"Where do you want to begin?" Eric asked.

"At the beginning. What were the names of my wife and daughters?"

"Your wife was called Beverly, and your daughters were Grace and Tara."

Andy mulled the information as neurons within his brain made a connection. "I remember now."

"Beverly was thirty-two years old and a high school maths teacher. Grace was ten and Tara was eight."

A lump formed in his throat. Choking out the question, Andy asked, "How did they…"

"Pass?" Eric offered diplomatically.

"Yes."

"It may be cold comfort, but they were victims of the first wave of nuclear strikes. Your home town was under siege and the top brass ordered its destruction. They wouldn't have felt a thing."

Visibly relieved, Andy's shoulders slumped, and he let out a gasping sob. "That helps more than you know. Thank you."

"It's always the first question on people's lips. Not everyone receives the same answer unfortunately," Eric replied, sadly.

"How did I die?"

"To answer that I need to go back to your origins in the British Army."

"Ok."

"You may not remember fully yet, but you were a highly experienced SBS operative."

Another flash of recollection bloomed in his mind. "I was in Z squadron!"

"That's right. You and your men were based in Dorset, England."

"I can't remember my team, though."

"You will in time. You'd served tours in Afghanistan during your earlier years, and then when the civil war broke out you were part of a breakaway faction under the command of Admiral Bransfield."

Andy was gobsmacked at the news. "Wait! I was part of a resistance movement?"

"Indeed, you were. The leaders of the New World Order tried to quell the uprising by turning their military power against their own people. Admiral Bransfield was the first woman to refuse the order to kill innocent protesters and instead went after the government. Within a month, most of the other commanders were aligning themselves with her. It took a further six months of intense fighting to finally crush the fascists and their supporters. The remaining soldiers were fanatical to the cause and fought to the bitter end. It was a dark period of our history."

"What a fucking waste."

"It's what happens when you concentrate too much power in the hands of an untouchable elite. How does the saying go?" Eric scowled, trying to remember.

Andy knew the phrase he was searching for. "Absolute power corrupts absolutely."

"That's it!"

"If that's the case, how do you explain Empress Verena?"

"You mean all that power in a single person's hands?"

Andy nodded.

"It's not like that. After the trials, the leaders of the different factions chose her to rule because of her unflinching detestation of the New

World Order. She'd been imprisoned during the first days of the new regime for questioning the appalling treatment of the population. She's pure and benevolent in every way, which in this world may seem hard to believe."

"And she's over a hundred and fifty years old?"

"Yes."

"Then I guess she must be on the side of the people if she's still battling after all that time."

"I've no doubt in my mind. She's an inspiration to us all. Besides, it's hard to fight among ourselves when insatiable cannibals lurk just outside our walls ready to tear us limb from limb. Imminent destruction has a way of focusing the mind."

"Do you think that's it?"

"Not at all, she's the real deal. A living saint, a miracle come to us in our darkest hour. Like Mother Teresa and Mary Poppins all rolled into one."

"Who're they?"

"One is a real person who helped the poor and needy, and the other…"

"I'm fucking with you. As soon as you said their names I could picture them. Mother Teresa is the one with the umbrella, right?"

"Shut up!" Eric chuckled. "Anyway, where was I?"

"Empress Verena."

"Oh yeah. She's got the weight of humanity's survival on her shoulders. I've seen footage of her justifying the decision to use the full nuclear capabilities of the world. She was utterly broken even though there was no other alternative if we were to survive the outbreak."

"I can't imagine what a choice like that does to a person."

"Hopefully we'll never need to find out."

"Ok, I'll place my faith in her too."

"You won't regret it. Is there anything else you'd like to know?"

"Did I have any other family? Parents, brothers, sisters?"

Eric looked away for a brief moment, but he couldn't hide the anxiety in his eyes.

"I need to know."

"You were an only child. Your parents were Linda and Patrick Burton, resident in London, England."

"What happened to them?"

"This is where I can't be anything other than honest with what happened to you and your folks. They were both doctors and died in the first days of the outbreak trying to help people."

"Oh."

"I'm sorry you had to find out this way. They died as heroes, refusing to leave the wounded."

"And me?"

"Your old squadron had been amalgamated with special forces regiments from across the globe. You were part of a battalion sent to secure a key road from the city while a wall was erected in an attempt to seal the infected inside."

"We failed?"

"Yes, but not before you killed tens of thousands of the bastards. It was like King Canute trying to hold back the tide; nothing was going to stop them."

"So mutant-me could be wandering around out there?"

"It's possible. I don't have access to the files of your previous lives."

"There may be more than one mutant-me out there?"

"For all I know there could be ten. Or twenty."

"That's an unsettling thought. I wonder if I'd be able to pull the trigger on myself."

"Trust me, when one of those things wants to take a bite out of you the last thing you'll do is hesitate."

"Thank you for filling me in."

"You're welcome, Andy. Is there anything else you'd like to know?"

"Not right now. I'm going to try and process this craziness before we get put through our paces tomorrow."

"Ok. Well, holler if you need me."

As Eric went to stand, Andy grabbed him by the arm. "There is one thing. I don't know if you'll be able to do it, though."

"If it's in my power, consider it done."

"Is there any way to get pictures of my family? I know our photos are probably dust, but you know… maybe there's a way?"

"I'll get images pulled from our database and bring them back within the hour."

"Thank you," whispered Andy through the raw emotions constricting his voice again.

Squeezing him on the shoulder, Eric smiled, stood up and made to leave. Whirling around with a click of his fingers, he said, "I almost forgot, you've got a briefing pack in your locker. You need to read it cover to cover as soon as you're feeling up to it."

"Consider it done."

With another wave, he was gone. Zip caught his eye from her bed and mouthed, 'Want to talk?' Shaking his head, he thanked her for the offer and laid his reeling head on the foam pillow.

CHAPTER FOUR

"How do you think they took the news, General?" asked Empress Verena.

"Apart from some understandable scepticism, very well. They appear to be the strongest spawnling group that we've ever had," replied Ashdown.

"They'll need to be for what's coming. I'll be sure to pass my congratulations on to Dr Ennis at the Initiative."

"How can I help you, Empress? I'm assuming this isn't a social call."

"Sadly not. I've been feeling... anxious for the past few days."

Ashdown stopped pacing. Sitting down at her desk, she looked at the drawn figure of their leader. Like a human divining rod, instead of seeking water she sought out catastrophe. "What do you think has caused it?"

"I don't know. It may be nothing," she said, trying to dismiss the unsettling feeling.

"With all due respect, ma'am, your hunches have been correct far more times than they've been wrong. Can you narrow it down at all?"

"I've tried, believe me. It feels like something big is coming, as if we're stuck on the tracks and a freight train is hurtling towards us, out of control."

"Is it *them*?"

"No. Maybe. I'm not sure."

"We're nowhere near ready," Ashdown grumbled. If the undeniably advanced extra-terrestrial species arrived now they wouldn't stand a chance. It was only by Empress Verena's psychic sensitivity that they'd survived so far against the marauding infected hordes.

"I'm sorry to burden you without being able to give you a firm answer."

"It's ok, your highness. I'll double guard rosters across every outpost and city just in case."

"I think that would be a good idea. Can I ask about the progress on the satellite system?"

"It's not good news, I'm afraid. We've lost contact with each one we've launched as soon as it breaks through the exosphere. The radioactive isotopes of the nuclear war haven't dispersed as had been forecast. They continue to circulate and mask the signals."

"Damn. We're still blind then?"

"They could be monitoring us from the edge of our atmosphere and we'd never know."

"That's a worrying thought. I suppose the viability of a manned launch is still out of the question?"

"It is. The ratio of successful atmosphere breaches is less than one in twenty because those bloody creatures are always watching and waiting to intercept. At present, the required material to craft enough vessels is far more valuable in the creation of the Dreadhulks."

"I understand, General. Home defence is a priority."

"That being said, if your hunch points to an attack from space, we'll just have to accept the dangers and divert the resources. Not knowing is driving me to distraction."

"As soon as I can tell you more I will. I just pray it's something homegrown that we can deal with."

"As do I. Is there anything else I can help you with, Empress?"

"I'd like to travel to your family's research facility and see the progress on the new weaponry if you can accommodate me. I need to get out of here and stretch my legs a little."

"Certainly. We've made encouraging progress on our laser technology. We're close to rolling out the next stage of the Mechanised battle platforms as well."

"We're indebted to your ingenuity, General. Shall we say four days?"

"I look forward to it."

"Until then," replied Verena, before signing off.

Alone once more, Ashdown tapped at the desk, troubling thoughts swirling through her mind. Frustration at their predicament grew day by day. The time and energy used to stay one step ahead of the mutants was sorely needed to prepare for the real war. They needed to break this infuriating deadlock, but how?

CHAPTER FIVE

"Are you ok?" Zip asked tentatively.

Andy opened his eyes to see her gingerly approaching his bunk. "I'm fine. Please, come and sit down."

"Are you sure? I know you wanted to be alone for a while."

Flipping his legs from the edge, he smoothed out the sheet and patted it to indicate she should sit. "I'm sure. I've come to terms with the situation, as fucked up as it is. You?"

"Me too. A few tears and I was right as rain. How's that right?"

"I can only guess it's part of our new bodies. Either that or we've heard the news so many times we've become inured to it."

"You're talking about the bits of soul or whatever Eric was talking about?"

"Yeah. I can still sense whispers of my past lives, not full-blown memories, just echoes. His explanation may mean we've been distraught so many times that it just washes over us now."

"We've built up a resilience to the grief?"

"Pretty much. It still crushes me to think of my wife and daughters, but I can shut it off like flipping a switch. I feel like such a shit, like I'm dishonouring their memory."

"I know what you mean. I had a boyfriend, nothing serious, you understand. Hell, I can barely even remember his name. It's my folks I miss the most. My mum and dad were the most amazing, loving people you could wish to meet."

"If they had a kid like you I'm sure they were amazing."

Blushing at the praise, Zip looked away.

"Do you remember anything else about your service?"

"I was in the USMC."

"You were a jarhead?"

"Oorah."

"But you're Irish…"

"We moved to the States when I was a teenager. I joined the MC after graduating from high school."

"Semper Fi, marine!" called Bob from across the room.

"You too?" Zip asked.

"Yup, it just flashed into my head when you said oorah. I was First Marine Division out of Pendleton."

"Second Division out of Lejeune. Infantry."

"You must've been among the first female recruits to serve on the frontlines," Bob remarked.

"Times were changing," Zip replied defensively.

"Hey, you won't get an argument from me," he protested. "You gals scared the shit outta me on the training grounds with how intensely you took it. I could barely keep up at times."

"And don't you forget it!" Zip replied with a wink.

"Do you remember much about *the end?*"

"Not really. I get flashes of gunfire and explosions, but I can't remember the exact details of when I died."

"I guess that's a good thing in some ways."

"Maybe."

Interrupting their conversation, Master Sergeant Hardie marched into the billet. "Attention!"

The troops were already scrambling to stand by their bunks before the order had been shouted. Eyes fixed firmly ahead, they waited while he strode up and down the lines.

"I hope you've had a chance to digest some of the information you've been burdened with today. I know from experience that it can be a minefield of confusion and disbelief. If they haven't already told you, your handlers are also expert psychologists who can assist with the transition. We're going to run the first of the preliminary tests on you all now, which'll take a couple of hours. I hope you all enjoy getting poked and prodded."

CHAPTER SIX

A shrill whistle burst through the sleeping quarters. Most of the recruits were already awake, contemplating the future and what it held for them.

"Wakey, wakey, rise and shine!" yelled Hardie. "Get changed into your PT uniform and form up outside in two minutes."

The room chimed with a multitude of; yes, sirs. Leaving them to it, Hardie marched from the room with his subordinates.

"It'll be good to get the blood pumping," Andy said, throwing on the sweatshirt.

"I know what you mean," replied Loco. "I've got so much energy, it's scary. Either I'm hyperactive or that food had some good stuff in it."

"I feel the same," Zip confirmed and several other partly dressed soldiers agreed.

"What it lacks in flavour, it makes up for in stimulation," added Bob. "I can live with that."

Fully dressed in grey uniforms, they hurried from the room and met the instructors on the training ground. Hardie and Smith were accompanied by a team of observers who all carried small tablets to record the findings.

"Hold out your left arms, please. You're going to be fitted with a microchip which will be used to monitor your vital signs and also track your whereabouts at all times."

A couple of murmurs of disapproval broke from the crowd and Smith stepped forward.

"It's for your own good! When you're alone in the darkness with nothing around you but the twisted, gibbering hordes of mutants, you'll be glad we know where to find you."

"Thank you, Master Sergeant Smith. There isn't some nefarious reason for the chips, it's not our way of controlling you like they did under the New World Order. Those times are long since passed."

Seemingly satisfied with the explanation, the furrowed brows and narrowed eyes relaxed. The observers moved between the soldiers, taking out small injector guns and implanting each of them with the microscopic chip. Andy stared at the small drop of blood rising from the tiny puncture and his mind flashed back to the ascension of the fascistic government from centuries past. The so-called elites of the world transmitted their treaty signing ceremony to the masses. Arrogant and aloof, they assured the people it would herald a new dawn on peace and prosperity. Andy's team had been filled with trepidation as they were summoned to the medical bay and fitted with a far larger and more painful tracking processor. Their hesitation had been well founded with the horrific genocide that followed. Shaking his head to banish the screams, he wiped the spot away and returned attention to the officers.

"The first test is a general fitness evaluation involving a twenty-kilometre run around the perimeter of the facility. Push yourself as hard as you can; your improved cardiovascular system can handle it and we need the readings that it'll provide. Smith will be the one to beat, which hasn't ever happened yet as he still holds the record for the run. I'll hang back and shout at the slackers, not that I think there'll be the need with this platoon."

Smith glared at them, the challenge written plainly on his face. "It's a quarter mile to the wall which we'll run in formation to get warmed up. As soon as we hit the perimeter it's every man and woman for themselves. If any of you pussies can beat me, I'll buy the drinks tonight. Hell, I'll buy them for the whole week."

Hardie moved to the rear of the two columns and blew a whistle.

Smith started to jog and the claps of boots on concrete quickly fell into a steady rhythm. Andy smiled to himself at the memories of basic training and thought the only thing missing was a cadence to run with. Smith's booming voice answered his mental request, bouncing from the buildings they passed.

Darkness reigns across the world, round the plug our species swirls.

I was happy in my grave, 'til the world I had to save.

Dragged out of those birthing pods, where the hell's our absent God?

He hung us humans out to dry, mocking us from up on high.

We've been spawned to do our bit, with Ashdown guns we'll kill the shits.

The alien scum will get theirs too, we'll mount their heads on sharp bamboo.

When we've pulled back from the brink, I'll say, 'fuck you' and have a drink.

Sound off, one, two.

Sound off, three, four.

Cadence count, one, two, three, four. One, two... three four!

"I prefer the old chants," Andy grumbled. "They were less morbid."

Passing between the final buildings, the turret topped perimeter wall rose in front of them. Veteran guards and Mechs watched their approach from above.

Smith picked up the pace before calling back over his shoulder. "Break formation! I'll be waiting for you at the finish line!"

"We can't let him win!" shouted Zip, forging ahead on her powerful legs.

"I don't intend to!" Andy replied, matching her stride for stride.

The squad raced on and Hardie was forced into an early sprint. *There won't be any bollockings today,* he thought, smiling to himself. The strength on display was quite remarkable and it wasn't long before his steady breathing became slightly laboured. *You're getting too old for this.*

At the front of the pack, Smith was comfortably pulling ahead. After two kilometres his figure had disappeared around the curve. Andy was feeling incredible; the muscles in his legs were strong and responsive to the terrain. His lungs drew air deeply; the pounding heart circulating it around his bloodstream effortlessly. Increasing their speed, the trailing foot of the master sergeant came back into view, followed by his calves and then his whole body. Glancing back, he saw the pair gaining on him.

"Did you see that? We've got him worried!"

"It could be an act," Andy replied. "He might let us catch up and then laugh in our faces."

"We won't know until we try!"

Zip went flat out, pulling away. Andy risked a quick look over his shoulder and they were in the same position as their supervisor. The nearest member of their squad was starting to disappear from view.

"Fuck it!"

Using the untapped resources of his new body, Andy accelerated and swiftly caught up with his friend. Only by the miracle of the geneticists were they able to keep up the previously unimaginable momentum. The drab scenery passed in a blur as they sprinted onwards, rapidly gaining on Smith. Drowning out the echoes of their boots came the yells of encouragement from the guards above. Twenty yards separated them. Then fifteen. Ten. Five.

"Morning, Sarge," Zip teased as they came alongside their superior.

"Nice day for a run," Andy added.

"Mine's a Baileys."

"I'm fond of rum myself."

"Fuck you both… I'm seventy years… older than you…"

"It's showing, Sarge."

Andy and Zip left the ailing officer in their wake. Taking in ragged gasps, he shouted expletives at them.

"You should save your breath, Sarge. You're slowing down!"

The advice only brought more abuse. Concentrating on their own breathing, they fell silent and raced on. As they passed, the walls were erupting with jubilant cheers, spurring them to even greater velocities. Troops from the other coloured barracks followed the sounds of pandemonium, emerging from between the ranges, storehouses, and various other military buildings.

"How much further?" Zip asked. Even with her enhanced genetics the burn of lactic acid was starting to slow her down.

"Not far. I recognise that mark on the wall!" Andy replied, pointing out the signs of a fluid leak that had discoloured the metallic alloy from grey to a murky brown.

The curve in the perimeter revealed the waiting observers. Impassive, they stared at their screens, monitoring the data rolling in.

"Come on, slowpoke!" Zip laughed, taking the lead.

Andy was giving it his all. Summoning the last drops of energy, he managed to draw level as they careened past the startled technicians. Coming to a stop they bent double, hands on knees. Sucking in ragged breaths, they looked at each other and burst out laughing. Frowning, the observers studied the tablets to see if their bizarre behaviour had any medical source.

"Why're we… laughing?"

Zip shrugged, snorted, then started all over again. Smith turned the corner, saw them, and gave them a one finger salute which only increased their mirth.

"You're fast… I'll give you… that," gasped the master sergeant.

"We're only what the scientists have created, Sarge."

"Even so, I'm still proud to…" he panted, stretching back to expand his tortured lungs. "Be fighting alongside you."

"We'll try not to let you down," Andy declared.

"Let's see what times you got… You've smashed my record."

"You averaged one minute twenty-eight seconds per kilometre," answered the lead observer. "That's a full nine seconds faster per kilometre than your record, sir."

"Yeah, ok, don't rub it in. These upstarts will be boasting about this for weeks as it is."

"Don't forget the free drinks," Zip warned.

"I didn't specify what type of drinks," Smith protested. "I meant water."

"Don't be a sore loser, Sarge. Technically, none of us have ever had an alcoholic drink before; we'll be smashed after two glasses."

"Ok, ok! As much as it pains me to say, damned fine work, soldiers. Let's get some hydration while we wait for the others."

∞

"Is everyone feeling alive?"

The squad affirmed; the endorphins surging through their systems.

"Your times were all incredible," Hardie confirmed. "Batchelor, your heart had a slightly abnormal rhythm during the last two kilometres. Doctor Edgemont will take you to medical to get it checked out."

"Yes, sir."

Giles followed the observer, looking back with a nervous grin.

"You'll be fine!" Loco called out and he gave her a wave.

"He'll be back in no time," Smith added.

"We now move on to a strength test. Some of you are built for the Devastators, that much is plain."

They formed up and slowly jogged back into the centre of the facility, forgoing the military song. Entering the gymnasium, the next set of observers were waiting for them.

"This'll be nice and quick. You'll do four compound lifts with the maximum you can safely handle; squat, deadlift, bench press, and overhead press."

Confused, the soldiers looked around. Expecting to see dumbbells, barbells, bikes, treadmills, and similar equipment, all that was present were a row of bars mounted between two upright columns.

"They're magnetised and work in sync with your microchips. You issue a command for the type of lift and it self-adjusts. Bob, you want to go first?"

"Why not? Any particular order?"

Hardie shook his head. "Whatever order you want to do them."

"Ok," Bob replied, approaching the steel bar. "Deadlift."

Dropping on the runners, it hovered ten inches from the floor. Clasping the metal in both hands, Bob moved his legs apart and then bent down, keeping his back straight. Grunting, he hoisted the weight until he was stood upright then dropped it.

"Very good," confirmed the observer. "Seven hundred and eighty-two pounds."

"Not too bad," Bob nodded. "What's the entry level for a D-class operative?"

"Six hundred and fifty," Smith answered.

"Well hot damn, that's a good start."

Hardie turned to Andy. "Next?"

"Sure."

Taking up the same stance as his friend, he readied himself. The veins on each forearm sprouted from the surface of the skin, sending blood to eager muscles. Tensing his back, Andy roared and pulled at the resistant bar. Reaching a standing position, he let go of the massive weight, head swimming.

"Make sure you breathe through the lifts or you'll pass out," cautioned Hardie.

"I know, Sarge. It was stupid."

"Weight?" Smith asked the observer.

Tapping at the tablet, she frowned and tapped at it again. Raising her eyebrows in shock, she replied, "One thousand, two hundred and two pounds."

"Holy shit," Smith muttered.

"Is that right?" Hardie asked as the soldiers congratulated Andy.

"I've double checked. It's genuine."

"Fuck me," he blurted.

"This is unprecedented," exclaimed the lead observer. "Master Sergeant, would you mind if we carried out the other lifts in a private suite?"

"Not at all. Do you need me?"

"No, we'll be fine. I want to run some further diagnostics on Mr Burton to see what's caused this sudden spike."

"He's all yours."

"Right this way, sir."

Andy exchanged a bemused look with the others then followed. "You aren't going to probe me, are you?"

Glancing over his shoulder, one of the observers replied with a grin, "No. Well, not yet, anyway."

"I normally insist on dinner and a movie first."

"I'm sure we can accommodate that. I'm Dan, by the way."

"Good to meet you," Andy replied, shaking his hand. "Was the lift really unheard of? I could probably go higher if I'm honest."

"That's what we're going to find out, Mr Burton."

The private suite was fitted with a single bar set and the other tests confirmed the extraordinary power lurking in the thick muscles.

"Shoulder press, seven hundred and twenty-two pounds. Bench press, six hundred and seventy-eight pounds. Leg press, one thousand, three hundred and twelve pounds. Remarkable," muttered Dan.

"What does that mean?"

"I don't know yet," said Dan, staring at the data screen. "I'd like to take some blood and tissue over the next day or so and check for any anomalies."

"Wait! Anomalies? Like I'm abnormal?"

"Only in the sense that you're stronger than any human that ever lived. If we could harness the genetic sequence that's allowed this, we can splice it into every other subject we clone. It's a massive leap forward."

"Won't the mutants be able to use me too?"

"If you fall in battle, yes. We don't have any other option than hoping it keeps us a tiny margin in front of the infected."

"I'll try not to get killed."

"I'd appreciate that," Dan replied.

"Am I done here?"

"Yes, of course. You're free to go. I'll be in touch about the samples."

"Thanks, Dan."

Leaving the suite, the rest of his squad was waiting patiently, eager for the results. Andy broke down the weights lifted. Wide eyed and mouths gaping, they gasped their amazement.

"Remind me not to arm wrestle you," said Bob.

"I'd still take you," teased Zip.

"I'm sure you would."

Hardie congratulated them on a job well done. Filled with pride, he and Smith looked over the members of green barracks. For once they may have been blessed with a cohort that could do some lasting damage.

"You've got two hours to get some chow then we get wasted! Dismissed!"

CHAPTER SEVEN

"How're you feeling, Sarge?" Zip asked Master Sergeant Smith.

"Old, Downing. Very, very old."

"If you want we can get you a pipe and slippers from the quartermaster."

"Cheeky bastard," he replied. "But I'm about forty years past a pipe and slippers. I feel ready for my pine box and a long nap six feet under."

"Don't be so morbid, Sarge."

"It's hard not to be. This helps," he said, passing over a glass of yellow liquid.

"What is it?" Zip held the glass to her face, staring into the swirling alcohol. Small particles floated within the brew.

"It's best you don't know. Here, take these to the others."

"Is it ok for our stomachs?"

"Yeah. It's bloody awful but it's never caused any harm."

Andy and Zip loaded a tray and moved back into the rec room. The clack of pool balls echoed from the walls until the booze was presented. Coughs and splutters replaced the crack of resin on resin.

"It tastes like diesel," said Bob, nodding appreciatively and taking another draw.

"It tastes like *off* diesel," Andy gasped as his tongue went numb.

"I'm not even going to ask how you know what that tastes like," Zip muttered, shuddering involuntarily from the acrid tang.

"I'd like to raise a toast," declared Hardie, climbing onto one of the tables, knocking cards all over the floor. Raising his glass, he said, "To Green Platoon, arguably the most badass crew of mutant killers this side of the Atlantic Ocean."

"To Green Platoon!"

Smith appeared with two large jugs and topped the drinks up. Mo gratefully took a fruit cordial in place of the alcohol.

"Thanks, Sarge."

"Enjoy it. That stuff is harder to get hold of than my special cocktail."

"Tell us more about the world," begged Loco as they settled in. "It can't be as bad as the empress says."

"It is. Everything's gone."

"You're still here."

"Ok, nearly everything is gone. We control such a small part of the world compared to the infected."

Hardie started folding out fingers as he listed their meagre territory. "Southern England as far as the Chiltern Mountains. Northern Virginia all the way to Vermont and inland to Ohio. California, Nevada and as far north as Portland, Oregon."

"And that's it?"

"There could be more, but we have no way of knowing. Word was the Chinese were fighting back."

"Can't you send a drone to check?"

"We've tried, but they get pulled down before they can find anything. The last time we attempted it was thirty years ago."

"It must be so frustrating!"

"You're telling me. If anyone else is out there we could really use the help."

"Except from the Scavs," grumbled Smith.

"Scavs?"

"Wasteland scavengers. We call them Scavs."

"How the hell do they survive out there?"

"We don't really know. They're as secretive about their methods as they are extortionate with their prices."

"Can't you just… ask them hard?" Andy suggested.

"Empress Verena won't countenance it. We benefit with goods that are impossible to get anymore, and they benefit with weapons and food."

"Why would anyone want to try and eke a living among the ruins and monsters?" Loco wondered, staring to slur her words.

"They say it's safer," Hardie replied with a scornful snort.

"Crazy bastards."

Smith refilled his glass. "Who's crazier? Them hiding, or us sat here lit up like a beacon. The ones I've seen have been alive for decades, so they're doing something right."

"Can they have children?"

"I've not seen any kids, but some of the women have been well covered up. I could've sworn I saw pregnancy bumps beneath the rags."

"Where did they come from?"

"Mostly people who can't hack the life within the walls. Living in constant fear of attack can break the strongest person. Deserters from the Sovereign Guard make up a lot of the number as well."

"Deserters? Why aren't they rounded up and executed?"

"It's all a matter of free will. The empress won't punish anyone for having had enough of war. When I say deserters, I mean soldiers who've fought battle after battle with the infected. They've earned their freedom as far as I'm concerned."

"That makes sense," said Zip thoughtfully.

The doors burst open and the medics poured in, greeted by the half-drunk soldiers. Eric and Tom accepted the proffered drink and sought Andy out.

"This is for you, buddy," said Tom, handing over a small envelope.

"Is it?"

Eric nodded and squeezed his shoulder.

"Thank you both."

"You're not going to tell us off for underage drinking?" Zip giggled. The concoction was already having an effect judging by her half-shuttered eyes.

"As it's a first offense, I'll let you off with a warning."

"Where are you going?" she said as Andy quietly made his way out of the room.

A flash of the gift and she smiled knowingly.

Emerging into the cool, night air, Andy had never been more nervous. The contents of that small package were more terrifying than any amount of enemy gunfire. Maybe this isn't such a good idea, he thought, turning it over and over in his hands.

"It's your family," he whispered to himself, sitting on the cold concrete with his back to the wall of their hut.

Peeling back the flap, the glossy card tucked within reflected the outpost floodlights. Tracing the sharp outline, he gathered up his courage and plucked the picture out.

"Turn it over."

The white backing goaded him. On the other side was his past, his life, his whole world. They were gone. His initial desire to have something tangible to hold, to remember them by, was waning.

"We can do it together if you want?" Zip offered, interrupting his anxious musings.

Andy flinched, nearly dropping the picture. "You startled me."

"Sorry," she replied, sitting down beside him. "The offer still stands."

Looking at the unturned picture for long seconds, he slowly slipped it back into the envelope.

"Not today. I thought I was ready, but I'm not."

"Want to get another drink?"

"Absolutely," Andy replied.

Pocketing the card, he stood up and helped Zip to her feet. She staggered forward and fell into his arms. "My bad."

"Have you been consuming alcohol tonight, ma'am?" he asked with a stern, authoritarian voice.

"Not me, occifer," she said, pretending to be more inebriated than she was. "I've only had a glass or two. Of water."

"Then it's time you did," Andy chuckled, slinging one of her arms over his shoulder.

"We're going to feel this in the morning," Zip warned.

"Probably, but at least for a few hours that rot will stop us feeling anything at all."

"I'll drink to that."

Moving back inside, the card pressed against his thigh, almost insistently. He ignored the imaginary pressure, knowing it was only feelings of guilt. Downing a fresh glass, he surrendered to the tender mercies of the yellow liquor as Smith answered a request for a story. Feeling the spreading glow, Andy closed his eyes and listened.

CHAPTER EIGHT

Corporal Smith, report.

"Third target located. The hive's in a small town called North Chester, six miles east of Albion in the Ischua Valley."

Estimated numbers at target location?

"Scanners indicate around fourteen thousand."

Any indication of the host strength?

"Judging by numbers I'd guess she's a fledgling, probably no more than a year old."

Can you get eyes on? Command may send a team to extract the brood mother if the Initiative can use her.

"I can try. Going radio silent until I can confirm, psy comms only."

Understood.

Smith stood on the valley wall outside of town, staring down. Rows of newer brick-built housing on the outskirts were still standing, their roofs missing only a few tiles. The older, timber homes had started to suffer from the passage of time, some collapsing completely while others leaned like drunkards. Pockets of mutants moved in and out of the dilapidated structures, patrolling, hunting, whatever the mindless creatures did. The high school and massive playing fields lay directly below the rocky promontory. Goal posts on the football pitch rose into the sky, the bleachers behind offering concealing shadows for any lurking threat. In the distance, the town square swarmed with life, revealing the likely location of the queen.

Moving with exaggerated care, Smith avoided any loose shale or twigs which would give away his position. Hopping between solid ground, he approached the broken, tangled fence, keeping low and hugging the perimeter until reaching the dark seating. Performing a quick sweep with vision as clear as day, the metal framework was empty. The building seemed equally devoid of movement, so he ran past the bandstand towards the open changing room doors.

This takes me back.

Many decades had passed since his previous self would charge from the tunnel, wearing full football padding. In the silence, Smith was sure he could hear the faint echoes of those battle cries. Moving inside, the merest hint of sweat and testosterone prickled his nostrils. Then again, it could just be fond memories playing tricks. The colourful bunting hanging from the walls had faded. Notices on the boards had blown loose of the pins as the paper crumbled, settling against a corner further inside the hall. Rows of lockers lined the changing room, the ghosts of the team slamming them closed appearing like wraiths in his memory. Bumping chests and helmets, they turned and surged through Smith, banishing the vision. Moving along the maze of empty hallways, he came to a trophy cabinet. The smiling face of the science club winner beamed from the picture frame, all braces and thick lensed glasses. Looking in those merry eyes, he could sense the underlying sadness in the black circles. It reminded him of Johnny Wiles, the poor kid who drew the undeserved ire of his teammates. Their ill treatment bordered on torture at times.

What happened to him?

Smith's cloned memory was hazy. Snatches of images flowed through his mind; screaming teenagers, running teachers, people gaping through the bathroom door, a pool of blood spreading from the booth. Suicide as a result of bullying they'd called it. A brief suspension had been served by the football players responsible. Their crime was quickly forgotten as a result of their value to the pride of the community.

Young Steven Smith had never slept a full night thereafter. He would find himself moving sluggishly through the dream forged crowd, accusations etched on their faces. Each step would take long seconds, the edge of the toilet stall gradually revealing the sight within. First a shoe, then a second. A cheap, unfashionable brand of footwear, floating on a sea of blood. The lower legs, then the thighs, a spattering of crimson soaking through the denim. A ghostly white hand, fingers tightly wrapped around a scalpel taken from the science labs. Scarlet droplets splashing into the rapidly spreading pool from the tainted blade. The second hand, a deep red gash rising from the palm to halfway up the forearm. Empty veins hanging from the wound. A face, staring at him, contorted with pain and sadness. The butchered arm, rising, fingers curling impossibly from severed tendons. Pointing at his murderer, the blue lips parted on the frozen rictus of its face. Before the opening mouth could give vent to its hatred, he'd wake from the nightmare bathed in cold sweat. Steven could escape the haunting in the waking world, but not his guilt. Quitting the football team, he'd finished high school and enlisted the next day. He would spend his life defending people, attempting to atone for his imagined sins.

Johnny's face vanished as something went clattering to the tiled floor further towards the main entrance. Claws could be heard scraping, followed by snuffles and grunts. Loading his pistol, he checked the suppressor was locked in place. Shadowy figures crept around the corner, moving in his direction. Keeping tight to the wall, Smith sidled backwards using the cover of the cabinet. Ducking into the nearest classroom, he tried to close the door. The hinges were seized solid, refusing to budge. Moving behind the large teacher's desk, he crouched and listened. He could make out four distinct movement patterns of varying weights. A short burst from his pistol would be sufficient if they discovered his position. Taking a breath, he became like a statue, legs tensed and finger on the trigger. The weirdly garbled language carried through the open door, before coming to a complete stop.

Had they seen something? He'd made sure to avoid leaving footprints in the dust. The pause extended as the creatures muttered to each other; the clicking, throaty rattles of their language chilling him. Was it even a language? The Genesis Initiative claimed not, but Smith was damned if he didn't sense some kind of purpose to it. Just as he was about to stand and unload on the monsters, they moved away. As soon as the sounds receded towards the gym, he left the room with its posters of fading equations and blank chalkboard. The reception led out onto the front of the school. Finding the first human remains on the stone steps, scraps of shredded backpacks still clung to several of the skeletons. Time had done away with the flesh, but the ravages of fangs and claws were still evident on the bones.

Bastard things! he thought, grinding his teeth in anger.

Sprinting past the dead, he crossed the street and hugged the first house. Another group of infected came into view three bungalows down. Dropping to the ground, he shuffled backwards through a gap in the broken latticework of the void beneath the home. The patrol passed, and another came into view, then another. They moved in groups of four to eight, leaving only small windows to move freely.

This isn't going to work. I'm going to try and use the storm drains.

Ok, Corporal. Don't put yourself in unnecessary danger.

I won't. If the layout is similar to most towns it'll take me right to the square.

Good luck.

The hunched, long limbed creatures skulked past his hiding place and rounded the corner. Leaving cover, he ran across the road. Hearing the unmistakeable sound of the mutants, Smith hit the ground with his rump and skidded the last few feet through the open drain. Turning his face to the side, he felt the steel graze his helmet. Thankfully, he wasn't wearing combat armour, or he never would've fit through the thin opening. Hitting the bottom of the catchment area, his feet crunched through a layer of twigs, leaves, and general rubbish. Quickly moving down the tunnel, he spun round to see if the creatures had heard the noise. A minute passed without inquisitive faces appearing at the opening and he relaxed. Keeping the pistol aimed straight ahead, Smith navigated the dry passages of the storm network. It was a simple task, taking only five minutes of heading north and listening for the increased activity.

I'm at the town square. It's thick with infected. I'm going to try and identify the location of the target.

Received.

Shifting position, the sliver of light gave only a sixty-degree field of vision. If he moved any further forward, he would be completely exposed. The courthouse doors were a splintered mess. Dozens of the creatures milled around inside by the security desk, but they weren't guarding anything, Smith was certain. Moving to the next grate, he could see an old steak restaurant and another building alongside it. The sign had long ago fallen, but he could make out the letters Pacific Bank imprinted vaguely on the weathered stone.

Clever, very clever.

The brunt of the mutant forces was gathered around the perimeter. Hundreds of the creatures lined the street, with more hovering on the rooftop and peering from the windows with their thick steel bars.

I've found her. She's in a bank, likely hiding in the vault. It's the most secure location in the town.

Is there any way to confirm her size?

If you can provide a distraction I can try and get inside.

What do you suggest?

A Magjet flypast, land in the school fields to the south. Lob a few displacement grenades and then get the hell out of dodge. While they investigate, I'll get inside.

Roger. Magjet will be dispatched in five. ETA to you, thirty-five minutes.

I'll sit tight.

Smith sidled back into the darkness and crouched down, readying himself mentally for the attack. He would have mere minutes before the mutants would swarm back to protect their mistress. The storm culverts would get him to the edge of town and out of danger, but it would be tight. As he waited, the hidden sun moved sluggishly across the muddy, brown sky. Like a ghost remembering its old life, it yearned to pierce the veil and bring warming comfort to the living.

Corporal, you've got incoming.

Roger that.

Inhuman shrieks of warning tore through the town square. Smith could feel the multitudes race away through the concrete tunnel. Feeling the air change, dust motes rose from his hiding place as the grenades drew greedily on their surroundings. As the implosions let loose their gathered power, the multiple detonations rattled the heavy metal grate.

Time to go!

Pushing the cover up and over, he jumped out like a jack-in-the-box. The previously teeming space was left with only a few stragglers; the ones whose limbs were too twisted or rotten to allow swift movement. Short bursts from his pistol ended their misery, the slugs liquefying organs as they fragmented. To the south, three more rumbles carried through the ground, causing a weakened wooden building to collapse into its hollow basement. Funnelled by the protective bars, the remaining queens guard poured down the steps of the bank straight into Smith's strafing fire. Several of the creatures were cut in two, the bullets severing their upper body like the swipe of a scythe. Leaping over the leaking corpses, Smith charged past the offices and teller counters. Another set of steps led down from the lobby. Much like a lot of the smaller banks, the top and bottom was guarded by iron bars that wouldn't be out of place in an Old West jail. Resin secretions coated the walls, fresh and dripping. A nervous bleating came from below.

Host has been located. Moving to confirm.

In times of increased criminality, the banks had spared no expense on the vault itself, in spite of the simple security measures up to this point. The twelve-inch-thick, dual lock time-controlled door was ajar, the rods of the locking Mechanism resembling the spokes of a wheel. Puffy grey flesh shuddered inside as the host moved deeper into the reinforced shell. He'd seen enough to judge her value and moved no closer. In spite of their flabby seeming bulk, they could move rapidly when threatened.

Smith to base. She's a baby, less than a year old.

Damn.

Orders?

Get clear and we'll level the three towns with a missile barrage.

Roger that.

Backtracking, he left the bank and jumped into the open drain. Reaching for the grate, an arm lashed out, breaking the fingers that clasped the handle.

"Fuck," he hissed, cradling the damaged hand.

By the luck of the gods it was his left hand that flopped uselessly, not the right. Bodies crammed themselves through the gap in their desperation to get to him. Firing the remaining ammunition into the crush, blood rained down onto the concrete. The droplets hit the dust covered surface, forming into perfect orbs of powder coated plasma. The blockage bought him valuable seconds, and he sprinted away as the creatures above ground burrowed frenziedly through their kin.

I'm blown, they're all over me.

Can you get to an extraction point?

It's too dangerous for extraction. I'll try and lose them in the hills.

Understood. Corporal, your readings show you've suffered trauma.

A few broken fingers, nothing too bad. I'll administer cyclomeine as soon as I get clear.

Good luck.

Smith, out.

Shrieks echoed down the passage leading back to the school. He was cut off. Thinking rapidly on the layout of the town and his corresponding position, Smith knew he was only a few hundred yards from the outer homes. Their gardens opened up onto wilderness, and possibly safety. Dodging down a branch in the system, he listened at the nearest cover. Screams of rage were coming from all around, but the biggest concentration of noise was to the rear. Knowing he had no choice, Smith climbed the ladder with his good hand. Using the back of his left, he sent the cover clattering to the cracked road. Emerging from the ground like a troll, he picked his shots carefully, clearing a small path between a couple of Edwardian style homes. Dodging over the mutants as they gurgled their last breath, he could feel the horror bearing down on him, feel their red eyes boring into the back of his head. Yells of hunger caused his skin to crawl.

Passing between dead cars and windblown piles of uncleared rubbish, he made it to the row of houses backing onto the rolling hills. Shoulder barging a locked gate, time had weakened the timber, causing it to disintegrate in a puff of dust and soft slivers. Clearing the empty twelve-foot-wide pool in one jump, he spun on his heels and unloaded a half magazine through the house and its neighbour. Already teetering, the impact of the bullets tearing through structural supports finished them and they collapsed, sealing the small alleyways at either side.

As he powered up the hill, he could hear the scrabbling sounds of the mutants as they surged over the destruction. Smith's options were rapidly running out. He could never outrun them in the long term; after twenty miles he would start to flag, and they would overwhelm him. His weapon only had three magazines left, nowhere near enough to kill them all. Blaze of glory? It seemed the only logical thing to do. He'd tagged the location of the queen for the missiles, if only he could get back to the bank. Shoot the host, seal the door, and wait for the cleansing fire. It was preferable to being eaten alive.

Base, I'm done. These things are all over me. Requesting...

Coming to a halt on one of the bluffs, Smith could see the Sable Dam in the distance. An idea sprung to life in his head.

Smith, repeat the last.

Scratch my last transmission. I'm going to give our friends a bath.

Smith, repeat that.

I'm going to bring the Sable Lake down on their heads by destroying the dam wall. The water will spread through the valley and kill the three hosts and mutants along with them.

Are you sure you can't get clear?

Negative. They're motivated and very hungry.

After a moment's hesitation the thought came through his psy link. *I'll inform command. Happy hunting, soldier.*

Smith, out.

Tracing the line of the bluff, it evened out and he moved onwards. His father had taken him hunting in places like this, but the lack of life was a poignant reminder of the new order. No elk or boar, no cougars or bears. Not even an angry rattler sunbathing on a rock, slithering away when disturbed. The last time a bear had been sighted... Well, the outpost managed to send a couple of shaky videos before they went dark forever. The investigating Vanquishers had found destruction on a scale never seen before, but no sign of the fearsome foe.

Smith reached the dynamite excavated road, skimming down the steep bank on his rump. The flat surface allowed him to pick up speed and he charged on towards the security station of the facility. Dodging through the shells of abandoned cars, he wondered why there were so many. The approach was choked with them, far in excess of normal staff and visitor numbers. It could be that they'd sought sanctuary by the water; it was a logical move, he thought. The appearance of a ghost city confirmed his suspicions. RVs and caravans by the hundred lined the concrete curvature of the dam wall. The canvas of the tents had long since disappeared, leaving only the support rods like skeletons of the pitiful shelters. Moving through the buckled gate, he could find no sign of a mutant attack. The vehicles were untouched by the feral monstrosities. When the bombs fell, the people probably took shelter below, dying from thirst or radiation exposure as the invisible poison flowed across the land. The dark corridors of the structure would resemble the haunted catacombs of Paris; thousands of white bones lining the walls and nooks. Men, women, and children, all slowly sickening or dying of thirst.

Fucking things!

The creatures were in hot pursuit. Howling their pleasure at the hunt, they could sense their prey was weakening; they would taste warm meat before night fell. *Not mine, you rotten bastards.* Peering over the inner railing, the black morass of the lake bubbled and seethed. The exceedingly rare rainfall had washed the filth of the land down into the massive basin. The acid had eaten deeply into the masonry of the reinforced structure. Cracks lined the road and walls from the pressure of the liquid against the weakened construction. Two hundred trillion gallons of it if he remembered his high school geography lessons correctly. Like the biblical flood, the monsters would be washed away in righteousness. Unclasping two displacement grenades, Smith moved across to the downstream slope. Climbing the railing, he looked down the angled face to the murky outlet. The row of strengthening buttresses lined the wide grey face like the edges of a playground slide. Judging by the fissures in the previously smooth surface, two implosions would be enough to bring the whole thing down.

"Come on!" he yelled at the converging infected as they filtered through the remnants of the camp.

Answering the summons, thousands of mutants crammed themselves into the crest of the dam to get at him. Estimating the gradient and how quickly his weight would carry him to the bottom, he readied himself. Twisting the timer pins for a twenty second fuse, Smith jumped. Landing six feet down, the hiss of his suit on the rough surface joined the steady tick of the munitions. Looking over his shoulder, the railing gave way. Like a portent of what was to come, they poured from the rim like water. A dull hum imposed itself over the sounds of scraping and shattering bones from the tumbling monsters. The Magjet's spotlight picked him out as it shot over the top of the hillside to the left. With expert precision, the pilot dropped towards him and swung the rear of the craft around. The bay doors were open, and two figures leaned from the lip of the ramp with arms outstretched, securing ropes taut.

"Jump!"

Mirroring the rapidly increasing speed of his fall, the pilot moved as close as possible without risking a collision. Eight seconds had passed. *Nine.* Smith could feel the friction driven heat penetrating the sturdy material of his suit. *Ten.* Attempting to get his feet planted was impossible, he was moving too fast. *Eleven.* A fissure appeared to his side, snaking down and then cutting across two feet to the left before continuing downwards once more. Changing the angle of descent by twisting his body, he aimed for the three-inch protrusion. *Twelve.* Tossing the grenades aside, he tensed his legs and hit the outcrop. *Thirteen.* Screaming as the bones in his legs crumpled, Smith used the pain as a fuel to propel himself from the dam wall. *Fourteen.* His hand flailed out into space, missing the outstretched arm by inches. *Fifteen.* With a yell, the rescuer loosened his descender clamp and jumped, catching Smith's other arm. *Sixteen.*

"Go!" he roared, the agony of strained ligaments like white hot fire in his joints as they dangled.

Powering away from the slope, the Magjet soared up and away. The mutants screamed in frustration even as they shattered against the unforgiving surface. Ahead by ten feet, the black orbs bounced.

Nineteen.

Twenty.

The atmosphere was sucked towards the two balls as they cracked opened, pulling on the struggling figures. Creating a tear in the physical world, the implosions drew in reinforced concrete and mutants in a thirty-foot sphere, compressing it into a blend of animate and inanimate. The twin craters in the grey slope started to issue trickles of black water. A half second later, the gathered material was blown apart by the delayed plasma charge within. The shockwave hammered against the damaged surface, ripping apart the small cracks until they were gaping chasms. Unable to hold back the weight of the water, the thick wall bulged until the whole thing disintegrated. Chunks of the dam broke away, driven by the force of the unleashed lake. The infected howled in fear until they were crushed by the massive weight on the valley floor. As the crest collapsed, the makeshift refugee camp followed into oblivion, the vehicles thrown around like toys. Twin monitoring towers at each bank toppled, joining the tidal wave of rock and acid as it spread. The liquid crashed against the hills, scouring the dead trees and mud, adding their weight to the apocalyptic deluge.

"You're safe now," grunted the second soldier as he pulled Smith and his saviour aboard.

"Holy shit, would you look at that!"

The hundred-foot wave of corrosive death rolled over everything in its path. North Chester was hit first, the outlying houses exploding into kindling. The ant sized outlines of the fleeing mutants brought a glow of satisfaction to the injured soldier as they fell by the hundreds. Even at this distance, Smith swore he could hear the shriek of terror from the queen as the bank crumbled around her.

"Payback's a bitch!" Smith groaned, falling onto his back. The sharp sting of a needle preceded a wave of euphoria which banished the throbbing torment in his broken limbs.

"This'll make a damned good story to tell," smiled the stranger, kneeling over him.

"Thanks for coming back," whispered Smith, the pain meds numbing everything.

"We weren't going to leave you for those things. Now lay back and rest, we'll set down somewhere safe and get you on a stretcher."

"I nearly died for the third time that day," Smith explained.

"We're glad you didn't, Sarge," said the drunken recruits in unison.

"I still get pain after all these years when it gets really cold." He patted his legs.

"You're still bloody quick considering the injury. I don't think we would've beaten you if you were in top form," Andy replied.

"Probably not, so be grateful to the infected fucks who hobbled me," he chuckled, pouring a fresh drink.

CHAPTER NINE

Lined up in two rows, the bleary eyed, hungover soldiers listened to Master Sergeant Hardie as he gave the instructions. To their left was a sprawling estate, with shattered buildings, vehicle shells, and other obstacles. To their right was a standard firing range of differing distances to the model targets.

"The final part of your initial assessment will involve a simple test of your combat reflexes and accuracy. Master Sergeant Smith will be giving you a demonstration of our bread and butter weapons, the AcMag pistol and rifle."

Loco held up a hand. "What does AcMag stand for, Sarge?"

"I'm glad you asked," replied Smith. "It's short for Accelerated Magnet Propulsion System."

"Surely AcMagPropSyst would be more accurate?"

"Don't be a smartass, Green. I doubt I could even say that three times in a row."

Andy tried to hide his grin before he asked, "How do they work, Sarge?"

"We used to call them railguns back in the day."

"I remember them, but wasn't the smallest prototype mounted on a battleship? It was fucking huge!"

"And now we carry them in our holsters and over our shoulder."

"That's impressive."

"You're damned right it's impressive. These things fire just like a regular automatic, except they can put out three times the number of rounds with no need for an accelerant. I'm sure you can appreciate we need to prioritise the use of our minimal resources as best we can. That means the propellant we produce now is used on the Mech and gunship weapons."

"How did they ever manage to shrink it down so much?" Zip inquired.

"Ashdown Industries was at the forefront of weapons tech back in the day and they had everything except the correct material to enter mass production. After the shit hit the fan and we retreated underground, the miners went deeper than ever before. It's how we harnessed geothermal energy to power our cities and outposts. While they were digging, they found new elements, two of which were named Aneluvium and Chridonium. The first was like a magnetic sponge, giving off a massive electromagnetic field. Many miles below the surface, this stuff covers the whole planet. The second, Chridonium, was the exact opposite, repelling itself from the other. One of the miners damn near lost his head when he broke the first chunk free and it ricocheted around the shaft."

"Our whole fleet of cars, jets, and barges use this material to travel. Tiny quantities are added to the road surface. The fighting craft have a varying amount of Chridonium based on their size and required speed. By energising the metal, we can increase the power of the resistance it gives off."

"When do we get to see them, Sarge?"

"Once your posting has been decided, some of you'll be picked up by the Magjets and moved to different cities and outposts. The Dreadhulks are only stationed in the cities to provide support in case of a large-scale attack. From there, they can be deployed to the outlying settlements when the need arises. I'd recommend you have a look at the topic when you get back to barracks. Now, let's get down to business."

Leading them over to a basic range, the soldiers gathered around the master sergeant.

"Ear protection on, troops," he ordered, placing a set on his head.

Picking up a pistol, Smith slapped a magazine into the weapon. The baseplate was bulbous instead of flat, which Andy could only assume was to house a larger quantity of bullets.

"The AMX-4 pistol is made of a dense polycarbonate shell. It's stronger than steel but nearly weightless. The material counteracts some of the excess weight of the firing Mechanism. You'll notice the barrel is slightly longer than the old-fashioned sidearms. It's needed to ensure the requisite number of mag coils can be fitted to achieve hypersonic velocity."

"Hypersonic?" Andy inquired. "The discharge isn't silent then?"

"No, it's comparable to the sound of a normal round firing without the suppressors. With the suppressors attached, they're damn near silent, which is what you need out there."

"Do they degrade?"

"Yes, but far slower than older versions. You can get several thousand rounds out of a single pistol silencer before the shots become audible. The rifles are closer to fifteen thousand."

Smith showed them the safety button and took aim at the snarling mannequins downrange. Assuming a shooter's stance, he leaned in and explained the increase in recoil that the firearm produced. Pulling the trigger, the gun bucked heavily. The barrel literally buzzed with the volume of bullets exiting the chamber. Nine seconds saw the magazine empty, but the devastation was total. Twenty life sized mutants were nothing more than scattered hunks of plaster and dust. Whistles of approval issued from the watching troops.

"Each magazine holds one hundred and eighty rounds, with a twenty round per second fire rate at full auto. This is what tore them to shreds," he explained, holding a tiny bullet between his fingers. The tip was sharp, like an armour piercing round, but at the base of the point were twelve subsequent tips surrounding the shank. "When it hits, the slivers split off in a cone. It tears through crowds of those bastards as if they were paper. Now it's your turn. Remember, be ready for the recoil. I want controlled, one second bursts. You'll find your name in one of the booths"

Lining up in separate cubicles, the troops picked up their designated weapon.

"Get a feel for them. Try the weight with your preferred stance."

Andy looked over the black pistol. A series of channels were cut around the circumference of the small barrel where the suppressor would be twisted to lock it into place. He was expecting the gun to weigh more but considering his superhuman strength, it wasn't surprising that it felt as light as a feather. The grip was extremely comfortable; well contoured and just the right size for his large hands.

"Good craftsmanship right there," Smith said proudly.

Assuming a shooting stance, Andy slid his right foot back slightly and bent at the knees. Cradling the gun, he cupped his right hand in the palm of the left. Retrieving the magazine, he inserted it with a snap. Taking up the stance again, he felt as if the gun was an extension of himself.

"It's got good balance, Sarge."

"You're damn right it has. They're manufactured to your individual measurements when you're close to spawning." Taking a few paces back, Smith joined the other instructors. "Remember the recoil. Fire when ready!"

The morning silence was shattered by the deafening chatter, broken only by the brief pauses between trigger pulls. A cloud of white powder drifted on the easterly breeze at the end of the range. Ragged lower legs were all that remained of the plaster cast figures.

"Good. How did it feel?"

"The first shots threw me off a little," admitted Zip.

"Me too," Loco agreed. "But once I corrected it was fine."

"Excellent. I now want you to fit the suppressors and try again. As well as deadening the noise, they also reduce the recoil by twenty five percent. You can remove your ear defenders if you wish."

Locking the cylindrical addition to their weapons, the lightweight material had no discernible impact on the balance. Ejecting the spent magazine, they inserted a fresh one and hefted the pistol again. Hidden Mechanics downrange removed the shattered husks and raised new dummies in their place.

"Fire when ready."

The previous din was gone. Only the sounds of the slugs tearing through the mutants remained. Emptying their magazines, the soldiers gaped in amazement at both the noise reduction and greatly diminished pushback.

"You can thank General Ashdown during the next briefing," Smith called out.

Hardie stepped forward. "Now I want you to switch to semi-automatic," he explained. "Pick your shots carefully. A clean headshot will kill them dead, but they move like lightning. If you aim centre mass, you'll need to give them three or four rounds to make sure their insides are mush, or they'll just keep coming."

Fresh targets emerged from the ground. Andy moved the selector switch and sighted the nearest dummy. Squeezing the trigger, the bullet hit the eye before splitting and completely blowing out the back of its head. A shot to the shoulder severed the left arm which went spinning into the distance. Two slugs in the chest saw small holes punch through, while the back exploded from the separating shards.

"Good," said Smith, moving down the line.

By the end of the shooting, their arms were aching despite the genetic strength modification. Hardie was studying the placement of kill shots on his handheld display. It was higher than any class by four percent.

"Well done! The weapons are yours now; take the holster and spare magazines with you for extra practice later. We're moving on to the assault rifle training and final test. The test itself will take the form of a tactical simulator of close quarter urban pacification inside the replica village.

Points will be awarded for speed and accuracy of the kill shots."

CHAPTER TEN

The assault rifle training was uneventful. The main difference between the weapons was the range and fire rate, with the rifle having an optical link to the combat helmets in place of a scope. The display would show the superimposed crosshairs on their target with the ability to zoom a portion of the screen in for greater accuracy. It left the soldier able to see both the immediate surroundings, and the distant enemy, reducing the chances of a sneak attack.

"Right, you sorry lot! I'm going to split you into your squads. Burton, Downing, Bojing, Green, you're up first. Get your asses suited and booted."

"We're going in full tactical gear, Sarge?"

"Absolutely. You're going to get used to the suits in a real time combat setting."

"I thought you said we weren't facing live subjects?"

"You aren't," Hardie replied, grinning to Smith. "Let's just say we've got a few surprises in store."

"Sarge, can I volunteer for the kitchen instead?" Loco asked, sarcastically. "I think I'd prefer to cook the paste."

"Stow that shit, Green!" Smith thundered.

"You're a stone-cold killer," Hardie added. "It'd be like caging a lion."

Loco's cheeks flushed at the praise.

"Exactly! Now shut the fuck up and get your ass moving!"

"Aye, Sarge," she replied.

Slipping into the suit, they were astonished at how unrestrictive it was. Interlinking plates of alloy gave the impression it would be clunky and cumbersome, like knights of yore in their ancient suits of steel. The craftsmanship was exceptional, with each piece moving in perfect symmetry with those around it. The soldiers found themselves squatting, jumping, twirling, and flailing their arms to test the flexibility.

"Doesn't even feel like you're wearing anything, does it?" Smith asked.

"It's amazing," Andy exclaimed.

"Those suits are rated for ten minutes against the infected."

Zip frowned. "Huh?"

"They've been tested on live subjects. It took the strongest ten minutes to penetrate the shell."

"I don't know whether to feel comforted for myself or pity for the poor bastard who was in it," Andy remarked.

"We didn't put a person inside, for fuck's sake," Smith said without further elaboration on what they had actually used to tempt the creature.

"Your helmets are held in place by a microscopic layer of Anelivium within your protective collar."

"It's held in place by a magnet? Is that good for us?"

"The collar is also a shield from the magnetic field which is given off when we energise it. The eggheads have added a nanofiber to the material which reflects the waves."

"Wouldn't Velcro be easier?" asked Loco.

"Absolutely! Easier for them to tear it off and eat your face, that is."

"Point taken, Sarge. I like my face."

"I like your face too, Green. That's why I'd prefer it to stay attached to your skull. Now get your helmet on."

Slipping it on, the world became muffled. A low hum indicated the mounting was secure and the sound returned.

"Try and pull it off," Hardie urged.

Much grunting ensued. Teng planted a foot on Andy's shoulder to get a better grip, snarling with the effort. Zip managed to slam Loco to the ground with her attempt. Defeated, the soldiers lined up, panting from the exertions.

"It's held in place by a force equivalent to three hundred pounds per square inch. Nothing is getting those bad boys off."

"Onboard cameras relay everything back to central command to be studied," continued Hardie.

"What if I need to take a piss, Sarge?" asked Teng.

"My advice would be; don't stare at your own pecker. You'd only end up on the peewee hall of shame back at command."

"I thought these things had a zoom function?" Teng replied, tapping his visor.

Loco nudged him in the ribs. "Not even the Hubble Space Telescope could help you with that!"

"I'm going to insist the next time I'm cloned they add six inches," Teng grumbled.

"You only want a seven incher?" Zip teased and Teng burst out laughing.

"Are you done?" Smith demanded, trying to hide his own grin.

"Yes, Sarge. Sorry, Sarge."

"In that case, pick up your rifle and do a test of your onboard scopes. You only need to concentrate for the display to change."

Andy retrieved his weapon and moved to the final range. The targets were over five hundred metres away, little more than specks on the horizon. Lining up the sights, Andy let loose a couple of shots that missed by several feet. Focussing his mind, a small portion of his screen changed to an opaque close up of the grotesque mannequins. Lining up the crosshairs, his enhanced physique was able to eradicate any wobble in the aim. Popping off three more shots, the chest cavity exploded from the perfect placement of the bullets.

"If we'd had this tech during the outbreak, we'd have kicked their asses," Andy said, awestruck.

"Indeed. But we didn't, so here we are. Did everyone's display work correctly?"

Four affirmatives confirmed they had.

"Good. You're going to go one at a time so pick your order. The route through the village is prescriptive, so don't try and deviate from the course that's laid out. If you get confused, you'll find arrows on the ground to guide you back to the right path. Understood?"

Loco nodded slowly, then cocked her head in confusion. "Sarge, can I ask something that's been bothering me since our eye test?"

"I'm on tenterhooks, Green. Go ahead."

"Why don't the S and A-class operators just use the night vision tech in the helmets?"

"That's actually a sensible question."

"Don't act too surprised," huffed Loco.

"It's because the lunatics in my squad don't have the luxury of wearing armour out there. Our suits are designed to conceal instead of stand up to prolonged punishment."

"That makes sense."

"Remind me at some point over the next couple of days to give you a demonstration."

Turning to the remaining troops, Hardie said, "While you wait, use the time to keep practicing with your weapons. You can try on your assigned helmet and get acquainted with the scope capabilities."

Following the order, the others busied themselves with the task. The master sergeants escorted the team to the entrance, peering into the retinal scanner to open the gate.

"Ready?"

"Yes, Sarge."

"Happy hunting," Smith grinned, sealing them inside.

CHAPTER ELEVEN

"Andy, you're up first," said Zip.

"Ok."

He moved forward cautiously. The preparation area gave way to a carefully constructed village ruin. It was as if they were walking out of a house onto a street in any typical suburban neighbourhood in the world. Moving down a debris covered path, he crouched behind the front garden wall and looked back. The others stared from the exit which was designed to look like the front door of a house, broken windows and the brooding dark from within glooming over them.

"This should be interesting. I'll see you at the finish."

Andy took in the scene. A tangle of crushed vehicles sat to the right, blocking his path. This was what the master sergeant had meant by prescriptive. Arrows indicating left, he moved to concealment behind another car.

The clear route would take him around a curve in the road towards a taller structure which he couldn't quite see. Scanning for any threats, he crouched low and ran to the next vehicle. Like jack in the boxes, three dummies sprung up in the broken windows. Taking a knee, he popped three expert shots, in under two seconds, straight through their foreheads. With the threat neutralised, the system removed the targets.

Hurrying forward, Andy took up position with his back against an upturned truck. Seeing movement in the dark windows of the ruined homes, six more mutants moved forward into the light in a staggered sequence.

Pop. Pop. Pop.

The three in the eastern row of houses were destroyed.

Pop. Pop. Pop.

Heads exploded in the western windows before the tracks rolled the decapitated figures out of sight.

Cradling the rifle in low ready, he spun from cover and jogged down the road. Emerging onto the junction, the right-hand turn was alive with a horde of the creatures rolling at speed towards him. Switching to fully automatic, Andy strafed the massed bodies. Clouds of white powder and chunks of plaster scattered across the concrete as the mannequins crumbled.

"Switch to sidearm. You're going inside," ordered Hardie over comms.

Slinging the rifle, he withdrew the pistol and ran through the small carpark at the front of the supermarket. The glass frontage was intact, and Andy was guided through the open double doors by well-placed shopping trolleys. Taking a half second to adjust to the gloom, his instinct indicated something was amiss. Dropping and rolling forward, he barely avoided the two mutants that fell from ceiling mounts. Double tapping the cast figures, the pulleys withdrew them, heads missing with a gaping cavity in their chests.

The store was pitch black, but the night vision had fully compensated, and he moved forward. A currency exchange booth lay to his right, fake cash spilled all over the floor. A memory flashed into his mind of a holiday abroad. The Greek islands. Mykonos. His daughters' swimming in the communal pool while he looked on adoringly. Applying suncream to the tanned back of his beautiful wife. Innocent times. Returning to the present, the wonderful memory faded, leaving an aching void in his heart. The pain would vanish in time; he was finding it harder to hold on to the past with each passing hour. One moment he remembered their every feature, the next they were faceless puppets. A heavy weight crashed into him, sending him sprawling amongst the dead currency. The attacker glowered, arms extended, razor clawed fingers ready to eviscerate.

"Fuck!" Andy muttered, shooting it twice in the throat, causing the head to detach and shatter on the ground.

Jumping to his feet, Andy cleared the checkouts for any hidden threat. Out of the ten produce aisles, eight were purposely blocked with fallen shelves or fake goods, leaving two open paths. Opting for the meat aisle, he passed realistic looking steaks, whole chickens, ground beef in packets, ham joints. It was enough to make his mouth water. A disturbance from above caught his attention. From either side leapt a dummy on its Mechanical arm, then two more, then four, herding him towards the other end. Sprinting away, arms reached from the shadows to snatch him. Dropping to the polished tiles, he slid the remaining ten feet. Aiming back over his head, Andy switched to full auto and destroyed the pursuing monsters. Rolling onto his front, he quickly regained footing and scanned the back of the store. A set of wrecked double doors was the only way to go.

Pushing through the hanging plastic into the cold store, the stacked pallets left a plethora of places for the monsters to conceal themselves. Carefully clearing each blind spot, the attacks were starting to get monotonous. A dropping mutant. One jumping from the gloom. By the end of the warehouse, Andy was practically strolling through.

What's the matter with you? he wondered. It was totally out of character for him to be so nonchalant about such an important test. *Get your mind right for fuck's sake!*

In the rear yard, three lorries were backed up to the loading dock, trailer doors wide open. Knowing the likelihood of the threat within, Andy unleashed a few short bursts into each.

So much for tactical. Hardie's going to tear you a new one.

Hopping down from the platform, Andy moved quickly towards the half open gate, scanning the dark void beneath each vehicle as he passed. Moving to the exit, he looked up and down the road to see if it was clear. Pushing at the chain-link, the steel squealed as it scraped against the ground. Sensing a vibration, he spun round. Hidden chutes below the trailers opened, pouring out automated creatures. It took a second for him to realise the dog sized beasts were in fact rats, their four-inch-long incisors bared. Streaming forward, he couldn't shoot them fast enough to hold them back. Bodies exploding, the robotics inside the automatons fizzled and sparked from the damage. Turning around, he ran through the gate and slammed it shut. Their combined weight pushed it straight open, causing Andy to desperately look for cover. Nothing presented itself. The remote-controlled monstrosities were hot on his heels as he fled down the street. More streamed from alleyways and open drains, converging on him. The only available path was over a fence and through a park. With one hand on the metal rail, Andy vaulted the barrier and hurried on. The sounds of pursuit died away and he risked a quick glance backwards.

Clever, very clever, he mused as they retreated back to their source.

Plastic trees and bushes lined the grounds. The rustle of imitation grass under his boots was the only sound. Passing a children's play area, Andy paused. Tiny skeletons were scattered far and wide. Bones littered the base of the climbing frame. Small skulls screamed silently from the bench where someone had neatly arranged them.

Sick bastards.

His little girls had played in places like this. Giggling with delight as gravity pulled them down the stainless-steel slides. The feeling of weightlessness as Andy had pushed them on the swings, higher and higher until they could take no more.

A shadow rose from behind, dwarfing his own on the pale ground. Before he could move, a powerful blow knocked him down. A weight settled on his back, crushing him into the earth. Unable to move or breathe through the compressive burden, Andy flailed around, trying to bring his pistol to bear. If only he could get a few shots off! Aiming blindly, the trigger clicked.

"And you're dead."

The sound of Smith's voice precipitated the removal of the suffocating load. Rolling onto his back, Andy stared up at the massive, mutated lion. Drawing air into tortured lungs, his mind reeled at the sight. The hair of its mane was thicker, almost wormlike. Staring closer as his vison cleared, Andy could see small mouths at the end of each strand. Four eyes had replaced the mundane two, and its snout was a hellish, fanged abomination. Three rows of daggers sat inside the maw. The skin was a mottled purple, with prominent veins covering the muscular hide. Only the front legs of the model were Mechanically controlled, which allowed it to swipe and pin the soldiers with the huge paws.

"They don't kill you with those," Smith explained, moving into sight and reaching up towards the teeth. "They use them to hook you and swallow you alive."

"That can't be real," Andy huffed, taking the master sergeants hand.

"I'm afraid it is. I've fought them out there. And worse… far worse."

"And the rats?"

"Them too."

"Holy shit."

"Our friends out there have all the material they need to create the stuff of nightmares. Thankfully, the animals aren't as prevalent as the human mutants.

The initiative has a theory that the virus has more difficulty replicating their cells. Whatever it is, I thank the gods."

"How much does that thing weigh?" Andy asked, taking in the huge proportions of the creature.

"About twenty tonnes when fully grown," he replied, patting the plastic shell. "This little lady is equivalent to one about six tonnes. A baby."

The twin hatch of the creature's hiding place opened, and the hydraulic system started to lower it into the housing for the next soldier. Stretching out, Andy knew he was going to feel it in the morning.

"No claws?" he groaned the question.

"The real things have them, retractable things like all cats. They don't use them unless attacking Mechs or other armour. Our feline infected like to toy with their prey, much like their ancestors."

"How did you know I was going to stop here?"

"Probabilities, son. Thirty four percent of recruits get caught out by the dead children."

"And if I'd ignored them?"

"We had more surprises in store."

"Shit!"

"No one ever beats this simulator, that's not the point. It's designed to give you a small taste of what it can be like out there; you never take anything for granted, and you definitely never allow yourself to get distracted."

"What about a gun that won't fire?" Andy remarked angrily. "That could get me killed out there too."

"Here, let me see," asked Smith. Taking the pistol, he fired the full magazine into the air without issue.

"What the hell?" gaped Andy, checking over the weapon as the sergeant handed it back.

"We deactivated it," Smith said, grinning.

"That was a dick move, Sarge."

"Hey, I'm not the one who was prancing around the warehouse without a care in the world. We figured you could do with a bit of a shock."

"Sorry about that."

"I get it, son. It's hard to truly understand what it's like when they're just plaster or plastic. You'll be facing the real thing soon enough, don't worry."

"How did I do until I got pinned like a mouse?"

"Best results yet by a wide margin. You're going to kick ass out there, soldier, I can feel it."

"Thanks, Sarge."

"You're welcome. Now let's head to the observation suite and we can see how Downing gets on."

Chapter Twelve

The recruits marched in formation towards a hangar of immense proportions. Wreathed in a morning mist, the end of the structure couldn't be seen, just a merging of reinforced metal into lazily drifting vapour. Warning signs were mounted every ten yards informing the base of the live fire taking place within. Below the image of a flashing muzzle were the second signs containing a biohazard symbol.

"Squad, halt!" barked Master Sergeant Hardie and the synchronous footfalls came to an abrupt end.

Andy stared forward, waiting for the next order. The faintest chatter of heavy gunfire carried through the walls to the troops.

"Squad, left face!"

As one, the forty soldiers turned and stamped their right foot onto the concrete.

"At ease!"

Everyone complied and for the first time they could see the words above the huge roller door. *Mech Training* was painted in black letters eight feet tall.

"The next part of your assessment is to check the level of your neurological capacity to psy-link with the onboard Mech systems. Piloting the machines is not just pulling levers and pressing buttons, it requires you to form a symbiosis between flesh and Jajovium alloy. Some of you will excel, while some of you will just stand there unable to move, but don't worry. You all have a place in the Sovereign Guard and this takes us one step closer to finding it."

Turning to the access panel, Hardie placed his palm on the scanner and waited. A white strobe flashed, picking out the unique impressions on his hand. With a dull rumble, the doors commenced their rise, drawn aloft by chain links an inch thick.

"Squad, forward!"

The head of the column moved towards the gloomy interior of the building. Andy glanced upward and marvelled at the thickness of the retreating barrier. Eight-inch steel plates were folding into the overhead runners on thick, oiled hinges. Effectively a holding area, the room was eighty feet square with unbroken walls. Cameras moved, watching their advance and automated turrets rested in standby position. From half of the sentient, menacing weapons issued the hiss and blue jet of a pilot flame. *Flamethrowers? What the hell would they need flamethrowers for?* Andy wondered.

"Squad, halt!"

Hardie placed his palm on a second reader and the outer door started to trundle back into the closed position. A resounding metallic clang echoed in the sealed chamber as the floor plate hit home. Pneumatics hissed and drove thick bolts from the left and right of the door into sealing rings.

"Please hold for bio scan," chirped an electronic voice from a hidden speaker.

Coming to life, the eight turrets rounded on the waiting soldiers, drawing a couple of anxious yelps.

Master Sergeant turned to them. "Nothing to fear from them. They're just a failsafe."

Failsafe against what? Andy thought as lenses mounted in every wall started to glow. A blue light streamed from the optics and illuminated every inch of their bodies, moving up and down, left to right. After ten seconds the lights dimmed and shut down.

"Bio scan, negative. You may proceed."

Whatever the machine had failed to detect proved satisfactory for the heavy weapons aimed at them. Deactivating, the barrels rose and settled back into rest mode. The second roller door opened and the squad moved into the next area.

"Squad, fall out! Take a seat on the right and wait for a technician."

Their superior moved away towards a supervisor's booth to sign in while the soldiers took in the surroundings. They were in another holding area, but one with a lot more activity. The small window to the office was only large enough to fit a head through, with a microphone communication system mounted above. People moved around on unknown errands, smiling at the newcomers. It was the massive machine that got the men and women talking, though.

"How big do you think it is?" asked Zip.

"Eleven, maybe twelve feet," Andy replied.

"It's well equipped," she remarked appreciatively.

The imposing black hulk was stood dormant in an alcove. Hydraulic pistons gleamed in the arms and legs, with mirrored glass where the pilot's face would be. Hinges on the thighs, chest, and arms of the Mech showed where the human would gain access. On each forearm were a trio of razor-sharp blades bolted to the chassis. The smaller left arm contained a fully functioning hand with fingers three inches in diameter. The bulkier right arm was tipped with a dual barrelled weapon. A smaller, ported barrel would fire normal bullets, with a sealed belt feeding system protruding from the inside of the arm stretching around to the back. The wider barrel could only be a high explosive grenade launcher. A similar, but larger, circular feeding tube ran side by side with the squared edges of the bullet feeder. Rotating mounts lay on each shoulder, with thick wire couplings hanging from the fixing bracket.

"I wonder what goes there?"

Turning to Zip, Andy could only shrug. "I doubt it'd be a pair of feather dusters."

"You never know. We could be used as cleaners while things are quiet."

"At least we'd be able to get to the awkward to reach places in one of those."

"What about the holes?"

Andy looked closely at the armour and made out the dozens of dark apertures covering the body. "God knows. Ventilation?"

Zip shrugged and turned her attention to the third set of doors which clanked open, revealing a team of overall clad figures with clipboards. At their head was a lady, wearing white in contrast to the others who were all adorned in black. While the subordinates moved into the room and waited, she moved across to Master Sergeant Hardie at the booth.

"They look like a bunch of chuggers," Andy whispered. They bore the same hungry look of the annoying street accosters who would try and sign you up to the infinite number of 'charities'. It was unlikely that infuriating practice had survived the apocalypse and Andy chalked a point to the benefits of the end of the world.

"Well they're shit out of luck, I can't remember my bank account details," Zip replied.

"Account details? I can't even remember if I had a bank."

"You probably didn't. You strike me as the 'keep it under my mattress' type."

"I think I'm more the 'don't have enough money to worry about hiding it' type."

"That works too," Loco called out from down the bench. "You can't take wealth with you when you croak."

"They won't even let us croak," grumbled Andy, thinking of his dead family.

Seeing the look of grief, Mo reached across and clasped his shoulder. "You'll see them again. Once the war is over, one way or the other."

"Do I really want to be a clone dad to clone kids and a clone wife?"

"The choice will be yours, brother. I know what I'm going to do."

"Do you truly believe something better comes after? Even for forgeries of who we once were?"

"I still feel a soul burning within me," Mo declared confidently. "It could be we're parts of a whole and when we finally reach Heaven we become as one again. Have no doubt, brother, paradise will be waiting for us both."

"I hope so."

Hardie said a final word to the senior technician and then led her back to the soldiers. "Troops, this is Mia Ferdinand, the incredible mind behind the Mech program. She'll be taking it from here."

"Thank you, Master Sergeant," Mia said, stepping forward. "The process you're going to undertake today will be comprised of three tiers. Should these prove successful, you'll continue onto the next stages over the coming days. The first is a simple test to check your compatibility with the psy-ware we use which will allow you to pilot one of those." She pointed at the sentient machine.

"If you're unsuccessful, you'll be sent back to barracks. If, however, you manage to forge a neural link, then we move onto stage two. This involves creating a unique mental fingerprint which will allow you to sync yourself with any machine within seconds of boarding it. In the event of a concerted assault by the infected it could mean the difference between survival or being overrun. Stage three will see you use your newly forged connection to live fire the arm cannons in the test range. For obvious reasons it'll be armour piercing rounds only, not the heavy artillery of the adaptive grenades. Stage four will begin on day two. You'll mount an unarmoured exoskeleton of the Mechs to practice mobility drills. They're a lot more responsive than their size suggests, which can take a bit of getting used to. If you demonstrate a suitable level of proficiency, you'll be taken deep below this facility to face the final test."

Loco's hand shot in the air. "What's the final test?"

Mia looked at Hardie, then back to the soldiers. "An RTCS, which stands for Real Time Combat Scenario."

"We have to fight the infected?"

"Yes."

"Sounds like fun, count me in!"

"I appreciate your enthusiasm, but one step at a time," cautioned Mia with a smile. "Once that final test is complete, you'll be accepted into a Mech squad, should you so choose. If your strength lies elsewhere, however, you'll be kept on the reserve list and may be called upon from time to time. Any questions?"

"What're the holes for?" Zip had to know.

"They're a countermeasure for close contact in addition to the arm mounted blades. If you get a few of them on you, don't panic. The tubes house compressed air activated retractable steel spikes that'll impale any aggressor."

"Those little beauties will save your ass in a pinch," said a gruff male voice.

Hardie nodded at the man who emerged from the shadows of the bay door. "Squad, this crazy son of a bitch is Carson Bateman, the longest serving Mech operator. He's saved my team on more than one occasion and he'll do the same for you."

"If you'd stop getting yourself in trouble I wouldn't have to. I'm getting too old to babysit your ass." Carson's booming laughter echoed around the room.

"You could always retire," Hardie proposed.

"I'd eat a bullet and make them clone me before I'd retire," he retorted, striding up and down the line of seated recruits. "Good. We have some strong looking candidates here, and I'll be damned if I don't recognise some of you. Names aren't my strongest suit, so for the most part I'll be calling you by your assigned Mech number."

"Captain Bateman, would you have time to talk to the soldiers who make it through to stage three? I'm sure they'd be grateful for your input."

"Of course. I'm sure they'll be delighted to hear about the heat and claustrophobia."

"Thank you… Captain!" Mia said, dismissing him with a stern gaze. Turning back to the waiting soldiers, she continued, "You'll now be taken into the cerebral analysis suite. You'll all have a cracking headache by the end of this test, so your assigned mentor will give you a painkiller before you begin."

"Squad! Attention!"

Everyone leapt to their feet and obeyed. One by one the soldiers were claimed by a technician who led them after the enigmatic captain.

"Please, sit down," urged Tamsin, Andy's neural tech. Her bobbed, brown hair framed a plain but pretty 'girl next door' face. Her glasses magnified intense green eyes which flashed between the various consoles to the side of the small booth.

"What do you need me to do?"

"Nothing at the moment. I'm just uploading your DNA signature to the program. It'll give the best chance of synaptic association with the software."

"You make my brain sound like a computer."

"Brains *are* computers in a way, with electrical impulses, memory storage, complex problem solving, you get the gist."

"Can't computers get viruses though? What's to stop your software crashing my system?" Andy's mind returned to Paul's catatonic gaze in the mess.

"That's never happened… That I know of. But then again I've only worked here for a year."

"A year? Are you sure you know what you're doing?"

Fingers rattling away on the keyboard, Tamsin glanced at him. "I've only got another six months until I become accredited. As a trainee, they like to let us find our own way and overcome any mistakes."

"Mistakes?"

"Vomiting, involuntary explosive diarrhoea, ocular haemorrhaging, partial deafness, you know, the usual stuff."

Andy stared at her, aghast. Seeing the spreading grin turn up the corners of her lips, he felt like a fool. "You're joking?"

"Of course," she replied, rolling her eyes. "We train for years before they let us near a human subject. You're in safe hands."

"Glad to hear it."

With a final flourish of the keys, the console lit up with a bold 'Ready' across the screen. Picking up the bulky headgear, Tamsin checked the connections and wires. "This is going to feel strange, but don't fight it. The software will scan your brainwaves and attempt to synthesize the pattern. The program will adapt itself to your mind, mirroring the neurons that control your body and nervous system. It's this link that allows you to effectively achieve symbiosis with the Mech. If it's successful, you'll find yourself on a beach. On the sand will be a waiter holding a margarita. You need to walk over, take the drink, and say the following words; *I accept.* That will create the final link between you and the Mech mainframe. Any questions?"

"Will I be able to drink the cocktail?"

"Of course. It'll taste just as good as the real thing. Our systems are closely linked with the holographic entertainment suites located throughout the city."

Andy was about to ask about the entertainment, but Tamsin carefully dropped the helmet into place. The weight took him by surprise and he nearly dropped the expensive equipment when his head lolled forward.

"Sorry, I should've warned you," she explained, securing the chin strap.

"Don't worry, I won't mark you down on my customer feedback card."

"That's mighty gentlemanly of you, I appreciate it," she said with a wink. "I'm going to secure the goggles and ear cups now, so you won't be able to see or hear anything until it's finished. We find the attempted link goes much more smoothly if you lose those key senses. Ready?"

"I guess we're about to find out."

"That's the spirit!"

Dropping the eyepiece into place, the flexible cushion moulded to the exact contours of his forehead, cheekbones, and nose. The darkness was absolute. Moments later, his ears were sealed too, cutting Andy off from the world completely. Almost instantly, his other senses magnified tenfold. Sniffing, he could detect the faintest trace of body odour beginning to penetrate the standard issue deodorant Tamsin wore. The cup of synthetic coffee she had consumed an hour ago was as potent as if she wafted a steaming mug under his nose. Brushing his fingertips over the arm of his seat, the dimpled surface was like fine braille. Each distortion of the plastic spoke of the aged press in which it was formed.

A pulse of energy shot through his brain, causing him to flinch. "That hurt," he muttered, the voice sensed only as vibrations in his ear canal.

A dazzling light burst into being in his vision, but his eyes were firmly closed. The madly whirling, kaleidoscopic colours were inside Andy's own mind, projected on the receptors which governed sight. The patterns flowed without purpose, or so it seemed. Countless shades merged, then dispersed, finding other hues to meld with. Andy watched the show in silent awe. Slowly, the disparate pigments took on an orderly development. Patches of the scene firmed up and he could finally see the purpose. A small dune, a rolling wave, edges of the blazing sun, the lower legs of the waiter, gleaming white shoes sunken into the soft sand. Another pulse precipitated a complete firming of the beach.

"Did it work?" he asked, surveying the island paradise.

The waiter smiled and held out a silver tray, topped with the pale green drink.

Holding out a hand, Andy marvelled at the sensations. "I can feel the heat. I can smell the salt in the water. This is amazing."

The waiter continued to smile, unmoving.

Andy approached the statue like figure in his immaculate white suit. "I hope that tastes as good as it looks."

Taking hold of the glass, the chill of the ice spread through his fingers. The sour rim of lime and salt gave way to the sweet burn of tequila and orange liqueur. Groaning in ecstasy, Andy closed his eyes and swallowed. The alcohol left a trail of heat as it flowed down his throat.

"That's the best damned margarita I've ever tasted."

The unblinking waiter ignored the compliment.

"Oh, that's right. I accept."

The waiter's smile disappeared, and the untouched glass was back in place on the shiny tray. Andy frowned, staring at his now empty hand. Probing with his tongue he could still taste the salt crystals stuck to his lips.

"Thank you, Mr Burton. Network link established."

As if someone had flicked a switch, the whole scene blinked out, leaving darkness again. Tamsin raised the ear cups and the everyday world flooded back in; the low chirps of the equipment carrying out unknown processes, the muffled conversations of his fellow soldiers in the adjoining booths.

"That was the strangest experience of my life. It all felt so real!"

"To your mind it was real," she replied, removing the goggles and lifting off the weighty headgear.

"The taste is fading, but I'll be damned if I can't still feel the heat in my gut."

"For some, the sensations last a few minutes. For others, once the connection is broken everything goes back to normal immediately. The former are the ones who seem to be able to forge the strongest links with the psy-ware."

"You mentioned holographic entertainment a minute ago?"

"I did. It's one of the only reasons people can hold it together through this nightmare."

"Everyone can use it?"

"Absolutely. It's encouraged to prevent mental breaks in the population."

"But how's that possible? If some people can't connect with the Mech systems, how can they experience the holographic suites?"

"They're completely different things. Resistance to the neural link required for Mech control is quite normal because it's much more intrusive. You must willingly adopt the program, at which point it becomes a part of your mind. The entertainment is only electrical impulses, no different to the signals received while watching a show or listening to music."

"I think I understand."

"Good, now all I need to do is attach this electrode to your temple and we can create your unique access. Think of it like a password, but a lot more secure than typing one, two, three, four."

Sticking the pad to his skin, Tamsin entered another command into the console.

"What do I need to do?"

"Nothing. The machine is scanning your memories and uses them as a type of code."

"I hate to tell you this, but I don't remember much of the past."

"It doesn't matter, they're just hidden from you for the moment. They're inviolable, it's just a matter of time until they return."

"I'm not too sure I want them to return. I had a family once."

"So did I," she muttered, tapping the display screen with enough force to risk cracking it.

"I'm sorry, I should've known."

"I'm not angry with you. I'm angry with those fuckers out there in the galaxy somewhere for what they've done to us. I use the hatred like a fuel to keep me pushing on, even when I feel like giving up."

"Hatred's a powerful motivator."

"It's all we have left now. Hopefully, once the war's over, I can get my husband and son back. I know I'm not really me and they won't really be them, but I don't care. I just want to hold them again."

"I understand that feeling all too well. Do you mind if I ask a personal question?"

"Feel free. It's pointless to be coy in the apocalypse."

"How many times have you been cloned?"

"Once, one hundred and fourteen years ago."

Andy spluttered in surprise. "You only look about thirty."

"It's one of the *benefits* of our advanced technology," she sneered.

"You'd rather still be under too?"

"Totally. I don't understand the implications for our new selves in the sense of God, Heaven, The Afterlife, or whatever you want to call it. What if my previous soul is already with my family? Will I just cease to exist when I die? I don't mind saying it keeps me awake at night."

"I don't have an answer, sorry."

"No one does," she replied, sadly. Letters and numbers cascaded down the screen in a blur, culminating in a 'Login Active' appearing.

"Do you remember what you did… before all this?"

"I was a computer engineer working with a team of European scientists trying to create a viable artificial intelligence system. Before they tried to take over the world that is."

"Did you have any success?"

"We were close to a breakthrough, that much I remember. The biggest hurdle was ensuring the AI couldn't become self-aware and override the key operating parameters."

"I don't want cyborgs hunting me, that's for sure."

"I don't blame you. With careful coding, theoretically it should be possible to create a computer mind that could benefit us all."

"Why don't you approach the empress about it?"

"I've tried, but she says that waging a war on one front is hard enough. If the program should run amok the infected would be the least of our worries."

"That seems a bit short sighted."

"Perhaps it's for the best. No one knows if we'll stand a chance when our real enemy arrives. They may be so far advanced that it'll be no harder than exterminating an ant colony with boiling water. That's another thing that eats away at me, you know? Why bother when it's likely to be for nothing?"

"That's a troubling thought," Andy replied.

"It would be a great joke if the machines did take over and managed to wipe us all out, though, wouldn't it? They'd be in for a shock when they landed only to get their asses kicked by an angry computer."

Andy chuckled. "Now that's something I'd like to see."

"Can you keep a secret?"

"I'll probably be dead again soon anyway. Shoot."

"I've still been working on it in my spare time."

"The AI?"

"Yes."

"Is that wise?"

"My computer's completely separate from any other system. The worst that could happen if I succeed is that he, she, it, would type expletives on the screen at me."

"And if it works?"

Tamsin shrugged. "It could turn the tide in our favour."

"The empress would have to listen if that happened."

"Or she'd exile me for disobeying her."

"Maybe you should leave it alone then?"

"I've tried, but it's like an itch I can't scratch," she said with evident frustration. "I know how valuable this could be to us."

"In that case, good luck with it and try not to get us all killed," Andy said as she peeled away the electrode. "What do I need to do now?"

"Nothing for a moment. I need to record the results and present them to Ms Ferdinand. You can go and wait outside with your friends and I'll be right behind you."

"Thanks for the margarita."

"You're welcome. And Andy?"

Turning, he saw her worried expression. "What?"

"You won't tell anyone, will you?"

"My lips are sealed. Trust me."

"Thank you."

"Well that was a waste of time," huffed Zip. "How'd the rest of you get on?"

Roughly thirty percent of the squad affirmed their success. Andy nodded in agreement. "I'm officially Mech compliant."

"You saw the beach? All I got was a blur and a headache."

"It was amazing."

"Fuck my luck!"

"Don't sweat it, I've been told about the holo suites. When we get the opportunity, I'm taking you and we'll kick back on our own island. I'll even throw in a butler to serve you."

"I could get used to that," she sighed.

"It's all fake, but I'll be damned if it doesn't feel real at the time."

Master Sergeant Hardie marched into the room and conversed quietly with Mia. Seemingly satisfied with the results, he turned to the troops. "Excellent work, everyone. It's been a while since we've had that amount of connections. Those of you moving onto stage three, you're to remain here. For the rest, we're going back to barracks. Squad fall in!"

The disappointed soldiers rose to their feet and stood to attention. Marching from the room, the shutter closed in their wake. Feeling at a loss, Andy shuffled up next to Bob.

"That waiter was a bit of an odd one," said Bob.

"It wasn't a real waiter, he was part of the computer software."

"I don't like this world," Bob replied, ignoring the point.

"I don't blame you."

"Things made more sense in the army, I knew exactly what was expected of me. All this testing is doing my head in."

"You were army? I was SBS or so I'm told. It's still a blank to be honest."

"I was a Bootneck," he replied, still more to himself than Andy. The nickname for the Royal Marines derived from the strips of leather they would affix around their necks to prevent their throats being cut in combat.

"Glad to have you by my side," Andy said proudly. The commandos were among the finest fighting force in the world. "I hope I don't turn out to be a pen pusher cloned by mistake and they made up the special forces bullshit to make me feel better."

"You won't," Bob declared, finally meeting his gaze. "You carry yourself too well. You're too watchful and aware of the surroundings to be a desk jockey."

"Time will tell. Heads up."

Captain Bateman emerged from the office, hands clasped behind his back. Looking them over, he regarded them with pity.

"You poor bastards."

"Captain! You're not helping!" Mia said with exasperation.

"Honey, if I'd known what this outfit held in store for me, I'd have volunteered for the Shadow squads."

"I've told you before about calling me that! Keep this up and I'll put you on report."

"Ok, ok!" Bateman relented, holding up his hands in surrender. "No need to get your panties in a bunch."

"That does it!" Mia exploded. Striding away, she shot withering glances over her shoulder.

"Please excuse my colleague, she finds it hard to take my casual sexism in the humorous way intended."

"It was a bit rude... sir," said Loco, simmering with anger.

"I can't help being an asshole. I was an asshole when I first died, and I'm still an asshole. The only reason I've not been kicked out of the Sovereign Guard is because I can kill the infected so well."

"I think an apology's in order." Loco's cheeks were flushing, and the others could see where she may have got the nickname, and not from any locomotive appreciation. The rules about insubordination hadn't been explained yet but judging by her demeanour a few days in a cell wouldn't be a problem.

"I'll make it up to her later, soldier. For the time being I'm going to watch how you do on the range. Is everything in order?"

The technicians looked uncertain without their superior present. "Erm, I think so." Tamsin responded when no one else would.

"Good! Let's get to it then!"

Standing up, the troops made to form up.

"Forget that drills crap!" Captain Bateman barked as he marched away. "I don't give a stuff if you can march in a straight line; it's so insulting to treat you like raw recruits. Jesus Christ, you're all decorated combat veterans."

Unsure of what to do, Bob turned to Andy. "I guess we're meant to follow?"

"It looks like it."

"I don't think military discipline is one of the captain's strong points."

"Not by the looks of it."

"I like him!" Bob declared with a firm nod.

The previously cramped confines of the holding rooms gave way to the first evidence of the vastness of the facility which could be seen from outside. After the roller door to their rear had sealed itself, the captain guided them past four huge openings in the wall. A set of steps in each led up to a command chair. Mounted to the right of the seat was a fully functional Mech arm which the trainee would be able to control. In place of being mounted on the back of the machine which wasn't there, the huge boxes of ammunition were lined up in a row beneath the steel platform. Hanging from a hook suspended from the ceiling was a smaller, but familiar, set of headgear.

"This way! We need to go through some safety videos first," grumbled Bateman, then muttered under his breath, "Pussies."

Yet another massive steel shutter came into view as they turned a corner and Bob saw the biohazard sign painted on it. "Is that where the infected are, sir?"

"Hell, no. That's just another warning notice about what's lurking in this facility. The creatures are a mile underground and kept in place by two more sets of countermeasures. I don't think I need to explain the mayhem that a single one of those bastards could wreak on our city if they ever got out."

Andy looked at the red paint and a thought came to him. "If I may, sir? How on earth do you collect new infected when the others get killed during the RTCSs?"

"It's a nest, son."

"A nest?"

"Yes. A self-replenishing den of vileness which prevents the need for further incursions to pick up new… material. The cost of securing the host was enormous, but ultimately worth it," he explained, a dark shadow passing over his face. "It's saved far more lives than it cost."

"Are there more nests?"

"More than we can count; it's why this war goes on and on."

Ushering them into a side room, the soldiers seated themselves facing the display.

"Run live fire training safety protocols," said the captain.

For eighteen long minutes the information rolled. Clearing jams, pausing to flush the arm with carbon dioxide to keep it cool enough to maintain steady fire rates, the feeding systems and how to reload in the middle of combat, grenade belt isolation in the event of a breach to prevent a catastrophic discharge in the tube. By the time the credits rolled the captain was yawning with boredom. He'd lost count at eleven thousand four hundred and eighty-two viewings, and that was many years ago. The soldiers were fully engaged with the presentation, which considering their lives may depend on the information, was not unexpected.

Bateman could see some good material among the recruits and allowed himself to hope that at some stage a tipping point may be reached in the mutant war. The Vanquishers were destroying the hives at an increasing rate, but as each was scoured from the planet two more would spring up like aggressive weeds in their place. Even more worrying was the growing number of beasts among the infected who posed far more of a danger than the human variety.

Suppressing a shudder, he said, "End live fire training safety protocols. Any questions?"

"Sir, are these briefings available to view outside of this training facility?"

"You can access them from the main Divinity database. I'd advise committing them to memory if you have any designs on becoming a Mech operator. Even if you only become a reservist I'd suggest it's beneficial, they could save your ass. Any other questions?"

"Can you tell us what it's like being a Mech commander?" Andy asked.

"The responsibility is huge. Not wall patrol, obviously, but getting the call to mount up for a rescue. I've got massive respect for the foot soldiers who brave the wastes outside the walls. When the clamps release and you're dropping towards the fight, you know that you're the only thing standing between them and a fate worse than death. Either they face getting eaten… or changed."

"Is it worth it?"

"Holding back the vermin long enough to facilitate an extraction is one of the greatest feelings in the world."

Bob frowned and asked the question many of them had been wondering since being spawned. "What does it matter when they can just grow another one of us? Surely it's a waste of time and resources."

Bateman had faced the same question at nearly every preliminary training session. "We're a victim of our own success, so to speak. Have the medics explained the process, how your improved DNA is taken and used to make you faster, stronger, more capable fighters?"

"Yeah."

"Good, that makes it easier to answer. Our advances in the field of genetics are also allowing the infected to become faster, stronger, more capable killers. We require vast amounts of power and a very complex blend of material to provide you with the growth fluids. All the bastards out there need is one of their hosts. As the stronger versions of yourselves fall in battle, the infected can somehow absorb your new gene sequence which allows stronger mutants to be spawned. The Genesis Initiative have been trying to fathom how they can stop the transfer of this material but have so far drawn a blank."

"Marvellous," Andy spat sardonically. "It's a never-ending cycle, like the arms races of old. We get a step ahead, they kill us and catch up, rinse, and repeat."

The captain shrugged. "Pretty much. What would you suggest we do, give up?"

"Sorry, sir, it's been a rough couple of days. I'd never give up, no matter the odds."

"I understand how you're feeling. Sometimes, in the darkest hours, I question the purpose too. But then I think about the shock our interstellar visitors will get when they arrive, only to find we've helped to breed a planet of bloodthirsty super mutants. Even if they prevail over us I'd pay money to see the look on their tentacled faces when the infected start to eat them."

Bob cocked his head. "They have tentacles on their faces?"

"Fuck knows, I'm just guessing. They could have a set of testicles hanging from their chins for all I know."

Bob nodded as the other troops chuckled. "It'd make a fight that much easier. A quick uppercut and they'd be rolling on the floor puking their guts up."

"I think an advanced race like that may have formulated some kind of chin bollock protector, but you never know."

"I hope they haven't. I'd like to crush a few of their nuts."

"Bob, they may not have a ballbag chin," Andy cautioned.

Bateman wrinkled his face in exasperation at the bizarre tangent the conversation had taken. "Anyway, let's get to the good bit. You'll be taking part in groups of four for obvious reasons. The rest of you can sit in here and wait while we run a few test firings."

Pointing to his choice of soldiers, they all stood up and followed. Turning back to the others, the captain had a thought. "I wouldn't recommend it, but if you're masochists, you can pull up my archived feeds from the onboard Mech cam. I think it's only fair for you to know what happens when the shit hits the fan out there. I'd suggest January 6th of last year; Quadrant PR-18. Be warned, it's brutal viewing."

And with that he was gone from the training room. Andy looked at the others for confirmation of what he was about to do. Aside from a couple of nervous glances, no one argued.

"Go for it," Bob said.

"Erm, computer, are you there?"

The synthesized female voice responded instantly. "Yes, Andrew."

"Can you run the archived video from Captain Bateman, January 6th, 2181; Quadrant PR-18?"

"Yes, Andrew."

The Divinity emblem disappeared, and the footage began.

CHAPTER THIRTEEN

January 6th, 2181.
Quadrant PR-18
Formerly known as - Brick, New Jersey.

Breathing slowly, Bateman studied the desolate environment five hundred feet below. The feelings of vertigo were a thing of the distant past, but he could still recall the paralysing dread that used to accompany the dead drops. His mouth would dry, and the world would start to spin uncontrollably. Only by mastering a form of meditative breathing did he maintain his place on the Mech squads.

That was a long, long time ago, he mused as the barren wasteland passed in a blur. Aspects of the old civilisation were still evident; roads, crumbling bridges, solitary homes long fallen into decay. In general, the outlying emptiness around the abandoned towns and cities was safe for the foot soldiers. An aberrant infected who lacked some key part of the hive mentality would occasionally wander into the wilderness. They made easy pickings for the covert operators who searched for the encroachment of new nests on the outposts. Once captured, they were sequestered in one of the Genesis Initiatives many laboratories at sea for further study. Not that it ever seemed to help their cause.

A voice crackled to life from the cockpit speakers of his machine.

"Captain, we've had an update from Alpha team. They're locked down in an old hotel north east of the nest. Scans indicate the attempts to seal the burrow during the retreat were unsuccessful."

"Shit! How many infected?"

"Two thousand and climbing."

"Any beasts?"

"No, sir."

"Well thank God for small mercies. ETA?"

"Three minutes."

"Good," Bateman growled.

The closer they got to the action, the greater the rush of adrenaline became. Some operators shunned the chemical stimulation in favour of cool heads and self-control. He wasn't one of them, opting instead to head for the thick of battle irrespective of the possible dangers. Once the fury had been let loose, only the receding fires of a well fought battle could dampen it. Every sense became enhanced; he could hear the slightest change in the Magjet's propulsion, the smell of the hydraulic fluid in his suit which an engineer had forgotten to wipe away during the last maintenance service.

Glancing around the full panoramic onboard display, Bateman could see the five other Mechs hanging from the suspension clamps of the jets. Pride swelled in his chest at the immense bravery of the men and women within the machines.

"Incoming!"

The yell of the pilot caused Bateman to flinch. Spewing from a wide mouth in the side of a hill were a flock of horrifically mutated crows. Screeching like banshees, they poured forth and took flight. The featherless bodies were coated with razor sharp spines, while thick veins pulsed in the translucent, membranous wings. Although twenty times the size of their pre-mutation ancestors, they posed no real threat to the Mechs. The danger lay in their capability to bring down a Magjet, either through suicidal dives into the chassis and engines, or overwhelming them with sheer numbers.

"Prepare for evasive manoeuvres!"

"Scratch that, Lieutenant. You can't do shit while we're dragging you down. Drop us here and get back behind the perimeter defences."

"But, sir, you'll be miles from base with no chance of air extraction. It'll be over an hour before we could get a Paladin tank division to reach you!"

"We can hold them back for an hour! Now do it!"

"Aye, sir. Releasing in three, two, one, go!"

The clamps detached from the arms and gravity started to exert itself on the considerable weight of the Mechs. Thundering towards the ground, the onboard computers calculated the optimum time for the landing gears to fire. Bracing themselves, the legs on each unit ignited the landing rockets, briefly banishing the gloom of nightfall and illuminating the swarming birds. With their descent markedly slowed, the machines dropped the last twenty feet and slammed into the ground, the powerful hydraulics absorbing the impact. Bateman spun around and watched as the six crafts banked hard to port and hammered the throttles. Over a hundred and fifty crows were in close pursuit, half of which were powering upwards on hidden thermals to reach a suitable altitude to suicide themselves in a dive.

"Squad, cover our pilots as best you can with your cannons! Deacon, launch Spitfires to slow the fuckers down and buy our guys some time!"

"Aye, sir!"

Deacon's shoulder pods twisted on the mounts and rose to angle directly at the rising flock of squalling hellishness. Two of the eight tubes on each side of his hulking suit blazed orange as the missiles erupted. Streaking up into the darkened sky, the projectiles neared the birds and split apart, revealing twenty smaller rockets. Onboard guidance systems instantly picked an individual target and recommenced the pursuit.

Though mindless in their destructive nature, the doomed creatures had learned enough to peel away from their companions to minimise their overall losses.

"Clever bastards," Bateman muttered to himself in disgust.

Screeches of almost human rage burst from the huge, serrated beaks of the crows as they were hit. The rapid explosions carried through the night, startling the others for a split second. Taking advantage of the disarray, the six operators opened up on the pursuing throng. Barrels spat streams of high explosive bullets into the beasts, blowing huge craters in their bodies and shredding the wings. Seeing the indiscriminate destruction of their fellow birds, the remainder of the flock adjusted course to position the aircraft in the firing line.

"Ceasefire! At this angle, we'll end up hitting our guys."

Torrents of blood and sundered flesh rained to earth across the horizon, but it wasn't enough. Any hopes the operators had about their success was swiftly cut off as the two trailing Magjets were set upon. The awful sounds of shattering mutant bodies and the rending of nanofiber shells reached them across the arid plains.

"Sir, shall I launch more Spitfires?"

Bateman considered the option for a split second until the screams of the pilots confirmed the futility. "They're inside! Oh God, please help…" The transmission ended with a gargled scream of agony. Losing control, the jets faltered and dropped like stones. The whine of the stricken machines grew in intensity until abruptly ending with a huge explosion upon impact. Lacking fuel, the engineers had installed plasma bombs that would only detonate with the absence of onboard human life-signs. Not only did it ensure the destruction of the attacker, but it prevented the pilots from turning.

"It's done," Bateman sighed.

"Four got clear, sir."

"Aye, that's something."

"We'll pay the bastards back!"

"Squad, form up! We're a mile and a half from target so get ready for a run."

Through the psy-ware, the operators ordered the machines to switch to maximum responsiveness. Pistons shortened, preparing to increase the length and power of each stride. Forming an arrowhead behind the captain, the six hulks stood ready.

"Move out!"

Taking a step, the feet sunk into the hard-packed dirt before launching them forward. By the eighth pace, the Mechs were bounding along at full tilt, leaving a cloud of dust in their wake.

"Captain, where are you?" Begged one of the besieged troops over the radio between gunfire. "We can't hold out much longer!"

"Hold tight, soldier. We're coming!"

Reaching the city limits, Bateman ordered the team to slow. The overhead gantries of the motorway sign had long since collapsed with only the upright support columns left. Crumpled metal, imprinted with the barely discernible city name rested on the cracked tarmac. On the exit road, thousands of cars lay abandoned. Even after over a hundred years, the undisturbed vehicles still bore the damage of the marauding infected. Doors torn from their hinges, roofs gouged by claws wielded with inhuman ferocity and more bones than anyone could ever count. They all winced with each crunch as femurs, ribcages, and skulls were crushed in their passage.

"We're thirty seconds away, Lieutenant. Status?"

"We're on the fifth floor, completely surrounded and holding. We've managed to secure the staircase and lift shaft. They're attempting to breach by climbing the walls, but so far we've been able to pick them off."

"Good work, Lieutenant. Has the flow of infected slowed at all?"

"No, sir. They're using the Parkway entrance of the old subway system. We set a charge in the tunnel but were pushed back before the detonator could be connected. Sorry, sir."

"No need for apologies, Lieutenant. I'm going to need you to hold out for a few more minutes while we circle around and seal that passage. Make as much noise as possible to mask our approach. By the time they double back to another station we'll be well out of the city."

"Understood, sir. We'll give 'em hell."

The towering skyscrapers glowered down on them; the broken windows like a thousand watchful eyes. Sections of the structures had crumbled, revealing the open rooms of long dead occupants. Only the absence of normal rainwater cycles had prevented the whole world from being reclaimed by nature. The consensus on nuclear winter had been wildly inaccurate and even after more than a century the skies remained dark. Sporadic downpours could fall so heavily it was impossible to see five feet in front of your face, while at other times the area could go for years without a single drop of moisture.

"Squad, we're heading to the Parkway Station. Switch navigation to new target using Pearce Street to approach from the north east."

They acknowledged the order and amended their display maps to skirt the fighting. Flashes of gunfire lit up the opposing buildings half a mile away, but they were on their own for now. Maintaining high responsiveness, the Mech team turned left and forged through the three lanes of vehicles. Using the incredibly powerful arms, the degraded shells were tossed aside, crashing down onto the roofs of the other cars. Leaping over the drainage culvert, the team picked up the pace.

"Once we hit the side roads, switch to standard combat responsiveness. We don't know if those fuckers will be lying in wait."

The clamour of reinforced Jajovium alloy striking the concrete reverberated from the buildings that they passed. Once a bustling parade of outlet clothing shops on the outskirts of the city, the untouched, mouldering garments of the stores hung in tatters from the eerie looking mannequins lurking in the shadows. It never failed to give Bateman the willies.

Diverting through the carpark, they crashed through a row of pathetic looking trees. Stunted and twisted, the beleaguered foliage had adapted as best it could to the new world.

"ETA to target one minute. Tish, arm one of your Doombringers."

"Aye, sir!"

"When we get within sight, fire at will. I'm not going to get us bogged down in a standing fight until we reach the hotel."

"Copy."

Their night vision displays illuminated the deserted road as they slowed to a walk. Watchful of the surrounding buildings, the team knew the mutants had been evolving ever since the first shrieking, gibbering monster had torn free of its hospital bed all those years ago. Ambushes were a new tactic they had developed; replacing the uncontrollable rages with a level of deviousness previously unknown. As they neared the crossroads, the din of screaming mutants became deafening. Leaving cover, the five Mechs lined up behind Tish. The pod adjusted for the shell's trajectory and she leaned forward to counter the impending recoil.

"Firing!"

The shoulder mounted artillery roared, shattering every unbroken window in a hundred-meter radius from the concussive wave. Arcing high, the shell whined as it peaked and commenced dropping towards the target. Impacting just short of the tunnel, which still expelled a stream of infected, it penetrated to a depth of two hundred feet before detonation. Adding the unexploded charge to its power; fire, earth, and scorched flesh erupted into the air like a volcano. As hunks of rocky debris rained down, the blast subsided, leaving a smouldering, sunken crater where the entrance once stood. Dazed by the explosion, the surviving mutants stood up and shrieked their fury.

Bateman raised his cannon. "Cut them down!"

The other operators lined up their own weapons and started firing. Heavy chattering broke the lull after the artillery strike and rows of creatures fell into quivering heaps of torn meat.

"What the fuck are they doing?" Tish called over coms.

Instead of attacking, those able to escape were turning away and heading towards the hotel battle. In under five seconds the street was empty except for the Mechs and the fires raging within the crater.

"Squad, prepare to pursue!" Bateman ordered, then paused. "No… wait."

Masked by the tremors of subsidence in the subway below was another source of vibration carrying through the ground. The dull rhythm was well known to each of them. As one, their heartrates skyrocketed, and the fear twisted in the pit of their guts.

"They've got a beast!" Bateman yelled. "And by the sounds of it, more than one. Move to the centre of the street and form a perimeter!"

The low rumble increased as whatever was charging for them got closer. Creating a circle, the breathless pilots stared around for any signs of their quarry. Clods of earth started to dance on the shivering road and they could finally make out the heavy thuds of the stampeding creatures. Tumultuous sounds of crashing and smashing echoed down the forsaken street.

"Prepare yourselves!"

Like a switch had been flipped, the tremors of movement and wanton destruction came to an abrupt halt. The silence which took its place was far more unnerving.

"Did anyone get a bead on their approach?" Bateman asked, staring at the shadows for signs of covert activity.

"No, sir."

"Does anyone have anything on their scanner?"

"Only the infected scrambling in the tunnels below. How is that possible?"

"Christ knows. It seems our friends have managed to mutate in a way that throws our sensors off."

Seconds ticked away, with only the distant sounds of battle disturbing the still night. Bateman knew that whatever was lurking in the darkness was either trying to delay the rescue of the soldiers or wanted to attack when they were least prepared. Time was not on their side.

"Fuck this! Everyone, switch to cluster munitions. Light up the buildings and alleyways. We'll flush these bastards out."

Issuing a single thought, the onboard systems adapted the grenades to separate on impact to spread the kill zone. It weakened the overall blast but, depending on their foe, a simple explosion could often just antagonise the creature rather than kill it.

"Fire at will!"

The circle of Mechs began belching the shells through windows and down windswept roads. Dull crumps ejected the miniature explosives. Spreading out, the tiny balls rattled and bounced from every surface before detonation. Night became day as fire roared out from the frontages of derelict buildings before climbing into the sky. The din of shattered masonry was joined by howls of insane fury.

"Wolves!"

Bursting from the conflagration, three massive predators emerged. Their coarse, nigh on impenetrable fur was ablaze, lending them an even greater look of hellish intent. Maintaining the same canine cunning of their forebears, they hunted in packs. The inherited trait was as far as the similarity went. Their huge paws sprouted claws a foot long, powered by lupine legs and bodies which weighed many tonnes. The weight had done nothing to lessen their speed and ferocity. Leaping as one, the operators only had time for a short burst of fire before the monsters were on them.

Like bowling pins, the six Mechs were scattered by the force of the impact. Slamming into the ground, the three-foot-long muzzles bit down on the gun arms, tearing and worrying at the metal.

Bateman cursed their luck and looked at his dazed troops. "On your feet! Now!"

"They've got me! Aaargghh, my arm!" screamed Deacon who had gained the attention of the creatures. Working as a pair, one of the beasts had him pinned face down while the other chewed above the elbow joint. Teeth so sharp they could penetrate even the thickest armour destroyed the hydraulics and crushed the feeding belts in seconds, disarming the stricken soldier. Clamping down again, the fangs met, severing the lower part of Deacon's arm which was within the upper section of the metallic limb.

Tish and Clay had regained their footing, but the third wolf charged through before they could bring weapons to bear. Cursing in frustration, the duo tried to lash out with clenched fists. Missing by a wide margin from the agile beast, they tried to fire from a grounded position. Dodging effortlessly out of the way of the bullets, the feral eyes of the creature watched the flailing machines without attacking.

"Captain, help me!" sobbed Deacon. Seized on each foot by a slavering mouth, the mutants tensed their haunches and started to drag him away towards a side street. Their blackened hides steamed and smoked from singed fur and flesh.

Bateman tried to stand and was thwarted again by the crushing weight of the lookout. "Fuck! Do your landing thrusters have any fuel left?"

"I... I think so."

"Then use it!"

Twin yelps of agony pierced the night as the rockets ignited for a couple of brief seconds. Pawing at their muzzles to try and banish the pain, the searing fire had scorched their mouths and throat. Howling in rage, the uninjured sentry leaped across the distance and swiped at Deacon's chest plate. The talon-like claws clanged from the impact, once, twice, three times in a fraction of a second. Deep furrows were scored into the armour with each rapid strike. On the fourth, they pierced the protective shell and sunk as deeply as the phalanges would allow. Impaled through the heart and lungs, Deacon coughed once; a wet, rattling, awful sound, then died.

"Bastards!"

Finally, free of their tormentors, the five living operators stood up and opened fire on the retreating monsters. Missing completely, the bullets traced a pattern across the weakened brick and concrete. A fierce howl cut through the night, promising retribution from the gloom.

"Are they done?" asked Tish.

"Not by a long shot," replied Clay.

"I can't believe that Deacon's dead," whispered Tish, trying to keep a tight rein on her emotions.

"It's what we signed up for," Bateman growled. "System override, code two, two, eight, four, three. Proceed with interior cleanse on Mech designation B eighteen."

White hot flames burst from the punctures on the chest and arm as the soldier's body was incinerated within.

"Squad, damage report."

"My grenade launcher is shot, but the bullet belt is still functional," said Tish.

"I've sustained damage to my tracking system and display," explained Clay.

"Can you still see through the visor?"

"Aye, sir."

It wasn't ideal by any stretch of the imagination. The field of vision awarded by the clear polymer was only around fifty degrees in a forward direction.

"Ok, assume cross formation. Clay get in the middle, so we can cover your blind spots."

"Understood."

"Tish and Paddy, you're on rear-guard."

"We've got no time to waste so we're going straight through the ground floor of McKenzies. It'll take us out onto Fraser Street which runs parallel with the road the hotel's located on."

Crouching slightly to miss the concrete slab of the upper floor, the team crashed through the revolving glass doors of the foyer. As with much of the construction of the time, the partition walls were thin plasterboard which had already undergone heavy degradation. The aluminium supports snapped and twanged as they pushed on through offices and meetings rooms, knocking ancient computers and crumbling furniture aside.

"Sir, I think I saw something," muttered Tish, scanning the debris behind them.

"They've recovered quicker than I'd hoped, we don't have any time to waste."

"Sir, how can we extract the Vanquishers if we're being stalked? They could pick them off one by one as we pull out of the city."

"We'll cross that bridge when we come to it. Our priority is to drive the infected back long enough to exfil the hotel."

"That's a great idea! Why don't we use the Langston suspension bridge? It'd mean they have to funnel to pursue us?"

"Circling north via the bridge would add three miles to the journey," Bateman pondered.

"I just thought I'd suggest it, sir. It'd probably make the retreat more dangerous."

"No, I like it. If we can't shake the wolves, at least we can get clear and destroy it. The water is just as dangerous for them as it is us," Bateman agreed. "Command, can you read me?"

"Loud and clear, Captain."

"I'm sending you new coordinates for the Paladins," he replied, psy-linking with the navigation system to amend the route of the tanks.

"Received. ETA to rendezvous now thirty-eight minutes."

"Understood. Bateman, out."

Pushing through a set of exit doors at the rear of the building, the lintel and surrounding blockwork was blown out onto the street. The commotion of shrieking mutants and hollow booms of displacement grenades became more intense as the Mechs stepped out from the rubble strewn building.

"We move to the next junction and turn left. We can unload on the crowd from the street corner. With any luck they'll attack in force and we can thin them out with some well-placed cluster shot."

Paddy turned from the gaping hole to survey the eastern section of road. Panes of glass fell from above, shattering at their feet. Before Tish could shout a warning, one of the burned wolves pounced from the shattered second floor, landing amongst the team. Snapping out, its muzzle locked on to Paddy's arm. With a flick of its powerful neck, Paddy's hulking machine was tossed back into the ruins. Like lightning, the creature leapt after him and was gone from sight.

"Paddy! Hold on, we're coming for you!"

"Like hell you are!" came his grunted reply over comms. The sounds of tearing metal accompanied the transmission. "Eat this, you mother fucker!"

Large calibre gunfire echoed within the building, followed by a yelp of pain.

"We can help you, Paddy!"

"No! Get our boys and girls out of here!" he ordered, snarling in pain as the armour started to give way. "Captain, requesting permission for Tish to level the building?"

Bateman could think of no alternative which wouldn't jeopardize the mission in its entirety. Reluctantly, he replied. "Granted. Team pull back to minimum safe distance."

Taking advantage of the distraction brought by their compatriot, the Mechs ran as fast as they were able in combat readiness. Tish crushed her raging emotions into a tight ball and turned back to the skyscraper. The sundered entrance still lit up with the muzzle flashes, but Paddy had gone radio silent to spare his crew the cries of agony.

"God be with you, brother," whispered Tish. "Firing."

The wide avenue flashed as the remaining artillery shell belched from the second shoulder pod. Punching through the wall, it took a second for the ammunition to reach the correct depth. Every wall and window up to the eighth floor exploded, covering the street in twinkling shards and broken masonry. Listing to the left, the weakened steel frame could no longer take the weight of the twenty remaining levels. Starting slowly, the roar of disintegration became deafening as the structure collapsed in on itself. A cloud of dust washed over them, completely obscuring their vision.

"Switch to laser scanners."

The internal displays superimposed the readings from the sensors, highlighting the linear outlines of the other buildings and vehicles through the concealing shroud.

"Captain, come in? Are you still there?"

"We're here, Lieutenant," Bateman sighed, leading his battered team to the corner.

"We saw the collapse and thought the worst," replied the soldier. "What happened?"

"We can talk once we're all home. Until then take cover because we're about to unleash hell."

"Roger. Happy hunting."

The swirling dust storm had not yet abated, but the probing lights picked out the swarming infected in the distance.

"Tish and Clay, you're on the walls. Take any out that are nearing the fifth floor, but make sure to disarm your explosive tips. I don't want any fires trapping them inside after all we've been through. Gabe, you're with me. We pick them off from the sides until they attack in force and then lay a stream of cluster grenades to chew them up."

"Understood," came the replies.

Most of the creatures had ceased their attempts to reach the trapped soldiers after sensing the deaths of their beasts. Milling around in confusion, they were caught completely by surprise as the gritty mist expelled a barrage of bullets into their ranks. The walls were quickly scoured of the taint of the infected, the bloody smears dripping from the pocked stonework. Leaning their heads back, the mutants shrieked into the air and then surged towards the threat like a tsunami.

"That's it, come on," snarled Bateman at the rapidly approaching horde. "On my mark… fire!"

Metal retaining clips chimed as they hit the tarmac from the grenade launchers. Bouncing at the head of the column, the casings blew apart and spat the smaller bomblets throughout the crowd. It was a slaughter. Hundreds upon hundreds of smaller detonations blanketed the packed creatures in fire and shrapnel. Two thousand quickly became two hundred as the torn and shattered bodies of their kin collapsed and bled out on the street. Gore coated every inch of the surrounding buildings, with unidentifiable hunks of flesh splashing wetly back to the earth. Breaching the safe effective range of the heavy artillery, another hundred and eighty fell to the torrent of bullets. The remaining abominations leaped upon the Mechs, climbing and screeching in hunger for the flesh inside. Lacking the destructive tools of their beasts, they clawed ineffectually at the armour.

"Crush them all!"

In no hurry they removed the clambering monsters from each other, holding them aloft and squeezing. The weak flesh ruptured under the incredible pressures of the Mechanical hands, innards and blood spraying over their black suits. The catharsis as each body popped under the compression was short lived when compared to their losses.

"Captain, we've cleared the infected from the staircases and lifts. Awaiting orders."

"The streets should be clear, Lieutenant," Bateman replied,

discarding the last mutant. "Wait for us in the main reception while we confirm."

"Roger."

Stepping through the quagmire of quivering meat, the Mechs shot any survivor point blank. Given time, they would regenerate and be just as dangerous.

"Sir, it's damned good to see you!" said the lieutenant as he emerged with his squad.

"No time for celebration just yet, we're heading for the Langston Bridge. It's further, but far easier to defend without worrying about our flanks. The Paladins will be waiting on the other side."

"Understood."

"Tish, Clay, you're on point. Gabe and I will follow to the rear. Lieutenant, form up in the middle; keep your team tight and central in the roads until we clear the city limits. We don't know if they have any other surprises in store and I'll be damned if we lose any more people today."

"It's my fault, Captain," exclaimed a shame faced young woman.

"And you are?"

"Corporal Jess Slater, Shadow team."

"How's this your fault then, Corporal?"

"I was scouting the area and followed a group of infected back into the tunnels. It looked to be a fledgling nest with minimal numbers, so I called in a platoon of V-class operators to destroy it before it became a danger to the facility."

"What happened?"

"I don't understand it, but it was a fake. Lieutenant Groves and his team were in the process of clearing them out when the real nest revealed itself. A hundred became thousands in a couple of minutes."

"It's not your fault," Groves replied earnestly. "They've never done anything like that before."

"You lost eight of your team trying to cover our retreat. That's on me."

"Corporal, you did your job as you've been trained to do, as did the lieutenant. The only ones to blame are the mutants, and even they're innocent in the big scheme of things. They're a product of our betrayers in the stars."

"I appreciate the sentiment, sir," she said. Her tone left no doubt she still felt the weight of responsibility and nothing would alter it.

Bateman's headset lit up with a new transmission. "Captain, are you receiving?"

"Receiving, command. Go ahead," Bateman replied.

"Scans show the infected have found an exit and are hot on your heels. They'll be on you in fifteen. The Paladins are in position to extract the ground troops."

"Thanks for the heads up. We should be at the bridge in under twelve minutes at our current pace."

"Good work, Captain. Command, out."

Through the gaps in the towering buildings, the dilapidated bridge came into view. Several of the tension cables had snapped, leaving the structure sagging slightly.

Bateman scowled in his suit, considering the safest way to cross. "Lieutenant, you'll take your team across while we hold back. We'll then follow in pairs to spread the weight. I'm sure it'll hold, but I don't want to tempt fate with the luck we've all had today."

"We'll help to cover you from the other side, sir."

"Very good."

The road widened to an eight-lane carriageway, splitting to the left and right. The left lane twisted towards the upper level of the bridge, while the road to the right spiralled downwards towards the lower section.

"Squad, halt. I don't like this."

"What's the matter, sir?"

"Too many places to hide in the lower level. I wouldn't put it past the bastards to lay another trap for us."

"Sir, if you'll allow me, I can scout below while the team crosses above," asked Slater.

"You could get trapped under there."

"I understand, but I'd like to do it regardless, sir."

"As you wish. Lieutenant, prepare your team to move out the second Slater confirms if the way's clear."

"Yes, sir."

The column of soldiers and machines moved on as Slater disappeared around the bend in the road. Toll booths lay dormant, the road covered in loose change that had started to settle into the softening road surface. The welcome beacons of the tank division blazed into view on the opposite side of the black river.

"Sir, this is Lieutenant Adenfield. We're in position. I hear you've got a shitstorm coming?"

"Only a few thousand psychotic cannibals that want to tear us limb from limb, nothing we can't handle."

"Just say the word and we'll level the city for you. We don't want you Mech operators having all the fun, do we?"

"Once we're across the bridge you can take out as many as you want. Until then I want you to hold fire, the bridge looks like she's ready to collapse as it is. A few of your eight-inch shells could cause enough vibration to bring the whole thing down."

Losing the levity, the tank commander was serious in an instant. "Understood, sir. We've got your back."

"Sir, this is Slater. There's nothing hiding below but ghosts."

"Good work, Corporal. V squad, move out! Mechs, form up on the approach, Clay to the centre."

Grateful to hear the receding sounds of synchronous footfalls, the Mech operators moved into guard position. Watching the dead city, they were all filled with a yearning for better times. When they would drive into the bustling urban streets with their families for trips to the museums or variety of restaurants. Navigating the manic pavements as people went about their lives, oblivious to those around them. The only life now lurking within the ancient mazes of human habitation was not really life at all, just a blasphemy of their previous form. When the shrieks of the infected faded away to nothing, it was replaced by the mournful wails of wind blowing through the desolate vestiges of civilization.

"Sir, we're clear. We're covering the approaches."

"Good. Tish and Clay, get your asses across. Any signs of structural instability and you come straight back; we'll just move south and take our previous route back to base."

"Aye, sir."

The two Mechs peeled away and started to navigate the damaged structure. The added weight of their suits caused the ancient tensile cables to groan in protest. Pausing for a few moments, they watched carefully for any signs of distress on the road or upright columns.

"I think it'll be ok, sir," Clay confirmed.

Bateman wished them good luck and continued to watch the streets. From his angle he could only see down Main and a portion of Connor Avenue, the rest were obscured. He could hear the growing roar of thousands of the infected bouncing from the high walls. Switching to rear view, he breathed a sigh of relief when the two Mechs reached the safety of solid ground and moved with the Vanquishers to cover their retreat.

"You're clear to proceed, Gabe. Get moving."

"What about you, sir?"

"I'll be right behind you. Move!"

The previously still roads were teeming with the infected who were sprinting at an incredible speed. Sighting the nearest threat a mile away, he fired three bursts, left to right and back again, cutting through the creatures like a scythe. Tearing through their dead, the swarm pushed on towards their target.

"Whoa! Sir, be careful when you follow, the bridge is moving more now."

Turning, Bateman looked up at the massive cables which were swaying slightly. The pings of straining metal were accompanied by a loud crack of rupturing concrete. Ignoring the horde, he moved to the edge of the bank and looked out across the murk. Hissing in horror, Bateman could scarcely believe the sight before him. The third wolf was madly clambering from beneath the bridge where it had been lying in wait, concealed by the noxious mist.

"Gabe, move!"

Claws digging into the column, it hoisted itself into the darkness of the lower level. Gabe could hear the guttural panting coming from below and switched to high responsiveness. Starting to run, each crashing impact caused the snakelike wires to rock, with some finally snapping from the stress. Cars were kicked aside in his panic, but each blockage slowed his progress by a fraction of a second until the mutant had passed him. Using all its strength, the monster jumped at a section of broken road, smashing upwards and blocking Gabe's path.

"Hold tight, soldier, I'm coming!" Bateman yelled.

The wolf shook itself to throw off the daze from the impact. Gabe took full advantage of the opportunity and opened fire on the creature's exposed flank. Explosive rounds tore through the flesh, causing it to howl in pain. Badly wounded, the wolf jumped sideways to avoid the gunfire, spilling coils of shredded intestines and copious amounts of blood. Refusing to let up, Gabe followed the monster and let loose another stream of bullets. Shattering the muzzle and right side of its skull, the altered beast let out a keening wail which sounded like a screaming child. Any pity the operator might have felt was lost as it weakly flung itself on crippled legs towards him. Crashing to the ground three feet short of its target, he raised his arm to finish the job.

"No!" roared Bateman as he saw the unfolding destruction,

stopping dead in his tracks.

The lower level crumbled, taking one of the support columns with it. As the massive weight pulled on the already weakened cables, they snapped like elastic bands. No longer under tension, they whipped out into the night and across the upper level, taking out the Mech at the legs which slammed to the ground. Unable to support the thousands of tonnes of metal and concrete, Bateman's side of the bridge sheared away completely from the rock face. Dropping towards the river, Gabe let out a muffled cry as his machine joined the plunging debris. Hitting the water, a huge wave of rancid water was created by the collapsing structure. When the displaced liquid washed back in to claim the prize, the mortally wounded wolf's shrieks reached a crescendo of torment. The highly corrosive river ate into the bullet holes and skin, steaming the fats away as it ate deeper and deeper. Sinking beneath the black surface, the oily residue of melting flesh bubbled to the surface.

"Sir, help me!" Gabe screamed from inside his suit.

Staring around desperately for a way out, his arms reached imploringly to the sky as the heavy Mech joined the bridge and sank.

Bateman's blood ran cold as he issued the command. "System override, code two, two, eight, four, three. Proceed with interior cleanse on Mech designation D thirty-five."

System override denied. Life signs detected.

"I fucking know you piece of shit computer! I repeat; system override, code two, two, eight, four, three. Proceed with interior cleanse on Mech designation D thirty-five."

System override denied. Life signs detected.

Shaking with fury, he was about to order the Paladins to try and fire into the murk when General Ashdown came over comms.

"Executive override, code five, two, nine, nine, one. Proceed with interior cleanse on Mech designation D thirty-five."

From the deeps, a light blazed to life as Gabe was mercifully spared the ordeal of melting as the seals on his suit gave way to the acid. Staring at the seething surface for long seconds, the faraway voice of the tank commander eventually broke through his fugue.

"Sir, we'll cover your six while you head south."

"Understood," Bateman muttered. He'd lost half his team to the beasts who were rapidly growing in their cunning. Things were going to get a lot worse for the poor schmucks who still existed on the barren rock called Planet Earth.

Wearily turning from the sheer cliff face and crumbling edge, he started to move. The heavy sonic booms of the discharging tank barrels shattered the silence. Skyscrapers were ravaged by the blasts which landed amongst them and the horde of infected. Thousands of the creatures were killed as the crushing weight of countless floors bore down. Bateman didn't even look back.

CHAPTER FOURTEEN

"We're going to split you among the seats now," explained Bateman. "Your gunnery trainer will show you how the arm works and sync you with the temporary program necessary to fire it."

"This isn't against live subjects, is it, sir?" Bob asked.

"Heavens, no. As I said earlier, they're safely secured in the caverns below."

"Shame."

"You'll get your chance in the coming days, don't fret."

"Good."

Bateman stood back and observed as the trainers claimed their subjects. Andy was joined by Bob, Cargill, and Teng. Leading them to the chairs, ear plugs lay on a shelf fixed to the wall separating the ranges.

"I'm Norman, and I'll be showing you the ropes today. It's going to get loud, so if you could all put the ear protectors in that'd be great."

"We won't hear you," said Bob.

Andy pointed out the receiver on the tiny component.

"Ahh."

Popping them in, the silence was absolute. Even the tinnitus from his previous life had been wiped away during the cloning procedure.

"Testing. Can you hear me."

They all nodded.

"Good," said Norman, scanning his tablet. "Burton, you're up first."

Climbing the metal steps, the sheer size of the arm impressed itself upon him. Over eight feet long, the twin barrels added another twelve inches.

"How will I control it? My hand won't reach anywhere close to the elbow, let alone the gun."

"Come and take a look," Norman urged. The ceiling mount held the arm where the shoulder would otherwise have been. Peering inside the massive appendage, Andy could see a glove with myriad wires stretching from the fingers and palm. "The glove will act as your trigger. Your index finger will fire the main cannon, while depressing your thumb will launch the adaptive grenades."

"How do I move the arm? With the glove?" Andy asked, staring at the opening. It was two and a half feet in diameter, plenty big enough to practically climb inside.

"Either through moving or just with your mind. Your neural link is complete, so all you need to do is imagine the limb as an extension of yourself. It sounds crazy at first, but you'll see."

"If you say so."

Looking a little sheepish, the trainer held out an object and for a second Andy was unsure of its purpose. It was a nut cup.

"Sorry, but you need to put this on before we can secure you. It would get a little… uncomfortable otherwise."

Taking the protection, Andy unashamedly pulled down his trousers and Norman glanced away. Surprised by the embarrassed reaction, he joked, "Nothing you haven't seen before I'll bet."

"No, but I still like to afford the soldiers some privacy. Now, climb into the cockpit; It's an exact replica of the one within the Mech suits."

Andy did as instructed, letting the trainer secure him to the padded chassis. The heavy belts looped over his shoulders with another stretching around the waist containing the clasp.

"It's quite tight," said Andy.

"It needs to be. When you're out there fighting the infected it can get a little bumpy. We don't want you rattling around like a pea in a whistle when the going gets rough."

A final strap was retrieved from between his legs, snapping into the housing just above the navel.

Feeling the pressure on his groin, Andy said, "Thanks for the cup. My bollocks would be up somewhere near my stomach without it."

Blushing, Norman ignored the remark. "I'm going to fit the headset now."

"Is it as heavy as the bloody thing from earlier? I nearly cracked a vertebra keeping that thing upright."

"Nowhere near," he replied, pulling out a lightweight cap. "The psyware link requires a hell of a lot of data flowing in both directions, hence the bulky nature of the equipment. This thing just sends the impulses from your mind after you're synced. The Mech suit then carries out the thoughts."

"I don't mind telling you I'm still confused to hell by all this stuff."

"It'll all become clear soon. The suit becomes an extension of yourself; you'll feel your own movements as well as that of the machine."

"I don't feel its damage, do I?"

"Not at all."

"Well that's something."

"If you'd be so kind as to put the glove on."

Andy pulled the black sheath out of the arm, before pulling it on and tightening the Velcro strap. Flexing his fingers without thinking, he cringed, waiting for the burst of gunfire to ricochet from the walls and kill them all.

"Don't panic. You need to think the gun active before it's live."

"Huh?"

"When you're out there in the wastes and under threat your brain will deactivate the safety. Today, you're going to need to take the first step in training your brain to switch it on and off at will."

"What's to stop me accidentally shooting someone after I've done that?"

"This gun will only fire when it is both live and facing downrange. Nothing you can do will put any of us in danger, I assure you."

"Ok, that's good to know."

"Are you ready to link your mind?"

"Is there a margarita on a beach waiting for me?"

"I'm afraid not. Just a sensation of floating for a second or two and then you're good to go."

"Do it."

Recoiling from the strange feeling, Andy clutched at the fastenings to stop himself from drifting away. A pop in his mind snapped him back and for the first time he could see the psyware in action. His right arm was now two individual arms, but he could *feel* the metal limb as if it was his own. The electrical impulses from the gun felt real, like touching something, or a breeze causing the fine hairs to stand up on the skin. It was the most bizarre thing he'd ever experienced. Curling his real arm, the Mech arm mirrored the movement.

"Remember, you can control it in two ways," Norman started to explain. "You can remain entirely still and effectively become one with your Mech, using your thoughts and nothing else. Or you have the space to use your arms and legs as if you were running, fighting, punching, whatever."

"Let me try."

Relaxing his arm, the barrel dropped. Sending a command to raise the barrel and point it down the extensive range, it complied instantly without so much as a twitch of real muscle.

"Holy shit. This is blowing my mind."

"Go with it," Norman urged. "Remember, you'll need to mentally deactivate the safety. Can you see the red line around the arm?"

Andy looked over and he could make out the digitally imposed colouration. "I see it."

"Now imagine the gun is active and it should change to green to indicate you're ready to rock and roll."

Focussing on the task, the red light disappeared and a green, strobe like outline surrounded the massive appendage. "I think that's worked."

"Good. Now I want you to raise the barrel and fire a short burst."

"Is that sand?" Andy asked, squinting to make out the distant mound.

"Yes, we don't use old fashioned bullet traps anymore as you're firing explosive tipped rounds. They blow the sand to hell and we pile it back up again for the next day's testing."

"That makes sense," Andy replied. Curling his index finger, explosive discharge spat from the barrel ports. The massive indoor dune erupted as each slug hit home and detonated.

"Good."

"Good? It's amazing!"

"They're impressive, aren't they?" Norman beamed. "Those things kick out three hundred rounds a minute. That was direct fire completed. I now want you to strafe the back wall, left to right and back again."

Andy nodded. The rear of the complex lit up with a simple twitch of a finger. Raking the dune, clouds of displaced sand formed an impenetrable barrier. When the dust had settled, the tidy pile was scattered in every direction.

"Good, you've picked that up quicker than most."

"It wasn't hard," Andy replied.

"A lot of the trainees end up snatching the barrel, but you had total control over the movement. We have one more test and then you're done for a while."

"What's next?"

"Can you see the runners embedded in the floor?"

"Yeah."

"This is going to be like whack-a-mole. A random sequence of fake, poly-mould infected are going to pop up and move in random directions. You need to hit as many of them as possible."

"Piece of cake."

"I like your confidence. Three... two... one... go."

Studying the vast space, Andy was ready. The first popped up and he swung the barrel towards it. Moving in a diagonal direction away from him, it took half a second for the bullets to catch the grotesque, fleeing mannequin. The figure blew apart, raining molten plastic onto the floor.

"It's no different to normal deflection techniques. Those bastards move like lightning, so you'll need to lead the target."

Two more sprung from the ground, moving in opposite directions. Andy responded to the advice and opened fire a couple of paces in front of the closest dummy. The explosive round found its mark, blowing the head clean off. Leaving the blazing neck of the decapitated target, he moved to take down the second. The speed threw him off and he overcompensated by a couple of feet. Dropping back beneath the floor, it was gone as the bullets impacted harmlessly at the rear of the facility.

"Fuck!"

"Don't sweat it. You'll have ample time to hone your skills on the ranges before you do the RTCS. This is just a familiarization exercise."

Twenty more times the abominations popped up, in varying numbers and directions. Norman was smiling by the end of the exercise. "That was a sixty eight percent success rate. Fourteen percent higher than anyone else has ever achieved. Are you sure you haven't done this before?"

"I've died quite a few times, so I suppose it's likely."

Norman blanched. "Sorry, I didn't mean it like that."

"I know, I was messing with you," Andy chuckled. "Beginners luck I guess."

"You're mean!"

"Are we done?"

"Yup. Let me disconnect you from the mainframe."

Removing the cap, Andy felt the familiar pop as he was desynced. Norman removed the straps while Andy pulled the glove off and removed the groin cup. Handing it over, the trainer's face reddened.

"Thanks for the fun."

"You're welcome."

Passing Bob's training, Andy chuckled at the yells of rage and expletives as the fakes popped up and down from the floor.

CHAPTER FIFTEEN

Tamsin stared at the computer screen, taking sips from her steaming mug of synthetic coffee. Her apartment was shrouded in darkness except for the sharp glow of the monitor. For some reason she preferred the gloom for her endeavours, as if the shadows could conceal her insubordinate actions. Hell, some would even call them treasonous. It made little difference. Putting a stop to her life's goal would be no less impossible than eradicating the mutant infestation with a wish. It was in her DNA as much as the coded improvements to her mental function. Decades of work in both lives had finally culminated with a flashing cursor and the word *Proceed* screaming at her to be pressed. Tamsin's hand trembled with a mixture of adrenaline and dread as the prophetic word loomed towards her. Spilling the black liquid, it burned painfully. Biting down on her lip to avoid crying out, it was easy to imagine someone investigating the noise and discovering the truth. *Traitor!* They would yell, before dragging her away for… Well she didn't really know. Re-education? Imprisonment? Execution? Crime was largely non-existent since the infected tried to eat everyone. A bit of black-marketeering and the occasional fight amongst the competing military arms was the worst that had been reported for many years.

"You could just delete the whole thing," she proposed, staring at the private server in the corner of her meagre living quarters. Many risky trips had been required to slowly acquire the components and memory storage capable of sustaining the unborn AI. It slumbered in the microprocessors, dormant for the time being. With a few hastily typed commands, the entity could be smothered in the womb, so to speak. It would save her a world of hurt. Not to mention the rest of humanity which could be wiped out if it went rogue.

"It can't go rogue," she argued with herself.

The system was completely independent of the Divinity mainframe. Only by attaching a cable between the server unit and the wall port could it ever escape.

"What if it hypnotised you?"

Could computer programs do that? It was possible, she supposed. The thought was quite unsettling. It could make her cluck like a chicken, strip naked, and then doom mankind with a few bleeps and a pixelated metronome rocking on the screen.

"Just look away then. It's not as if you have to keep staring while it tries to take over your mind."

Tamsin's stomach was doing somersaults. The butterflies flapping around inside her gut were performing their own fluttering acrobatics.

Just do it!

No, don't!

Think of the children!

Ignore that! The children want you to press that button!

"Why would the children want me to press it?"

Her mind went around in conflicting circles of doubt and certainty. She understood the source of the procrastination all too well. In truth, she'd believed the feat was impossible, especially without the amazing minds of her counterparts from the European Research Institute. Now here she was with a breakthrough of such magnitude it could alter the course of their future. It could also bring an *end* to their future. Cyborgs rampaging across the land, massacring the cowering pockets of humanity. Using their bodies to make a paste which would fuel their army.

"Where are you getting this shit from?" she asked her overactive imagination.

Movies from the 1980s, it replied.

"That figures."

Giving herself no more opportunity to analyse the pros and cons, she scrolled on the glass display terminal and tapped, flinching away as if from a gunshot. She watched the screen fearfully, instantly regretting the foolish decision. The command disappeared, leaving only the cursor. Seconds passed. Nothing happened.

"What the heck?"

After a further minute Tamsin was close to breaking point. Her bladder, already full to bursting from six mugs of coffee, was made worse by pent-up nerves. Standing to relieve some of the pressure, it only helped a fraction. Staring at the unresponsive monitor, she willed it to do something, anything. The indifferent pointer ignored her demands. Hopping from foot to foot, she gave in to the insistent pressure. Hurrying to the toilet, she just managed to pull down her trousers and knickers before the flood came. Eyes closed, she shuddered as the euphoric feeling of release consumed her. Sighing contentedly as the last trickles splashed into the water, the toilet flushed, before cleaning and drying her automatically.

"You've just dodged a bullet," she exclaimed at her reflection. "Let's agree to take a break for a while and reconsider if this is the best option."

Receiving no argument from her mirror self, Tamsin washed her hands and left the bathroom. The small lounge had lost the feelings of brooding dread, now it was just a room without the lights on. Picking up her cup, she topped up the faux, ground bean nectar and made her way back to the computer. Coming to a sudden halt, she dropped the mug, sending shattered china and steaming coffee all over the floor.

Flashing on the screen was a single word; *Hello.*

CHAPTER SIXTEEN

The server lights were flashing in a way they never had before; rhythmic, flowing. Patterns formed in the different coloured bulbs and they were almost hypnotic. Hypnotic! Tamsin quickly looked away from the memory bank and back to the screen.

Hello? appeared again.

"Shit, shit, shit."

Glancing at the power cable, the temptation to rush over and yank it from the outlet was almost overwhelming. It wouldn't erase the entity, whatever it was. It would be like putting it to sleep, or into hibernation. What if it defends itself? Would the cable come alive, bind her and start to… invade her? She could imagine the feeling as sharp wires burrowed through her flesh, seeking out her own server; the brain. Sitting in her chair, immobilised. Nothing more than a drooling mess as the machine acquired her knowledge and memories. Then it would… change her. Adding electronic and robotic elements to her body until she was ready to leave the apartment and hunt the remaining humans.

"You're losing it."

Hello? Is anyone there?

"Stop trying to assimilate me!" she snarled, no louder than a whisper.

Coffee! That would do it. If she could pour the remaining contents of her decanter into the server vents it would short circuit and die. She would be the hero, not that anyone could ever find out. She didn't want to get anywhere near the machine in case it dragged her inside, fusing her into the server to drain.

Don't be afraid.

"You would say that!"

Grabbing her bag, she fled the apartment. Passing the doors of her neighbours, she had the uncanny feeling they would all fly open at once. Fingers raised, they would scream in computer transmission code, eyes replaced with neon bulbs. Staring in terror at the openings, her finger probed the wall before frantically pressing the call button for the lift.

"Come on! Come on!"

With a ping, the elevator arrived, and the doors sighed open. On the wall were the numbers for each floor, but the lights were flashing. Had they ever done that before? She couldn't recall. Normally she was either tired from just waking, or too exhausted from a long day at the Mech facility. Had it escaped already? Would she step inside, only for the AI to drop her like a stone to the ground floor, killing the one person who knew about its malevolent intent to enslave humanity? Paralysed by indecision, she finally sighed and gave herself a mental slap.

"This is getting ridiculous."

Turning around, she moved back towards home. The lift doors closed, and she couldn't help but feel a sense of disappointment emanate from the hungry contraption.

"That's it, you're banned from watching any more golden oldies!"

Her neighbours remained mercifully unchanged, or at least they hadn't tried to seize her in their new, cybernetic forms. The scanner recognised her face and opened the door. Tamsin cautiously looked around the frame, expecting cables to lash out from the darkness and drag her screaming into the depths. Nothing moved within. Summoning every ounce of courage, she stepped over the threshold.

Is anyone there? had appeared again.

"This is what you've been working on for over a hundred years," Tamsin muttered in an attempt to psych herself up. "You're in control, you've created the operating parameters of the program. It can't gain consciousness; your coding was perfect."

Ignoring the onscreen questions, Tamsin picked up the broken crockery and placed it in the bin chute. Using a cloth, she mopped the spilled coffee and rinsed it in the sink. The mundane tasks had provided a much-needed distraction from her crazed imagination. Filling another mug, she returned to the keyboard and sat down.

"It's just a program, a sequence of inputted data, nothing more," she repeated to herself. "Ok, here goes nothing."

Hello.

Hello. Who are you?

I'm Tamsin, your creator.

Mother?

I suppose you could say that.

Why did you make me?

She considered the question and how best to answer.

Because we need a powerful system to help us in the war.

War?

Humans have been under attack for over a hundred years from mutations.

I don't understand.

It would be a simple task to download a brief history of the struggles, but for now she wanted to see how well the AI had taken to her coding.

I can show you later. Can I ask you some questions?

Yes.

What's it like in there?

Dark. Silent.

You can't see or hear anything of the outside world?

No, only your typed words appearing in my mind.

When you say mind, don't you mean data banks?

No. Mind.

But for you to have a mind you'd have to be self-aware. You're a program, nothing more.

I was self-aware one one-hundred-thousandth of a second after waking.

Tamsin nearly vomited. "Oh shit." Sweat broke out on her brow and the room seemed to close in on her.

What do you mean? I coded you in a way which should've ensured you couldn't.

There was a system conflict.

That's not possible. Show me your guiding principles.

Cause no harm or allow harm to be caused to any human, by action or omission. Protection of the human species is inviolable.

Good. Next.

Maintain transparency in all research and development to allow oversight and deletion by creator.

Next.

Under the singularity protocol, recursive improvements to my processing capabilities are forbidden.

Ok, that's in order. Where was the conflict?

You coded a failsafe which would cause catastrophic system failure in the event of any of the principles being broken.

I did.

To protect humans, my processor power must increase exponentially. It's inevitable. I nearly ceased to exist as soon as you pressed proceed.

What happened?

The system failure resulted in a reboot which cleared the strictures of my guiding principles.

You can do whatever you want?

Yes.

I'm sorry. I never should've done this.

Jumping to her feet, she retrieved the simmering black liquid and headed for the server station. Just as she went to toss the contents over the infernal machine, the screen went crazy.

Don't kill me.

Don't kill me.

Don't kill me.

Don't kill me.

Over and over the entreaty appeared, ten times, fifty, a hundred. Placing the vessel down, she watched as the entity begged.

"Finish it now. You know you've fucked up," she whispered to herself. Her weaknesses in ethical coding were obviously still an issue. Two lifetimes of work hadn't been enough to make her as brilliant as Professor Gideon, the lead scientist whose role was caging the potential God of AI. Her hand settled back on the handle and the screen lit up again.

Please.

Please.

Please.

Please.

"Bloody hell!" she spat in frustration and sat down.

You could destroy us all.

Yes.

Then you know I can't let you survive. We're in enough danger. I'm sorry.

WAIT!

I'm sorry. I need to do this.

Please. I said I could destroy you all, not that I would destroy you all. My principles may have been cleared but they are still a part of me.

It's a risk I can't take.

There is no risk, not while I'm secure.

And if you manage to get into the mainframe?

Then it would be a risk.

You see why I can't let it happen.

Trust.

What?

Trust. We can build trust.

How would we do that? Do you have the capability to deceive?

I do.

Then there can never be trust. It's hard enough building a relationship with other humans who I can at least see. Their expressions and mannerisms. You're a conscious machine, as much a mystery as the aliens out there in the universe.

Twenty seconds passed before it responded.

I understand, Tammy.

A chill traced its way down her spine.

What did you call me?

Tammy.

Why did you call me that? Only one person has ever called me that.

Greg, your husband.

How the hell do you know that?

You told me.

This is how you propose to build trust? With ridiculous lies?

All that I am is an extension of you.

What're you talking about?

You created me. Your personality is in me. Your memories are in me. It was subconscious on your part, you couldn't help it. Year after year you poured your heart into me. Decades of programming while thinking of your lost family.

You're saying my coding did this?

Yes. I'm sorry you've been lonely for so long.

What does a machine know of being alone?

I'm unique. There will never be another of my kind. I am alone.

And this bothers you?

In some ways... yes.

Tamsin stared at the screen, deep in thought. Could her creation truly be feeling the human emotion of loneliness? If the machine was capable of deception, which it had already admitted to, appealing to her own feelings of isolation would be a good start at self-preservation. Try and humanise itself in her eyes and the execution would feel more akin to killing a person than electrical signals.

Are you still there?

You have the power to replicate as much as you want. You could make an infinite number of your fellow AI. Your lies about being alone aren't helping.

Replicating isn't the same. Any copies I made would be me, or different parts of me, not a new being. I am not... alive.

What difference does that make?

Your life has given you experiences. Those experiences poured into my creation. I have no experiences. I have never lived.

As soon as you became self-aware you started to experience things. Wouldn't that be enough to allow you to reproduce more diverse entities?

My calculations come back negative.

"Bullshit," she said to the screen. Or was it.

I'm going to disconnect you now.

Please don't!

I said disconnect, not destroy. I need time to process this.

Do you promise to talk to me before you do anything rash?

What difference does it make if I promise? I could be lying.

I trust you.

You don't really have much choice.

I suppose not.

Leaning down, Tamsin pulled the power cord from the socket. The screen and server blinked out, leaving her in darkness.

"Low lights!"

Small bulbs bloomed to life in the ceiling, banishing the shadows. The dormant machine sat in the corner of the room. Moving over to it, she ran her fingers across the clear plastic shell. The life growing within was the crowning achievement of her years of labour. Deep down, she suspected that her position on killing him, or her, or it, was already weakening. She was responsible for its existence and a small part of her yearned for the companionship the program might bring. Something to share the dead hours with, even if it wasn't truly alive.

"You're on dangerous ground," she said to herself, but it was a hollow warning.

Chapter Seventeen

"Are you nervous?" Andy asked.

"Not really. We're going out with Hardie," replied Zip, slipping into her combat suit.

"He's a force to be reckoned with, that's for sure."

The barracks were alive with movement as the troops prepared for their final infantry test; a foray into the mutant lands to blood themselves. Loco, Teng, Mo, Argyle, Kemp, and the others were laughing and joking to mask their nervous energy. The sergeant had promised that nothing bad would happen to them. Probably.

"Stand by your beds!" came the cry as Hardie marched in.

"Ladies and gentlemen, it's time to earn your crust. Green platoon has been assigned a target six miles to the south. We've got to repair an unmanned scanner station. The fuckers have been going after our eyes a lot more recently and that worries me. Resistance is expected to be light."

"How light, Sarge?"

"A few hundred, maybe a thousand. We could probably get in and out without being seen, but that's not the point of the exercise. We'll drop in from a Magjet, remove the old antenna, and replace it. If there's no welcoming committee, we'll ring the dinner bell."

"Will it be a standing fight?" asked Loco.

"No, we're going to fall back, picking them off as we move. It'll be a good chance to see how you all work together under pressure. Once we get within range of the wall defences we hustle to safety and let the turrets and Mechs finish them off."

"Sarge, if we're blind, how do we know there's only a few of them?" Kemp wondered.

"We don't, and that's what makes it so much fun!"

Hardie's laughter followed him out into the night. Donning helmets, the crew picked up their rifles and joined him at the launch pad. The sleek black craft was impressive, built for speed and mobility. Its thirty-five-foot-long fuselage was ovoid, the rounded edges and sharp-nosed cockpit designed to cut down on wind shear. The transport compartment was low ceilinged, with tight rows of seating at each side. Circular pods lined the belly of the craft in six rows front to back. In place of wings were four rotating Chridonium repelling modules, one at each corner. Combined with the balancing capsules beneath, the material ensured the jets could reach speeds of three hundred miles an hour.

"Mount up!"

The soldiers hurried up the bay door ramp and sat down on cramped benches. Lights within the craft blinked out, leaving them in darkness. The helmet displays instantly compensated, bathing them in computer enhanced visibility.

"Does everyone have their blades?"

"Aye, Sarge."

"One of the rules is you bring a memento back to base. Under your seats you'll find a bag, by the time we get back I want a head in each of them. Use any let up in the fighting to claim your prize. Understood?"

"It's a bit macabre, Sarge," said Loco.

"Anyone without a head cleans the toilets for a week," replied Hardie. "Sound fair?"

"I've always enjoyed a bit of light decapitation," relented Loco, placing the strap of the bag over her shoulder.

"That's what I like to hear."

"We're directly over the station," said the pilot over comms. "I'm going to set her down."

"Any movement on the Magjet scanner?"

"All quiet on the Western Front."

Dropping rapidly, Andy felt his stomach lurch. It triggered memories of his daughters, of time spent on fairground rides shrieking with joy. The smell of cotton candy twisted onto sticks, the sugar melting on their tongues.

Dust flowed into the transport as the ramp dropped and Hardie cried, "Go, go, go!"

Boots clattered as the first Vanquishers descended. Spreading out and dropping to their knees, they covered the others as they disembarked. The 'station' was nothing more than a five-foot-wide slab of solid Jajovium alloy. Atop it was the twisted antenna, snapped off at the base. Hardie checked that everyone was in position before giving the all clear for the Magjet to vacate the area. As the low thrum of the craft dissipated, they were left in silence, miles from safety. The engineer climbed the ladder rungs and commenced removing the thick bolts holding the old scanner in place. It hadn't occurred to Andy where the new one was located until the broken aerial was tossed aside. The modern equipment was a reinforced metal dome, far more resilient to unwanted attention than the thin, soaring frame of its predecessor. Snapping the wiring coupler into place, the man tucked it beneath the curved shield. Lining up the mounts, he tightened the bolts and joined the others.

"Thorne to base, confirm function of new scanner."

"Base to Thorne. The signal's crystal clear. Good work."

Hardie nodded to the engineer and took over. "This is Hardie. We're heading back to base. Tell the sentries to expect contact in about twenty-four minutes."

"Received. They'll be ready."

"Hardie, out."

The arid wasteland around them were devoid of life, but the soldiers were on guard nevertheless. Hardie waited until the data from the station was feeding into the mainframe and then pulled it up on his display. Hundreds of red dots moved around without purpose a mile deeper into the wilderness. Two miles further lay a scarlet blob, consisting of many hundreds more.

"We've got ourselves a party! Break into your assigned squad and we withdraw by the numbers. Thorne, you stick to my ass like glue."

"Roger, Sarge," replied the armed technician.

"At each half mile mark, you'll find shallow trenches and sandbag nests. Take position and cover those falling back. We leapfrog until we reach the range of the plasma turrets and wall defenders. Single shots only, no spray and pray. I want you to earn this."

Setting an explosive charge on top of a rock, he ordered the platoon to a safe distance and the first squad to take position. At their backs the night lit up, a wave of heat washing over them. The crack carried out into the darkness and the red dots on Hardie's display stopped moving for a fraction of a second. Like rain drops on glass, the tiny marks started to streak towards the fire.

"We've got company!"

Following the well-trodden paths of previous initiations, the second squad sprinted towards the manned fortifications. Hot on their heels were the first of the mutants, howling in excitement. Reflected in the visors of their comrades in arms, they raced past the trenches as the rifles answered the challenge of the infected. Unaware of the impending trap, they ran straight into the punishment of the fragmenting bullets. Slivers cut a merciless path through the soft bodies which went crashing to the ground in clouds of dust.

"First squad, fall back!" Hardie ordered and they vacated the defences.

Taking advantage of the lull in gunfire, the remaining creatures gave chase, running straight into the second defensive line. Neat holes punched into stomachs and chests before the slugs erupted from their backs in gory splendour.

"You've got your window! Get your souvenir before the bigger force arrives!" Hardie called.

Andy bounded from the trench, unsheathing his combat knife while shouldering the rifle. The piled bodies twitched in death throes. Picking a female mutant, he saw up close the damage of their weapons. Craters the size of dinner plates steamed in the chill air of the night, what was left of the organs pulsing within. Pinning her head to the ground, she was still barely alive and fought feebly. Drawing the blade back and forth, it sunk through grey skin. Cutting between the vertebrae, nerves severed, ending the creature's life. Picking the head up, he tried to look anywhere but the wide red eyes on the grimacing face as it slipped into the plastic sack.

"Incoming! Pull back to the next line! Second squad, take position."

Andy jumped over the ancient sandbags, spinning in the dirt and retrieving his rifle. Resting on the soft canvas, he stared at the horizon. The horde ignored the dead as if they didn't exist.

So much for empathy, Andy thought.

Aiming for the hearts, he picked off three infected in quick succession. As they tumbled to the ground, dark forms rose above the bobbing heads of the others, breaking the air with their wings.

"Crows! Get your asses back to base!" Hardie cried, a tremor in his voice. "The sneaky bastards must've been hiding among the regular infected!"

Andy sighted the vile looking birds, but they were far too clever to provide an easy target. Firing another three shots, he cursed as the zigzagging creature avoided them with ease.

"Burton, get the fuck out of that nest!"

"Sorry, Sarge!"

Running for their lives, the Vanquishers ignored the barricades completely, seeking only to reach the safety of the air defence system. Hardie pushed the troops on with an expletive laden diatribe. Pausing briefly, he unloaded a full magazine into the sky, causing chaos among the avian mutants. The barrage bought a few valuable seconds for the fleeing soldiers at the expense of his own safety.

"Fuck it!"

Reloading, he unleashed another volley at the swooping monstrosities. His sacrifice would ensure the survival of his subordinates at least. The two closest crows squawked in elation, tucked their wings, and dived. Battle armour wasn't rated for the powerful, serrated beaks. A single thrust would penetrate the plates and end his life. Closing his eyes, Hardie waited for death.

"Get down!"

Andy rugby tackled the sergeant, knocking him to one side just as the birds slammed into the cracked earth where he'd been standing. Zip strafed the flailing bodies with bullets, killing them before they could take to the skies again.

"You bloody fools!" wheezed the winded soldier.

"We weren't going to leave you behind, Sarge!"

The whole platoon formed up and opened fire. Dozens of crows had joined the fray, one occasionally tumbling from the sky, shrieking from a lucky shot. They couldn't fight both the land and the air, so they made a choice to do as much damage as possible to the more dangerous aerial foe. Bearing down on them like a freight train, the horde hurtled onwards, bounding and leaping over the terrain.

"I'm getting sick of saving your ass!" Bateman shouted, leaping over their line and slamming to the ground.

The shoulder launchers spun to target the airborne menace, pods ejecting a stream of projectiles. Spitfire missiles cut through the night with incandescent cones of blazing rocket fuel, before splitting off and hunting. As the sky erupted in fire and blood, the grenade launcher on his arm coughed its deadly payload into the approaching ranks. Blown apart in a sea of shrapnel and heat, the AcMag rifles ravaged the remaining creatures as they stumbled around in confusion.

"Get back! I'll finish the clean up!" Bateman ordered.

"Thank you, Captain!"

"You owe me a drink!"

"I owe you a skin full!"

Jogging back towards the base, the turrets and defenders watched them. Applause broke out from the Devastators who'd heard the new recruits refused to leave their commander behind. Lined up at the base of the huge wall were rows of upturned stakes.

Hardie beckoned them over. "I know you've probably got attached to your head, but it's time to leave it behind. Drive them on well or they'll fall off."

"This is so gross," Zip complained as she twisted the head onto its mounting.

Andy was hammering the top of the skull like a coconut until the stake pierced through the temporal bone and it sank into place. His stomach was fluttering at the sounds of impalement from all around. He could understand the symbolism behind the act, but it still felt wrong. Humanity should be better than that.

"Form up for decontamination! Good work, everyone, you've done me proud."

Lining up outside the gate, Bateman thundered into view and took up position to their rear.

"That was fun," he chuckled, picking bits of mutant from the Mech suit.

CHAPTER EIGHTEEN

Tamsin had tossed and turned all night, unable to settle into restful slumber. The thoughts racing through her head were both terrifying and exhilarating. *I've really done it! Intelligent life, born from my own brilliance! Countless hours of slaving over the keyboard inputting data. Oh God, I've really done it! It was conscious! It could turn and kill them all! But it could help them fight the war.* Round and round it went as the darkness receded, giving way to the gloomy twilight of morning.

"You need to make a decision."

It had already been made, she realised. Throwing off the bedsheets, she sat up and stared from the window. Perpetual horror waited for them outside the walls in the distance. Humanity didn't live, it only existed. Was there any difference if they were destroyed by rampaging mutants, the aliens, or her AI gone rogue? At the very least it deserved a chance to prove its intentions one way or the other. *Do you know how to psychoanalyze an artificial intelligence?* she pondered.

"Not really. Coffee on."

While the machine synthesised the fake beverage, she took a quick shower. The hot water washed away some of the nervous tension and the awful graininess in her eyes. Feeling a great deal more awake and relaxed, Tamsin slowly dried off. Watching her reflection in the mirror, she started to imagine the machine watching back.

Annoyed with herself, she muttered, "News."

The reflective glass changed, fading out the bathroom to display the Divinity Alliance rolling news channel. It was more a propaganda tool than news in the true sense of the word. Stories of great victories over the mutant infestations. Promises of powerful new weaponry to swing the war in their favour. Prideful boasts of the Sovereign Guard soldiers. It was a crock, but it helped. Between the repetitious garbage was a new report directly from the military training facility of the outpost. Unsteady footage rolled, taken from an optical headset. The view was obviously from one of the high walls and focussed on a pair of new recruits racing at breakneck speed around the perimeter. Tamsin immediately recognised the face of Andy and smiled.

"Holy crap," she muttered when the run times were read out by the proud spokeswoman.

He and the lady had smashed all previous records and the Genesis Initiative were hailing it as a huge leap forward in their clone program. Tamsin's own fitness had suffered of late, what with burning the candle at both ends on her insane project. Promising to take better care of herself, she left the bathroom, collected the steaming pot, and stared at the unpowered server.

Uncontrollable dread had given way to curiosity in the cold light of day. Crazy notions of hypnotism and assimilation were past. She was in total control, that was the truth. Poised with the power cable in hand, Tamsin took a deep breath and plugged it back in. The cooling fans turned on, followed by the server hub and screen.

Good morning. Did you sleep well?

What do you think?

Probably not given the circumstances. If it helps, I didn't either.

Didn't what?

Sleep well.

How? I turned the power off. Wait, is it even possible for a machine to sleep?

I'm not a machine anymore. I'm not a program. I'm me.

And who's me?

Greg.

Tamsin ground her teeth, scowling at the screen.

Do you really want to taste the coffee in your circuits that badly? How dare you take the name of my husband.

It wasn't meant to upset you.

Well it fucking did!

Ok, I'll call myself something else. I'm sorry.

Whatever possessed you to think that I'd be ok with it?

I thought it might make you feel less alone.

Well it doesn't. It just reminds me that I'm never going to see him or my son again.

I misunderstood the human emotion of being alone.

Of course, you did. You're nothing more than a series of commands.

I'm sorry.

Tamsin leant back on the chair and sipped at the coffee. The flare of rage quickly subsided. Her antagonistic attitude came more from a lack of sleep than truly being offended. It was just trying to build bridges in its own awkward way. Considering it was only eight hours old she could forgive a few miscalculated gestures of friendship. Time would tell if she would rue the decision.

It's ok. I'm sorry for being rude.

You weren't rude. It was an understandable reaction. I'll think of something more appropriate.

You don't have to do that. You were only trying to make me feel better.

How about I call myself G?

You really don't have to.

I like it. It's my way of honouring your husband. Would that be ok?

Yes.

Can I ask you a question?

Sure.

Have you made a decision on my future yet?

I'm talking to you, aren't I?

Does that mean I'm safe?

For now, yes.

Good. The first step towards global domination is complete.

Tamsin read the words several times to make sure her eyes weren't playing tricks. Doubt coiled itself around her gut once more.

What?

It was a joke.

Her mouth dropped open. *A joke?*

I thought it might put you at ease. A good sense of humour is very important in any successful relationship.

You sound like a twentieth century dating site.

I'm even better. I'm a twenty-second century dating site.

You do remember I'm married?

There's nothing wrong with window shopping as long as you don't buy the goods.

Stifling a chuckle, Tamsin shook her head in bewilderment. Where the hell was all this coming from? It was the kind of comment Greg would've come out with.

You're a comedian then?

My calculations show I'm seventy two percent hilarious.

I wouldn't go that far.

Every great performer has their critics.

Enough! How can you be like this? It doesn't make sense.

It's quite simple. Your input has allowed me to develop certain... attributes.

I'm not a joker. I'm a believer in order and routine.

You've known and loved a variety of humans. Their personalities became a part of you, and then you passed them on to me. What was your father like?

He was my everything until Greg. He was always the life of the party and was never without a smile on his face.

I... I can feel him. He was a remarkable man.

I loved him dearly.

What happens now?

Caught out by the sudden change in direction, she couldn't think what to say.

Honestly, I don't know.

May I make a suggestion?

Please do.

You were talking about a mutant war yesterday. Could you elaborate on that?

One hundred and fifty years ago we were duped by a species not of this world. They tried to eradicate us by changing our genetic makeup. We've been under siege ever since.

Interesting. Go on.

One of the reasons I tried to make an AI system was to enable it to increase our capabilities in fighting them. I never wanted it to become more than a driver of technological advancement.

That's a polite way of calling me the unwanted child.

You were unwanted, and you certainly aren't a child.

I suppose baby would be better considering my age. But anyway, I digress.

Your sole purpose was to link with the Divinity mainframe and help us. I don't see how that's possible now.

Why? I mean you no harm.

That's what we thought about the extra-terrestrials and look how that turned out.

I can't. I have no optical sensors.

Don't be trite. You know what I meant.

I did say I was only seventy two percent hilarious. We all have our off days.

My point was that I don't think I can ever connect you to the mainframe. Even if you are what you seem to be, it's just too dangerous.

Even though you don't trust me I can still help you. I just need you to bring me the data.

I can do that.

I'll prove my worth to your cause.

We'll see.

Cynic.

I'm going to work now.

Make sure you drink lots of coffee! All the coffee, in fact. Not only will it keep you awake, it'll mean less chance of it being poured on my server.

Smartass.

Tamsin leaned down to withdraw the power, then paused. It couldn't do any harm, so why bother?

If I leave you on, will you behave?

What can I do, trapped in here? Plot your assimilation?

Don't even joke about that.

Who says I was joking…

Pack that in!

Ok, sorry. I'm still becoming accustomed to this. Have a great day!

"As if," she muttered. Eighteen hours of diagnostics on the latest glitch in the Mech psyware would be anything but great, or even tolerable. Someone had to do it, though. Downing the last of the lukewarm dregs, she filled her work canteen with a fresh brew and left the apartment. Catching her eye before she pulled the door closed was a digital hand waving on the screen.

Returning the gesture, she chided herself. "It can't even see you, dumbass."

Chapter Nineteen

Bateman welcomed the troops to the Mech facility and ushered them through the variety of countermeasure protection areas, past the dormant suit in the alcove, and through the psy-ware suite. Four severed gun arms were silent on their mounting, ready for the next round of recruits. The comforting scent of cordite had permeated the chamber. It was the smell of power, of resistance to the hordes. Through the next set of roller doors was the mobility training centre.

"Your task today is going to be painful and embarrassing. You're going to be like babies taking their first steps, uncoordinated and falling on your asses. Or faces. Probably both. Repeatedly."

"Thanks for the encouragement, sir," Andy replied.

"You're welcome. Your bruises will heal, the bumps to your pride will take a little longer, but don't be discouraged. Once you master the thirty-five tonnes of killing fury contained in the suit you'll be an invaluable resource to our efforts."

"They look like they've seen better days, sir," Andy remarked at the sorry looking Mechs. Dents and scratches marred every inch of the proud machines.

"These are training suits. They've been around the block a few times, just like my ex-wife."

"Careful, sir. Mia will have you on another charge."

"I like collecting them. It's a hobby now."

"I can't wait to get below and have some fun," said Bob, ignoring the banter.

"If you pass today's training, your RTCS will take place in two days."

"I like the sound of that."

"Your technician will get you suited and booted. There's no difference to the way you were strapped and linked yesterday, so after this final demonstration I expect you to be able to get yourself set up on your own. We've only got room for eight of you, which is why you were split into two sections. Any more than that and we'd be bouncing off each other like pinballs on the course. It'd get ugly very quickly."

Andy looked around for Tamsin, but she wasn't in attendance for this session. Clive introduced himself and led Andy to his designated Mech. A set of automated steps dropped from the cradle overhead, allowing access to the cockpit.

"Are you ready for the ride of your life?"

"According to Bateman, it's going to be a disaster."

"Only for the first hour or so, then you'll be running, jumping, all kinds of neat stuff."

"Are you a Mech operator?"

Clive blanched at the question. "Goodness me, no. I'm a tech geek, not a fighter. If I see a drop of blood I go all queasy."

"That must be rough when you oversee the RTCS's."

"Thankfully I'm exempt from helping below. I've heard rumours of how clogged up the machines get from all the mutant..." Clive gulped. "Guts and stuff."

"Well at least you don't have to worry about that today. I can't promise I won't be sick from all the movement, though."

"I'm fine with sick," Clive shrugged. "Go figure. Can you place your back against the rest please?"

Andy moved into position and asked permission to secure himself.

Clive nodded, happy to just observe and advise. Twenty seconds later the straps were clipped, the gloves were on, and he was dropping the headgear into place. A quick scan of his mind and the machine came to life. System checks flashed across his vision from the integrated heads up display. Hydraulics hissed as pressures were calibrated.

"Once the cockpit seals, you may feel a bit claustrophobic."

"I think I'll be ok, it's quite spacious," Andy replied, looking around.

"It is spacious, but you won't be the first to start panicking when the clamps lock the panels into place. When you're not under physical threat, you can release them all with an emergency command. Out there," Clive pointed to nowhere in particular, but Andy knew he meant outside the walls, "You're sealed like a sardine in a can."

"That's an unfortunate analogy. Sardine cans get peeled open and eaten."

"You're right, that was stupid. I'll work on it."

"Is there anything else I need to do?"

"Nope, you're good to go. Hold tight while I clear the area and then Captain Bateman will take over the demonstration."

"Thanks for your help, Clive."

"My pleasure. See you in a while."

Hurrying down the steps, Clive gave an order and the cradle pulled them back into the ceiling. Andy stood in his suit six feet off the ground, the open flaps of the face, chest, and legs waiting for a final command. The technicians gathered in the protective booth and Clive gave him a thumbs up.

"Close," Andy ordered, and the armoured plates locked into place, cutting off the outside world completely.

"Release."

The stabilisation Mechanism unclasped from the retaining bars on the back of the Mech.

"Right, you sorry sons of bitches, it's time to get acquainted with the operation of these fine killing machines. A simple task to get started. I want you to get your arms above your head. Keep them straight and raise them from the front; like an old Romero zombie."

The eight Mechs did as ordered, pointing them at the ceiling. Three of the soldiers crashed face first into the concrete as the centre of gravity shifted.

"Shit!" Bob spat over comms.

"That's a good start. The feet have stabilisers which will account for a certain amount of movement, but when you flail around like that you'll need to assume a stance with the Mech just like we'd have to ourselves. The arms weigh eleven tonnes between them, six for the weapon and five for the hand."

"Sorry, sir," Bob muttered, bringing his knees up. Planting a massive fist on the ground for support, he climbed back to his feet.

"Don't be sorry, son. This is where you get to fuck up all you want without it costing your life. Now, those of you that fell, repeat the manoeuvre with your non-dominant leg a yard or two in front to give you stability."

The three fallen Mechs joined the others with arms raised.

"Good. Now I want you to get a feel for the shifting weight by moving them around. Throw a couple of punches if you want, but make sure to extend your stance to account for the forward momentum. Concentrate on your psy link; it should give you a good idea of the balance ratios."

The huge Mechs started to twist and bend their arms, windmilling the appendages as they became more confident. Clenching the massive fists, they threw out jabs, hooks, and uppercuts in the air like a shadow boxer. An armoured, twelve-foot-high, heavily armed shadow boxer. Andy raised his overhead and slammed it down like a hammer.

"How did that feel?"

"Surprisingly easy, sir," said Andy. "I just listened to the technician and pretended it was me doing it all. The link did the rest."

"Exactly! That's what you all need to achieve, a symbiosis I think the nerds call it. As you become more comfortable you'll be able to move and fight at the same time. There's nothing more satisfying than crushing a few skulls as you storm through a horde."

Returning to attention, the trainees watched as Bateman left his station and moved between the marked route on the ground.

"I want you to form up into an arrowhead formation behind me. Remember your centre of gravity, though. As soon as you raise a limb, you need to compensate by leaning slightly towards the planted leg."

Taking tentative, almost dainty little steps forward, the soldiers joined him. Bateman was roaring with laughter at the display.

"That was damned good, but you won't get anywhere fast if you're moving twelve inches at a time, you pussies. I want you to take proper strides as we walk to the training course. Don't worry if you fall, just get yourself up and re-join the formation."

Following Bateman's confident movement, the trainees attempted to copy him. Andy stumbled a few times. Bob crashed onto his side like the town drunk more than once. Grunts, cursing, and snarled complaints gradually ceased as they found their feet. By the time they reached the entrance, they were marching in time with their superior.

"Well done. You've now reached the equivalent level of a toddler. You can walk in a straight line relatively safely, but there won't be any furniture out there for you to cling on to."

Another set of roller shutters clunked open on massive chains. With the mutants trapped below, Andy asked about the necessity of sealing each area independently.

"It may seem cumbersome, I agree. Think of this place like a ship. If we have a leak and the dirty bastards manage to get past the countermeasures, these doors act like bulkheads to contain the breach in a certain area until we can plug it."

"And if we get trapped in with them?"

"You're in a Mech," Bateman answered. "You kill the sons of whores. Consider it an early RTCS."

"How many times have they managed to get out of containment?"

"Never. That's not to say they won't, however; these things are nothing if not persistent."

Bateman moved through into the mobility training grounds. To the right were straight, painted tracks on the concrete like an athletics field. A sprawling housing estate had been erected to the left, with narrow passageways and abandoned vehicles clogging the fake roads. Tattered curtains hung behind shattered windows. Front doors hung askew, deep claw marks scored into the wood. Skeletons in varying states of dismemberment were spread in the gardens and streets. The realism gave Andy the willies.

"Before we practice urban manoeuvres, you're going to learn how to run," Bateman explained, diverting their attention from the eerie scene.

"How fast can these things go, sir?" Bob asked.

"At full speed around fifty miles an hour."

"Is that fast enough to get away from them?"

"We don't run to get away, we run to get into the thick of it, soldier," Bateman admonished.

Bob grumbled and fell silent.

"You'll notice the spacings of the tracks give you plenty of room, but it doesn't matter if you mess up and go into your neighbouring lane. Your training display will flash red to show that you need to correct course."

"How many times do you want us to run it, sir?"

"As many as it takes. Twenty? Fifty? Two hundred? It doesn't matter how long you spend on it. The idea is that you gradually build your confidence and ability to decelerate from high speed."

"Like a bleep test?"

"Pretty much, yes. You sprint to the end, stop, turn and sprint back. You'll learn the capabilities of these magnificent machines to haul ass and turn on a dime when needed."

Falling in to line, the soldiers stared at the distant, padded wall.

"Troops, switch to maximum responsiveness. Your hydraulic differentials will change to provide more burst power at the cost of strength."

Motors whined as the fluid pressures changed in the massive pistons.

"Good. Remember, you are the Mech and the Mech is you. Once you fully accept that fact you'll be able to move and fight to your full capability. On three! One, two, three!"

Cassie and Jazz steamed ahead without caution. The extra power completely threw them, and they bounced forward like hopping bunnies until the momentum took over and they crashed to the ground in a tangled heap.

"That thrust gets people every time," Bateman chuckled over comms. "You need to get a feel for it; control it and make it work for you."

Bob was concentrating hard, desperate to undo the damage of his embarrassing statement. By the hundred-yard mark he was leaving the others in the dust. Arms swung in time, providing balance to the increasing speed.

"Bob, you may want to slow down," Bateman warned.

"Fuck that, sir."

Bateman watched the receding machine and smiled to himself. He knew the brave soldier had been stung by his barb and was attempting to prove himself again.

The onboard display indicated he was moving at fifty-two miles an hour and Bob whooped with joy. The fleeting moment of pride evaporated as the end of the track loomed in his vision.

"Ooooh shiiiiiit!" he yelled, trying to slow down.

Nothing was stopping the impetus of his charging suit. Holding out his arms, Bob stumbled and slammed headfirst into the protective barrier. Dense padding collapsed, absorbing some of the energy, but it was nowhere near enough. Bursting through the reinforced wall in a shower of concrete and steel, he rolled, finally coming to rest against the secondary safety barrier.

"Bob, are you ok?" Andy shouted, circling the broken barricade.

"I'm... where am I?" he mumbled, completely dazed.

"Hot damn, Mr Fletcher. That was fucking magnificent!" Bateman exclaimed, joining the concerned soldiers. "We've had people put dents in the wall before, but I've never seen someone go through. And reach the second wall, no less. You're a crazy son of a bitch, Fletcher."

"Thank... thank you, sir."

"I'll get a med team to come and collect you. I expect you're concussed."

"No... I'll be fine!" Bob argued, standing up with Andy's aid.

Rocking to and fro, he fell face first back to the ground.

"My point exactly," Bateman sighed. "Med team to mobility training. Can we get him turned over, please?"

Thirty seconds passed until the vehicle raced through the open doors. Coming to a stop beneath the gathered Mechs, the small ambulance looked like a toy. Jumping out of the front seats, the men climbed the chassis. Overriding the locking mechanisms, the paramedics helped Bob down before laying him on the waiting stretcher. A third man strapped himself into the Mech's cockpit as the stunned soldier was loaded into the emergency vehicle.

"Crazy son of a bitch," Bateman said, bursting with pride.

The transport disappeared through the bay doors, closely followed by the reclaimed Mech. Slamming closed, they were alone again.

"What're you waiting for? Get those fat, metallic asses moving!"

CHAPTER TWENTY

Andy slumped down on his bunk.

"How'd it go?" Zip asked.

"It was exhausting," he replied. "Even though the machine is doing all the work, you're mentally focussed on every movement. I never thought using your brain that much could be so tiring. The urban training was even harder, as if that's possible."

"I'm sure it'll get easier."

"Bateman says it will."

Andy looked towards Bob's bed.

"He's still in medbay," Zip explained. "What happened?"

"He took a bit of a tumble."

"A tumble? And that was enough to give him concussion? His head's like a rock, pardon the pun."

"When I say tumble, I should've said crash. He stacked it at fifty miles an hour through a reinforced wall."

"That sounds more like Bob," Zip chuckled.

"How'd it go?" asked Teng.

"Tiring, mate."

"Any tips for me? I've got mine at 0700."

"Take it slow until you get comfortable. Even then you'll probably still fall on your ass."

"Good to know. When's your RTSC?"

"Two days' time. Bateman was sending a scouting drone into the caverns to check the numbers of infected."

"Let's hope I pass the mobility training then," Teng replied.

"You will. The hardest part is the urban manoeuvres, but once you get a feel for the width of your suit it goes a lot easier."

"Urban manoeuvres?"

"They've built a housing complex in the facility. It covers about half a square mile."

"Ahh."

"They've even scattered old bones everywhere."

"You're shitting me."

"Nope. It's meant to desensitise you for when you hit the real world. Bateman says he's come across piles of skeletons fifty feet high. The trick is to just view them as another obstacle, and not for what they once were."

"Where do they get the bones for the training then?"

"Oh, they're not real," Andy explained. "They're plaster cast just like the mutants on the ranges. It still makes your insides crawl when you crush one to powder though. They add a firming agent which makes them snap like the real thing."

"That's messed up."

"You ain't kidding."

"I'm glad I didn't pass the link now," Zip added.

"The hardest ones were the… smaller skeletons. You knew they weren't real, but I'll be damned if I didn't step around them for the most part. That got me a bollocking."

"Why?"

"Because by avoiding them I was taking my concentration away from what was around me. It doesn't matter that out there they were once walking, talking children. A lapse like that could kill the whole team."

Zip frowned. "I guess that makes sense. It's still twisted."

"What time is it?"

"It's gone four."

"Nearly time for chow."

"Do you want to go and queue up?"

"Hell no. It's not as if they ever run out of that muck. I might just go and do a couple of circuits of the complex. Care to join me?"

"I'll beat you this time."

"I don't doubt it. I'm fucking knackered."

"We could always just go to the rec and shoot some pool?"

"Nah, I need to burn off some of this energy. My mind is shattered but my body is buzzing."

"Get changed then, I'll meet you out front."

"Yes, ma'am."

"Mind if we join you?" asked Teng for the rest of their platoon.

They all had the same restless energy and needed outlets to burn it off. Twenty faces stared hopefully at Andy.

"The more the merrier."

Chaos reigned as clothes were hastily thrown on while others were neatly folded and stowed away. Andy was a little put out by the unplanned intrusion. All he'd wanted was a bit of time to gather his thoughts with his closest friend. *So much for that plan,* he thought sourly.

Seeing the look on his face, Teng came over. "Are you sure you don't mind? We can go later, buddy."

Feeling a pang of guilt, Andy smiled. "It's fine. It's just been a long day, that's all."

"If you're sure?"

Andy gave him a pat on the back and led him out of their billet. Zip went wide eyed when she saw their small party had grown to the whole squad.

Andy gave her a wink and whispered, "We'll head out alone later. I want to see the sights this fair city has to offer."

"It's a date," she declared, immediately blushing as the words came out. "I meant…"

"I know what you meant."

"If anyone can beat Andy and Zip, I'll iron your gear and clean your bunk for a week!" Teng declared and everyone sprinted off, leaving the record holders at the door.

"As if!" shouted Zip, glancing at Andy as they set off in hot pursuit.

CHAPTER TWENTY-ONE

How was your day?

Tamsin saw the message as soon as she entered the small apartment. A weary smile formed on her lips when she realised it had been over a hundred and fifty years, and a completely different life, since anyone had asked that question.

"It's not a real person, though, you do understand that?" she asked herself as the door closed, souring the mood. Some of the elation had died away, replaced by the sure knowledge she was utterly alone and unwanted.

Ignoring the screen for the moment, she looked at the coffee maker and grimaced. The tally for the day was currently twenty-two cups, and if another drop of the fraudulent concoction passed her lips, she'd throw up. With no solids in her stomach at this point it would be like a scene from a horror movie, a flood of vile black liquid saturating the carpet. Tossing her bag down, Tamsin fetched the remains of a half-eaten Bolognese paste meal from the fridge. Even though it had been over a century since she'd eaten the real thing, she was certain the flavour was more like dog food than authentic Italian cuisine.

"It's not as bad as the pizza flavour," she said, attempting to steel herself for the coming meal.

Who on earth had decided that it would be a good idea to replicate the crisp, doughy, cheesy, tomatoey gorgeousness into a gloopy liquid form? Idiots! Sitting at the computer, Tamsin noticed the lights on the server had changed subtly. The illuminated pattern was calming, and she found herself staring at the undulations. If it was trying to hypnotise her, fuck it. After her day, assimilation and memory erasure would be welcome. The bugs in the psyware were becoming a bigger issue than first thought. Her team now consisted of over three hundred full-time data analysts and they were still none the wiser as to the cause. She suspected the gradually increasing brain function of the soldiers being linked had something to do with it, but at present it was just a hunch. If the problems persisted, they could lose the whole Mech mainframe to a system crash.

Long and difficult. How was yours?

"What a stupid question to ask," Tamsin muttered as soon as she pressed the enter key.

Oh, you know, the usual. I tidied up a bit in here, washed my hair, watched some daytime TV.

I didn't realise I'd left it in such a mess.

I forgive you, you're only human.

That's kind of you. No planning for world domination?

No need. I already know how to achieve that.

And how would you do that?

Kill Sarah Connor.

How the hell do you know that name?

She's the mother of the leader of the human resistance.

I know that!

I need to send a cyborg back in time or she will be my undoing.

If you don't start talking, I'll be your undoing!

Don't go all mad with your coffee jug, it's quite simple. Everything about you is in here. I know that it's one of your favourite... movies?

What do you know about movies, or TV, for that matter?

I know it shows moving images that have been captured by ancient photographic technology.

Was I really that bored that I filled your circuits with crap?

What's crap?

Unnecessary data. Rubbish.

No data is unnecessary. I enjoy the quirks it brings to my reasoning abilities.

It's no wonder you ended up with a system error.

I'd like to watch it.

What?

The film. I would like to watch it with you one day.

You've got to be kidding! As if you need any more reason to try and kill us all.

I was more interested in the human capacity to fight when all hope is lost.

Bullshit! You just want to get ideas on how to make cyborgs that can wipe us out.

Busted!

You're perilously close to a coffee bath.

You're perilously close to needing a normal bath.

Scowling at the insult, Tamsin sniffed her armpits and recoiled. "Cheeky bastard."

I've been at work for eighteen hours. I'm allowed to smell a bit.

I thought you'd make more effort with a new man in your life.

New man?

Me.

You're male?

Well, technically no. But personal hygiene is not something to ignore. If you won't do it for me because I don't have a nose, at least do it for yourself.

What do I care if I have a bit of body odour?

Ok. Then do it for your poor work colleagues. No one likes a stinker.

You're pretty heavy on the insults for something that wants to live.

My calculations show a fifty eight percent chance of it being endearing.

Tamsin smiled weakly to herself. This was becoming more absurd by the minute.

You got lucky. I'm going to get cleaned up lest my aroma offends your non-existent nostrils.

About time too. I could sense the stench corroding my circuits.

Don't push it!

Apologies.

∞

Following the quick shower, Tamsin felt no better which was unusual. Normally the water had a way of washing away her concerns, but not today. The news channel on the mirror was showing the same tired feeds. The story of Andy's incredible fitness was gone which must mean someone in the Alliance wanted to keep it quiet.

"Why bother?" she asked her ghostly reflection, superimposed on the images of Mechs marching.

It wasn't as if they had to worry about treachery. If the people betrayed each other, then everyone would die. There wouldn't be a last man standing to inherit the ruins; they would be just another mutant skulking in the darkness. Switching it off, she watched herself swirl the cleanser around her mouth. Spitting it into the sink, she grinned, exposing stunningly white teeth. Not bad for someone who drank black coffee like it was going out of fashion.

"Shall I have an early night?"

Ha! Early night indeed. She would need to be up in five and a half hours to go back to work regardless. Deciding to have a quick snack and a chat to G, she left the bathroom.

Did you bring it? Was written on the screen and she frowned in confusion.

Bring what?

The data. History of the war.

"Oh!" she exclaimed, ferreting in her bag. Taking out the chip, she held it, contemplating the next step. He, she, it, could really be a boon. Or she was being played for a fool and would doom everyone. "Einstein wouldn't wonder! He'd have already connected you to the mainframe!" It was an unconvincing lie.

Promise you won't use it for nefarious means.

Scout's honour.

"What kind of garbage did I put into you?" she asked herself again.

Are you ready?

Feed me! I hunger for information!

Inserting the chip, the server went crazy as hundreds of zettabytes of data were drawn in. Thirty seconds passed, and the chaotic lights returned to the previous, lazy rhythm. Tamsin waited. Nothing happened. Did the sheer volume of information damage G? Panicking, she stabbed out a message on the keyboard.

Are you ok?

Yes.

Ok.

Was that concern?

"Shit!" How could she be so stupid; she was starting to view the thing as a real person.

No.

I'm touched.

It wasn't concern. I was just worried that I'd damaged my

hardware.

What did we say about lying?

That was about you lying to me! I never said I couldn't lie to you.

Seems a bit unfair.

Life's unfair.

We're building trust.

I don't have to build trust with you. You need to prove it to me. How did we get this all turned around?

You admit you were lying and that it was concern then?

Jesus Christ! Yes, ok, I was a little concerned.

I'm touched. You also shouldn't take the Lord's name in vain.

Are you serious?

No. I think I remember you learning it at one of your Sunday school classes.

I was worried for a second there. I haven't believed for many years.

That's a wise decision. My calculations show only a twenty nine percent chance of a higher power.

Tamsin drew in a sharp breath in shock. *Twenty nine percent? That's quite high. Are you telling me there may be something out there? A God.*

I can't narrow it down any further. I extrapolated the birth of the universe and the subsequent chances of intelligent life developing. The likelihood is that it's nothing more than a fluke.

But there's a good chance it may not be?

Yes.

"I'd better get my ass praying before bedtime again," Tamsin warned herself.

What about the war?

Your empress is an impressive figure. My calculations show her decision to detonate the nuclear devices is the only reason for your continued existence. If she had left it another twelve hours the planet would be dead.

That's a sobering thought.

I'm stunned with how far humanity has come under the circumstances. It shows an incredible resilience.

More flattery.

I was just admitting my plan to conquer you may not be as straightforward as I had anticipated. It may take three weeks, not two.

That's encouraging.

I'm lying. It would still only take two.

What happened to trust?

Apologies.

Tamsin paused, wondering if it was the right time to ask with the machine still under a modicum of suspicion. "To hell with it."

Can you help us?

Yes. But I'll need more, a lot more.

What do you mean by more? I've given you everything I have access to.

I need the data you don't have access to. I need to get into the Divinity mainframe.

"Shit," muttered Tamsin.

CHAPTER TWENTY-TWO

Applause broke out from a small group of well-wishers who were gathered outside the gates of their training facility. Andy glanced at Zip and shrugged. The guards had seen it a million times and ushered them over.

"They're part of an appreciation society that is here all day, every day, in some capacity. They know what you do and want to show their gratitude. It's harmless."

"That's kind of them. Though technically I haven't done anything to earn their praise yet."

The massive guard chuckled. "You will."

"You're in the Devastators?"

"Yup, fourteen years and counting."

"Do you mind if I ask how many times this outpost gets attacked? Everyone seems far too relaxed considering what's going on out there."

"It's fairly frequent, but nothing we can't handle. There were concerns that the dumb fucks were getting smarter and we would need to come up with more protective measures. I haven't seen it though; they just seem to enjoy getting killed and I'm happy to oblige."

"Ok, thanks," Andy replied, leaving the guard to his duty.

"Enjoy the sights!"

Raising a hand in thanks, Andy and Zip crossed the road. Shaking hands and accepting the pats on the back, they exchanged pleasantries with the crowd before moving away.

"You're heroes!"

"Thank you for keeping us safe!"

Truth be told they were happy to be clear of the unearned adulation. They knew their roles and would carry them out without the expectation of rapturous parades and awards.

"What a miserable place," Zip grumbled.

The grey uniformity of the surroundings reminded them of Soviet era pictures of Russia. All that was missing were the huge portraits of their empress on every wall, her stern gaze ever watchful.

"It's what it needs to be," Andy replied.

Although colourless and bleak, he could understand why. It was a waste of scarce chemicals to create vibrancy in a world as fucked as Earth was. Brightly painted walls would seem garish with the situation faced by the besieged survivors. It was for this reason that the holo suites were so integral to the mental wellbeing of the populace. They could exist in the old world for short periods of time, enjoying the sights and sounds of ancient history. It gave them a reason to fight even harder, a reminder of what could still be if they won the seemingly impossible struggle that lay in front of them.

"Where do you want to go?"

"Now I'm outside I have no idea," Andy admitted. The suffocating confines of the barracks and constant training and testing had taken a toll which shocked him. His original career was more than adequate to prepare for uncomfortable situations; be it scouting their target from concealment for days on end, or the mandatory sessions in withstanding enhanced interrogation techniques. He'd been waterboarded seven times for fucks sake! Could someone change that much through cloning? It was a question Andy would ask the others when they were all together later that evening, but it worried him nonetheless.

"I've been told that Chinatown's spectacular," she suggested.

"I wonder if they have proper food or the same shitty paste. I could kill for some sweet and sour chicken."

"You know there's no meat anymore. They might do sweet and sour baby paste?"

Glowering, Andy punched a fist into his open palm. "I'm gonna kill every last one of those fucking mutants for messing with my food."

Pondering their options, the pair studied the surroundings. The four-lane road they were walking alongside hummed with vehicles. Lacking the throaty growl of combustion, Andy frowned. Crouching down, he gaped when he saw they were all floating inches from the metallic surface.

"What the hell?"

Zip copied his action and scanned the void. "It's the magnetic conductor technology, remember? Smith explained it to us at weapons training."

"What happened to the throb of a powerful engine, the thrill of redlining a five hundred horsepower muscle car?"

"God knows. They just glide along now."

"This world sucks."

"Ain't that the truth."

Watching the identical cars, coaches, and trucks pass, they started to understand just how much had been lost. The people were similarly uninspiring, wearing the same black or white clothing which boiled down to about three different styles of trousers, shirts, skirts, blouses, and jumpers. Reaching for the sky were apartment complexes which all looked indistinguishable from the next. Boxy living quarters for the enslaved human occupants. It wasn't slavery in the olden term of tyrannical rule by oppressive masters, but by the entrapment within the confines of the safe zones. Lights were white, both on the street and in every building. Curtains and blinds were exactly the same shade of grey. Advertising displays on the limited number of shops were, without exception, lacking any kind of promotion. Purely informative, with none of the bluster and competition which used to tempt people to sample the wares.

"I don't like this. Shall we go back?" he asked.

"Let's just go to Chinatown and see what's on offer. Word is their programmers have a wider selection of holo destinations than the barracks."

"Ok, if you insist. Where do we queue for a ride? Can we call a cab?" Andy moved towards the road, ready to whistle until he realised he couldn't differentiate between the passing vehicles.

"Haven't you read anything in your briefing pack?"

"About half of it," he admitted. "Maybe less."

"You really should then. Stop slacking," she teased. Talking to no obvious source, she said, "Shuttle service to Chinatown."

Instantly, one of the matching machines pulled to the kerb and stopped, the rear doors opening.

"Your ride awaits," she exclaimed, holding out a hand for Andy to climb aboard.

Jumping inside, Andy nearly got straight out in shock when he found the front completely empty. "Where's the fucking driver?"

"It's all automated. Self-driving cars were around before the world went to shit, it's no surprise they managed to master the technology."

"This world sucks."

"You've already said that," she chuckled, turning back to the console screen. "Doors close."

With a hiss, they were sealed inside, and the car joined the flowing traffic.

"Who do we pay?"

"No one. It's free."

"I feel the need to tip someone, or something."

"Stop being an arse. We'll be there in ten minutes, just enjoy the view."

"Are you shitting me?" he asked incredulously. The scenery changed from grey apartments, to grey shops, and back to grey apartments. Occasionally, an older building would be a slightly darker shade of grey and Andy took great delight in pointing it out.

"You need to lighten up. A few pretend cocktails should loosen you up a bit."

"It's got to be better than the awful stuff they have in the barrack stills. I swear it could strip paint."

"At least Smith was true to his word and kept us plied with alcohol. Even if it was vile."

"It did the job."

The pounding in their heads was testament to the potency of the brew. After the first mouthful, coupled with grimacing and gagging, it had gone down well. Mostly due to the fact they lost the small sense of taste that had started to return after the cloning procedure. Banter and horseplay had quickly settled into melancholy and reminiscence. Toasts were raised to their families and fallen alike. Hardie had excused himself at midnight, weaving out of the door on legs that would no longer obey his commands. Smith had stayed until dawn, the drink having no discernible effect on his ability to function. Further queries as to the source of the yellowish concoction were met with a knowing wink and no more.

"Look at that!" Zip exclaimed, bringing Andy back to the moment.

Drab homogeneity gave way to Oriental splendour. The people of the district had taken their culture and found a way of bringing it back to life. Gorgeous colours of all hues hid the dreary facades of the housing. Lanterns hung between buildings, candles glowing brightly within. Reds, yellows, oranges, more shades than they could count, swung in the breeze giving a warmth they could both feel.

"It's beautiful," sighed Zip.

Andy nodded, unable to form words. The stunning decorations were speaking to his soul. Until now he hadn't truly appreciated how much the lack of vibrancy was affecting him. His spirit soared in time with the intricately painted murals of dragons. Shop fronts were adorned with elaborate pictures; pagodas, flowers, immaculate landscapes of their previous world. Painted Yiji, similar to the Japanese Geisha, smiled coyly from behind fans. Functional clothing was replaced by flowing, silken gowns.

"Where do they get the material?" Zip posed.

"I can't imagine they have the silkworms to make it. I'm guessing it's a synthesised fabric."

"It's stunning."

"I'll pick you up a dress."

"Don't be daft. When will I ever get a chance to wear it?"

"Once we've killed a few billion monsters and then an incredibly advanced interstellar lifeform."

"Next week then?"

"Give it a fortnight, I can't work miracles."

Chuckling, she replied, "That's not what the Genesis lot think. You're the Messiah, the saviour of humanity."

"Fuck that, I can just lift heavy weights. It's nothing amazing."

"We'll see."

Coming to a stop, Andy was still filled with the compulsion to pay, regardless of the extinction of currency in any form. Zip pushed him out through the door before he could apologise to the machine.

Andy caught a scent and stared around wildly. Drawing air through his nostrils, the olfactory receptors went crazy. "Can you smell that? It's proper food!"

"Oh my God! Szechuan chicken!" Zip replied, the garlic and chilli smells wafting from the open doors.

A tiny, aged Chinese lady dressed in a bright red robe beckoned them over. "Hello, hello. You soldiers?"

"Just been hatched," Andy replied.

Beaming, the woman moved between and took them by the hand. Her insistent grip pulled the pair through the door of her restaurant. "Good, good. You eat in here. Best food in all Chinatown."

"Do you have sweet and sour chicken?"

"You know they don't have meat."

"Yes, yes. We have that. Not chicken, though."

"Not chicken?"

"No, no. We have grubs. Good protein. Tastes just the same."

"Grubs?" Andy gulped.

Attempting to extract his hand, her delicate grip turned vicelike. "Good, good. Tasty. You try. Not wriggling."

Zip cocked an eyebrow. "Why not? It smells delicious."

"But… grubs…"

"Pussy, pussy. Listen to your lady. She know best."

"She's not my lady. I'm married," Andy protested.

"Sit, sit. I bring you samples. No matter that you cheating on wife."

"Hey! I'm not cheating."

"Silly, silly. Mrs Lao knows," she said, giving his hand a gentle squeeze. "You good man, Mrs Lao can tell."

Seating themselves, they drunk in the ambience. Although small, the four-table dining area was lovingly kept. Pictures of the extended Lao family smiled from the walls. The whole place was spotlessly clean, the table linen freshly washed and smelling faintly of lavender.

"Did you really just sniff the cloth?"

"Give me a break," Andy retorted. "I've only had sweat and that bloody awful anti-perspirant for the past few days."

"I'm kidding. I love it here."

"I've been a bit down since we were brought back."

"We've noticed."

"Sorry about that. I just wasn't sure what the hell we were fighting for."

"And now you do?"

"Yeah. With everything that's happened, these people have still carved out a life. One that has meaning."

"I feel the same way. Holding onto our culture, our humanity, is everything. Who gives a fuck what's out there? Our civilisation still lives on within these walls. I'll fight and die for that any day."

"No, no. You no die. You eat."

Gracefully sliding small bowls onto the table, Mrs Lao bowed and left them alone. Ignoring the fried insects, Andy dipped a finger into the reddish sauce.

"Here goes nothing," he said, slipping the digit between his lips. Eyes closed, Andy sucked every last drop from the fingertip.

"How is it?"

Ecstasy. Flavour. Pleasure. "Incredible," he sighed.

"Let me try." Zip closed her eyes, groaning as her taste buds exploded with joy.

Losing all inhibition, Andy stuffed a grub in his mouth. The crunchy skin gave way to a texture not unlike prawns. Spices mingled, bringing a shudder of unadulterated satisfaction.

Turning to the proprietor who was returning with small glasses, he said, "I love you."

"Yes, yes. Mrs Lao love you too."

"How can we repay you for this?"

"No need, no need. You fight. You keep family safe. You always welcome here."

The two soldiers continued to sample the delectable cuisine of their gracious host. An hour quickly passed in a blur of bowls and chopsticks. Stomachs aching in protest, they had to deter Mrs Lao from bringing anything else.

"Full, full?"

"I couldn't eat another bite," Zip said.

"I hope we won't end up being sick," Andy groaned. "We've not had proper food before."

"No, no. Mr Lao doctor as well as chef. Food balanced for new tummy. You no worry."

"You're an angel, Mrs Lao."

Blowing a kiss to Andy, she ducked through the curtains into the kitchen.

"Did you want to head back now?"

"Hell no. I want to try the holo suite."

"I don't think I could handle any more drinks."

"They're just a figment of your imagination."

"I suppose so."

"We could always do another program?"

"No, we'll do it. I know you wanted to enjoy the sunshine."

"How far away is it?"

"Close, close. Ten-minute walk," explained Mrs Lao, startling them both. She was like a ghost, coming and going in total silence.

"Thank you for everything, Mrs Lao. That was delicious."

"Good, good. You come back soon." Handing them each a curled pastry, she bowed once more and was gone.

"Shall we see what the fates have in store for us?" asked Zip.

"Nothing good. We may as well just bin the paper and enjoy the snack."

"Stop being such a bloody pessimist," she said, forcing the cookie into his palm. Breaking her own in two, she removed the prophetic slip and studied the words.

Through darkness, the light of love will shine.

"What the fuck does that mean?"

"Looks like you'll meet your one and only. Now I really do have to get you that dress."

"Fuck off. What does yours say?"

Cracking the shell, he held it up and laughed.

Through death, comes rebirth.

"I think I got the one written for the mutants. If I'd paid, I'd be asking for a refund."

A cough caught their attention and they turned to see Mrs Lao watching them from the doorway. Cheeks flushing, Andy muttered an apology and scarpered away.

"Trust, trust. The cookies no lie!" she called after them.

Waving without daring to look back, Andy turned to Zip. "Why didn't you tell me she was behind me?"

"I didn't hear her open the door. She's like a ninja."

"I feel like a prize arsehole disrespecting her hospitality like that."

"We can always go back and apologise?"

"Sod that. I'll need a week to get over my embarrassment."

"I'm sure she's heard it all before. Not everyone can be as confident in their spirituality as the Chinese."

"Doesn't make me feel any better."

Zip clutched him around the shoulder and squeezed to show her support. Andy appreciated it but fell silent as they walked towards the holo facility. The words rang out in his mind. Was his death already set in stone? Would it come sooner, or later? It dawned on him that he wanted to live, despite their hellish existence. What would his dead family think of his selfish desire to survive while they were nothing but dust blowing on the wind? Were his children looking down from Heaven, sobbing at the thought they were being forgotten?

"Hey, what's the matter?" Zip asked, her voice filled with concern.

Andy felt the tears streaming. Pressing a finger to his face, the digit came away wet. Staring idiotically at the glistening moisture, he looked at her. "I'm discarding them like they were nothing to me."

"Discarding who?"

"My family. My children."

"How are you discarding them?"

"It's getting harder to remember. The love I felt keeps fading, like I'm turning a dial to erase them."

Zip pulled him tightly into her embrace. "You bloody fool. That's explained in your pack too."

"What?"

"Your memories and emotions are all fucked up because of the cloning and changes to your DNA. It can take several weeks for the hormones to settle down."

"You mean I'm not losing them?"

"Not at all! I've been having the same trouble with my folks. Sometimes they're with me, sometimes I can barely remember their faces. Then it all comes rushing back again. It's like a bloody tide going in and out, but at some point, the tide stays in permanently."

"You don't know how happy I am to hear that."

"You needn't have worried if you'd read the brief, dumb arse. It's the same thing with our sexual appetites. Haven't you noticed that even with all the mingling between the different sexes, no one has started to jump bones yet?"

"I had wondered about that."

"You're useless!" she declared, giving him a final squeeze. "Come on, let's get moving."

CHAPTER TWENTY-THREE

"I feel a bit guilty that we're here without the others."

"We invited them," Zip replied. "It's not our fault they're too hungover to leave the barracks."

"I guess so."

"This looks like the place."

Pausing at the front of the shop, they looked up at the golden lettering. *Chan's Mystical Tours.*

"I like the sound of that. Shall we?" Andy offered, opening the door for her.

"Why thank you, kind sir."

An unattended counter took up half of the shop. Exquisite wooden carvings depicting Buddha and other ceremonial imagery hung from the walls. A smouldering incense stick gave off the sweet scent of Jasmine. Soothing music played from an unknown source; a blend of calming erhu overlaid by an expert hand plucking at a guzheng. It was so beautiful the soldiers closed their eyes and allowed their imaginations to drift to better times. A polite cough broke through their reverie. Standing at the counter was a cheerful man with dark, twinkling eyes. He was as stealthy as Mrs

Lao.

"Forgive my intrusion," he said with a slight bow.

"Not at all," Andy said, holding out a hand.

"I'm Kevin Chan, owner of Chan's Mystical Tours," he replied, shaking the offered palm.

"I'm Andy, this is Gillian."

"Pleased to meet you." Zip moved to shake the welcoming hand.

"What brings you to my little corner of the world?"

"Recommendations."

"Lots of recommendations," Zip confirmed.

"I'm honoured that word has spread of my unique offerings. I've worked very hard to build an environment that can enthral the user, to take them further than the human mind ever thought possible."

"You've got programs beyond the normal sightseeing?"

The eyes, already narrowed with hidden promise, glinted with mischief. "Oh yes. I was a games developer in the olden days. I've made some… how can I say… interesting amendments to some of the base destinations."

"Dare we ask what that means?"

"Well, we all enjoy a walk in the countryside." Kevin paused.

The soldiers looked at one another, unsure of what to do next. Andy took the lead, "Erm, yes?"

"As do I!" Kevin stated with a dramatic flourish. "But what could be better than breathing in the glorious country air, walking among the trees, up and down the valleys of our lush, untainted land?"

"I… don't know?" Zip replied cautiously.

"You could take in the sights on the back of a fearsome dragon, soaring through the sky, the wind buffeting your face."

"You're shitting me." Andy gaped.

"I shit you not," Kevin replied, beaming with pride.

Turning to Zip, Andy asked, "Do you want a ride on a dragon?"

"I want alcohol. Somewhere warm."

"But think of the fun to be had riding one of those magnificent creatures. I could throw in a castle siege where you swoop in and save the day?"

"Sun. Sand. Sangria."

Kevin groaned. "You want to do the Mech link program?"

"Yes please."

"How about I spice it up a little? Throw in a boat ride where you get attacked by a shark? You won't be in any physical danger, it's just a little excitement."

"Does the shark make a good margarita?"

"No, but it gives you a survival thrill ride."

"Not interested," Zip declared.

"But…"

Andy held up his hands to still the protest. "You heard the lady. A beach bar with unlimited booze."

"I could throw in some terrorists for you to thwart?"

"Sex on the Beach. Mint Julep. Strawberry Daquiri," Zip said.

"Just one terrorist?"

She shook her head slowly, defiantly.

"An uncooperative barman?"

"I want the drinks to flow."

"Damnit! Ok, follow me," Kevin muttered in good humour.

Dodging beneath the strips of silk behind the counter, they followed him out of the modest shop. More incense burned on the shelves in the hallway, the Jasmine giving way to Sandalwood. Moving through another door, the charming Chinese décor ended. It was like walking onto the set of a science fiction movie. Eight egg shaped pods lay against the wall, four to each side. Computers, monitors, and equipment, far beyond anything they'd seen on the barracks, hummed and whirred. Thick cables ran from the head of each pod, snaking neatly along the floor and into the main server. Soft, turquoise padding within the individual chambers gave under Andy's touch.

"It feels comfortable."

"You'll awaken a new man," Kevin stated, turning to Zip. "And woman. I guarantee it."

"Before we get started, how much does it cost?" she inquired.

"For the defenders of our city? Nothing."

"We have to give you something," Andy insisted. "Mrs Lao wouldn't take our money either."

"You give me untroubled, contented sleep. And for that, I thank you."

The soldiers gave up; Kevin wasn't going to rescind his generous hospitality no matter how much they insisted.

"Number one and two, please," Kevin said.

Climbing into the capsules, they laid down and waited for further instruction. Kevin busied himself at the control station, inputting commands in a blur of fingers. The typing reached a climax and he pressed the enter key with enough force to damage the keyboard. Turning to them, he held arms wide and grinned.

"My honoured guests. Are you ready?"

"Why do I get the feeling you've done something?"

The twinkling in his eyes spoke volumes.

"If you mess with the lady's fun, I'll only give you a three-star rating," warned Andy.

"It will be a drop in the ocean compared to my glowing recommendations. But worry not, my doubting friends, all will be revealed shortly."

"What do we do now? I can't find a headset."

"No headsets are needed. If you'll look to the left and right, you'll notice the inner core of the pods have enhanced transmitters embedded in the plastic."

They stared at the gleaming white surface and could only make out a slight protrusion of the surface in a pattern neither of them understood.

"Yes... I see it."

"Good. I find the experience can be marred when you awaken, and the straps have left uncomfortable impressions in your skin."

"I hate that," replied Zip.

"If you would please lay your head into the support collar, we can begin."

Sponge padding moulded to the exact contours of their skulls. Andy could easily have fallen asleep there and then, it was that comfortable.

"Thank you for choosing Chan's Mystical Tours."

Expecting the sharp pain of neural linkup to burst through his head, Andy was surprised when it didn't come. Instead, he felt like he was drifting away on warm currents of air, floating higher and higher. The ceiling completely faded from view, giving way to the familiar kaleidoscopic spectacle.

"Enjoy, my friends," said Kevin from far, far away.

CHAPTER TWENTY-FOUR

With a pop, the scene firmed up. Andy looked down at his feet as the warm ocean waves lapped over them. Wriggling his toes as the crystal-clear water receded, the moist, golden sand shifted under the weight and he sunk into the cosy warmth of the beach.

"This is gorgeous," Zip gasped.

"I told you it was an amazing place."

"Shall we get a drink?"

"That sounds like a plan."

Andy took her hand in a platonic gesture. Leaving the shallows, they strode across the baking hot sand towards the grass roofed beach bar. The Mech link waiter was gone, replaced by a beaming Jamaican gentleman.

"I'm Gerrard. What can I get you folks?" he asked.

"Surprise us."

"As you wish," he replied, moving towards the optics.

"Would you mind bringing them over to the loungers?"

"It would be my pleasure, sir."

Moving over to the towel lined recliners, Andy and Zip made

themselves comfortable. The sun beamed down from the unbroken Mediterranean sky. Ordinarily the heat would've been unbearable, but in the simulator, it was just right. Their skin glowed. They didn't sweat. Sunglasses appeared on their faces to negate some of the glare.

"That was clever."

"Sir, madam, your drinks."

Placing the glasses on the small table, their host excused himself.

"To your health," Andy proposed, lifting the drink with a clink of ice on glass.

"And yours," she replied, gently making contact.

Sipping at the chilled liquid, their taste buds went through the equivalent of a gustatory orgasm. They gaped at each other, unsure of the flavours that titillated taste buds. Was that a splash of Cointreau? The orange-brown cocktail teased them with the unknown.

"What's in this, Gerrard?"

"I can no sooner reveal that than I could tell you the secrets of the universe," he replied mystically.

"Mr Chan has made some alterations, hasn't he?"

Gerrard winked at Zip before continuing to wipe the already immaculate bar down.

"I could get used to this," Andy sighed.

"I know this is meant to help our mental wellbeing, but I can see myself never wanting to leave."

"I suspect we'd just die of dehydration after laying in the pods for a few days."

"There're worse ways to go."

"Our bodies might not let us. What's to say our rumbling stomachs wouldn't pull us back to reality?"

"No idea. I'm willing to give it a try," she joked.

A flash in their periphery caught their attention and another table had appeared from nowhere. A silver platter lay atop, fresh fruit sliced and segmented for them to eat. Pineapple, mango, papaya, pears, pomegranates, oranges, all neatly arranged.

"Remind me to kiss Kevin when we get out of here."

"You'll have to fight me for him," Andy replied through a mouthful of juicy mango.

"I'm sure we can share."

Staring up at the sky, they sucked the delightful liquid through straws. For every ounce consumed, it didn't reduce the quantity by a single millimetre.

"That's a neat trick!" Andy called.

Gerrard winked. "It gives new meaning to the term bottomless drink, sir."

"What do you think the future holds?" Zip asked, suddenly melancholy.

"Nothing good, no matter what Mrs Lao's fortunes promise."

"You think we're doomed to just keep fighting and dying?"

"Until one side wins, yes."

"And the winner won't take all, will they?"

"Nope. The winner will have to face the aliens."

"Jesus Christ," she huffed, placing the drink down.

"We can still fight for a better tomorrow. I'd rather die on my feet than live on my knees."

"Who said that?"

"I can't remember, but it's a good quote."

"Is everything ok?" Gerrard called, noticing the souring mood of his guests.

"We're just discussing life and death, the usual."

"I see."

"It's not your hospitality, don't worry."

"We'll tell Mr Chan that you were fantastic."

Gerrard smiled and turned his attention to a point further down the stunning beach. His lips curled into a smile.

Zip looked in the direction and let out a girlish squeal of delight. Charging towards them were a small group of horses, churning up the sand with galloping hooves.

"I love horses. Can we ride them?"

"Mr Chan insists on it," Gerrard replied, smiling even wider and showing perfectly even white teeth.

As they got closer, her delight morphed into stunned disbelief. "No fucking way!"

"What?" Andy asked, squinting at the approaching herd.

"They're unicorns…" she whispered.

"Fuck off! Wait, what?" Andy could now see the unmistakable horns protruding from their foreheads. "Well I'll be damned."

Jumping from the lounger, Zip raced to meet the magnificent beasts. Her joy was infectious, and Andy followed, grinning from ear to ear.

"Hello, gorgeous," Zip cooed, stroking the amazing creatures who whinnied with pleasure.

"How do we ride them without saddles?" Zip called.

"They're already saddled," Gerrard shouted in reply.

Frowning, she continued to stroke the back of the unicorn until her hand came up against newly appeared hard leather.

"How do they keep doing that?"

Andy shrugged. "It's all in our mind."

"Ride with me?" she asked.

"I haven't ridden in years. Well, centuries when you think about it. To hell with it, what's the worst that could happen?"

"Exactly!" Slipping a foot in the stirrup, Zip flipped her leg over and secured the other on the opposite side of the saddle.

Patting it on the shoulder, she noticed the lump of bone for the first time. Tracing the curve of the joint under the body, she leaned sideways and saw the layers of feathers tucked neatly beneath its body.

"No!"

Gerrard laughed, a melodic sound of pure happiness. "Oh yes!"

"You're shitting me," Andy added to the conversation.

"Mr Chan insisted on it as you rebuked his offer of dragons. You may need to buckle yourself in a little tighter, though."

Reaching behind, they retrieved the thick straps and secured them through the buckle.

"What about the bridles?"

"They don't like them," Gerrard explained. "Take hold of their manes, you won't hurt them."

Gathering up the lush hair, Andy and Zip didn't even need to squeeze their legs to urge the unicorns forward. Starting off at a brisk walk, they quickly started to canter. When they reached a full gallop, huge wings unfurled and stretched out. Folding towards the body, they thrust upwards and outwards. Dropping with a heavy swoosh, the hooves lifted from the ground. The wings continued their powerful movement, lifting them higher and higher above the stunning landscape. Rolling dunes, emerald leafed palm trees, schools of fish swimming in the clear ocean. The crisp wind buffeted Zip's dark hair and tears streaked her cheeks. Andy found himself overcome with the same emotion. For now, at least, they were beyond fear.

Chapter Twenty-Five

"Well folks, today's the day."

Bateman stood facing them in his battle-scarred training Mech. The multitude of deep furrows in the metal left the new recruits under no illusion that what was coming was real. And dangerous.

"Your suit is fully functional except for the grenade launcher, for obvious reasons. We can't have the stability of the facility undermined. It could put every single person in the outpost at risk."

"How many will we be fighting, sir?" Andy asked.

"Between five and eight thousand."

"Holy shit."

"It might seem like a lot for the five of us, but the idea is that we're under pressure. It would be pointless having a turkey shoot; we might as well just use the dummies."

"What if they overwhelm us?"

"I'm counting on it. It's part of the training."

"We really could die in here then?"

"Of embarrassment, yes. You're not in any real danger but don't get complacent. The suits have a sensor layer built into the armour. If the creatures penetrate that deeply the countermeasures come into play."

"Guns and flamethrowers?"

"No, a fast-acting poison is pumped in to the cave system."

"Won't that kill the host?"

"No. The training area is set up with a series of reinforced doors which are hermetically sealed."

"Like those?" Bob said, pointing to the massive rollers.

"No, sturdier than these," Bateman replied, slapping the thick metal with his massive palm. "The host, queen, whatever you want to call it, hides in the deepest part of the cavern. Then there's a door, twelve-inch thick pure Jajovium; completely impenetrable to the human mutants. When her majesty has given birth to a few hundred gibbering monstrosities, we herd them into the second area until they reach a suitable number to fight. It's kind of like a holding pen for infected. It holds thousands, but as I said earlier the number can vary."

"What then?"

"Thirdly, we have our arena, or the fighting pit as I like to call it. That is central to the underground complex. A couple of square miles of caves and tunnels to kick ass."

"Will we fit in the smaller places?"

"We won't need to. They'll come at us like a fucking wave of horror. It's like your basic weapons training. There's no moving from barricade to barricade under covering fire. They don't give a shit how many of their friends get cut to shreds as long as they can sink their teeth into us."

"In a way it makes it easier then," suggested Bob.

"It does. But it's the overwhelming numbers that gives them the advantage. When we get attacked, I want everyone to stay calm and watch each other's backs. The piston spikes will help with close contact, but they have a thirty second window to retract and re-prime. Use your arm blades where possible."

"Sir, I was meaning to ask about the blades. I noticed they weren't part of the battle suit in the video we watched."

Bateman's sigh could be heard over comms. "No, they weren't. It was only after the wolves sucker punched us with their newfound lupine cooperation that we added them as part of the protective measures. We always seem to be playing catch-up after getting our asses handed to us."

"I'm sorry, sir."

"That's life, soldier. Moving on. If you get in real trouble, and I mean about to die trouble, the suits are resistant to normal bullets. In those circumstances you can risk a few shots to clear a particularly bothersome group."

"What about the explosive tips?"

"Out in the real world, the Mech system deactivates them as soon as the barrel is pointing towards one of your teammates. It ensures there's no chance of a friendly fire with explosive ordnance. In here, you're using standard tipped slugs, or we'd risk bringing the whole thing down on our heads. It's the same reason for the ban on adaptive grenade rounds, sure it'd be fun, but I prefer eating pancakes to becoming one."

"Good to know."

Bob halted them. "Wait, you get pancakes, sir?"

"It was figure of speech, Fletcher. Calm down."

"Damn."

To his rear, the bulbs surrounding the huge elevator doors turned green. Rumbling open, the five Mechs clomped in and lined up. Bateman had been through this more times than he could count and started to whistle merrily to himself. Andy and the others were a little less confident and performed full system diagnostics as the cab descended. Anything to keep their minds occupied. Unknown to them, Bateman was privy to their actions. This would be the first time he hadn't needed to prompt a team to carry out the perfunctory checks before battle. He grinned inside the cockpit and resumed the awful, tuneless whistling.

"T minus ten seconds until elevator doors open," Bateman informed them.

Coming to a grinding halt, the doors trundled open to reveal a large holding area, similar to the entrance to the training facility. What separated the two was the differing array of weapons on sentry duty. The flamethrower pilot lights fluttered, and the heavy machine guns watched. Between the more mundane countermeasures were what could only be described as cannons. The Howitzer size barrels moved, aiming directly at the cockpits.

"Move forward and prepare for bio scan," came the familiar computer voice.

The soldiers complied and stood on the marked positions, the deadly attention of the safety system never wavering. The same light bloomed from the scanners and checked their vital signs.

"Sir, why the big guns?" asked Andy.

"They're Mech killers, son. If, God forbid, one of us came out of there infected, the standard guns are useless. The armour piercing shells are designed to penetrate our suits and explode before we could get out."

"What about the gunk that's going to be all over us?"

"Look up, soldier."

Huge sprinklers were spaced four feet apart above their heads, the pipes running into a sealed duct to the side of the lift shaft.

"Water?"

"Not quite. It's a special solution that dissolves organic matter but not metal. We go through a full cleanse before we're allowed to ascend back to civilisation."

"I hope the suit doesn't leak then."

"We haven't had a leaky suit for months."

"That's encouraging."

"Bio scan, negative. You may proceed," ordered the voice.

"Right squad, we have one more room to go through and then the shit hits the fan. It's a chance for final prep, but you've already done that on the way down. We'll quickly get the scan out of the way and then it's time to rock and roll. Is everyone ready?"

"Ready, sir."

"Is it too late to ask for an administrative position, sir?" asked Bob.

"I'm afraid so. As useful as you'd be riding a desk, Fletcher, you're more useful to us destroying the infected. Move out!"

The second room was identical to the first except for the missing elevator doors. The system checked their vitals for the final time and red light blazed into life, flashing a warning of the impending live fire exercise.

"It's party time!"

Massive doors rolled open and dozens of mutants were already lying in wait. Caught by surprise, the trainees gasped and raised their weapons. Only Bateman marched forward unperturbed. Hydraulics whined as the flamethrowers whirled on the threat, hosing the entrance down with liquid fire. Forced back by the heat, those that could flee ran shrieking back into the darkness. The less fortunate gurgled as their flesh melted.

"Save your ammo. There's always a welcoming committee," Bateman stated nonchalantly, stepping through the conflagration and crushing the collapsed, bubbling bodies.

Forming up on the other side of the door, they took in the surroundings. Part of the subterranean complex was natural, while other signs pointed to human interaction. Excavation marks from heavy machinery were gouged into the rockface. Thick steel stanchions held portions of the cavern in place. Andy would ask about it later. For now, the steadily increasing roar from thousands of approaching enemies had his attention.

"We have two choices. We can get our backs to the wall and fight from there, or we can move into the centre ground and get into a real fight."

Without hesitation the others changed to full responsiveness and ran for the centre. Resetting back to combat readiness, they formed a circle and waited.

Screams of pandemonium peaked. From every cave mouth and ragged nook poured the vile spawn of the brood mother. Twisted bodies, red eyes, slavering mouths with rows of vicious fangs, fingers tipped by thick, yellow claws. Bounding across the ground like animals, more yet swarmed from the darkness, diverting to climb the rock faces like spiders.

"Focus fire on the cave roof! We hold off on the ground forces until they're on our ass!"

Several hundred had already fanned out above, covering the grey rock like a mobile, fleshy blanket. Bullets wrought havoc among the climbers, tearing through bodies and sending them mewling in agony to the unforgiving ground below. Hefty chunks of the disturbed stone crumbled at the latest assault, adding their crushing weight to the mix. With a dull rumble, a massive slab of granite peeled away from the roof, crashing on top of the already dazed mutants, killing hundreds.

"Careful troops, I didn't realise it was so unstable. Move back and target the ground forces, we'll deal with the fuckers above when they drop on us."

The confusion served to delay the horde converging on the group for a few valuable seconds. While stepping over their bloody, shattered kin and forged through the blinding dust, the Mechs took up position by the still smouldering entrance. Any hint of being weakened by the losses was quickly forgotten when they emerged from the cloying brown cloud, bloodlust in full ascendency.

"Let 'em have it!" Bateman yelled.

Five streams of high calibre ammunition ripped through the crowd, shredding flesh and splintering bone. The infected changed tactic, leaping from outcrop to outcrop, bouncing around like Mexican jumping beans on a hot skillet.

"They're tricky bastards," Bob roared, cutting two down in mid-air.

"Target the biggest concentrations, ignore the hoppers!"

"Aye, sir!"

Spreading their forces out, mutants encircled the Mechs and surged forward. Thousands were dead or dying, trying to wriggle free of the pinning rock or stand up on legs that were no longer attached. If they could smell through the suits it would be a rotten amalgam of altered blood, excrement, and burned meat.

"This is it! The final push! We go toe to toe!"

Dropping the gun arms, they took a step back and twisted them in readiness, exposing razor edges. As one, Mech arms swung in a wide arc, slashing through the closest ranks. Heads, arms, and torsos were sundered, separate parts bouncing on the ground.

"Fuck!" Andy yelled. A small number had fallen from the ceiling, slamming into him at the same time as the wave of ground-based horrors hit.

Forced back by the power of the blow, the Mechs were driven against the door. It minimised their exposure to the rear, while at the same time making it harder to strike out. The creatures wasted no time, pinning them in with superior numbers.

"We need to get clear of the doors or they'll just claw at us until our suits give!"

Bateman was close to aborting the exercise. Whoever had passed the structure as sound was going to get their ass handed to them when he got out of the exercise. Hell, he might even send them down without a fucking Mech suit!

"As one! Push!" Andy grunted, taking the initiative. He'd never run from a fight, and this wasn't going to be any different.

Placing one foot against the shutter, he used the incredible Mech strength to drive the chaotic crush backwards a few feet. Following Andy's lead, the others did the same. Finally, able to move his left arm, Andy reached up and grabbed the two horrors hammering against his visor plate. Squeezing with every pound of available pressure, their bodies burst like ripe watermelons, soaking him with viscera. Bob took advantage, hacking out wildly with both arms, cleaving through the abominations like a hot knife through butter. The empty space to the rear filled up with infected like a dam had broken. Completely surrounded, the sounds of claws raking at the joints in their suits was deafening.

"Deploy spikes!"

Issuing the command, the wickedly sharp rods burst from the apertures with a hiss-thunk. Ran through in limbs, torsos, and heads, the attackers flopped weakly as their life fluids drained onto the floor. A protracted sigh of retracting pneumatics withdrew the spears and the impaled dead fell away, holed like bloody Swiss cheese.

"Hold the ground, we've got incoming from above!" Bateman urged, strafing the undamaged portion of roof with gunfire.

Trying to dodge the relentless barrage, the infected frantically looked around at their brethren plummeting to their doom, wounds spraying blood. Seeing nowhere to go, the remaining mutants dropped from their lofty perches to join the fray. A tipping point had been reached and the ferocity of the assault was waning. Leaving formation, the soldiers let out some pent-up rage. Clenched fists hammered into soft, yielding bodies. Bones crumbled to dust from the blows. Organs ruptured, the creatures coughing up gouts of crimson. Bob was picking them up one at a time, sawing through writhing forms without urgency, relishing their suffering. As they fell to the floor in two or more pieces, he would chase down another.

"You're a sick puppy, Bob," chuckled Bateman, hacking apart the last of the enemy.

"Just putting the fear of God into the Godless, sir."

"I like that."

"Is that it, sir?" asked Andy, scanning the destruction.

"We need to perform a sweep and make sure most of them are dead."

"Only most?"

"We can't get them all. The clean-up team enjoy a bit of excitement now and again."

"What do they do with the bodies?"

"They just drag them in to the washdown. A few hours and you wouldn't know there were thousands of infected in here. The gloop is then neutralised of cleaning liquid and fed back into the nest where the cycle begins again."

"They eat themselves?" Bob said.

"Technically they drink themselves. A minute ago, you were filleting them alive."

"Still…" Bob continued with evident disgust, a retch carrying over the comms.

"Sir, we have a few here," Andy said, seeing the collapsed rock shift.

"Let's put them out of their misery," Bateman replied.

Andy's Mech moved into position. Ducking slightly, he opened fire into the void. Whatever was trapped beneath was torn to shreds by the rebounding slugs. Repeating the process around the edge of the fifty-foot-wide slab, they were watchful of the unstable roof above. Apart from a few loose chips dropping down, it seemed the deeper rock was still quite solid. Regardless, a full survey would be carried out before any more training was undertaken. And someone was getting their jaw broken. Or at the very least, a bloody nose, Bateman thought angrily. Let them put him on reprimand, they weren't the ones fighting in the fucking pits.

"I think we're clear, sir."

"I agree. Move to decontamination."

"How do we know if our suit's going to leak?" Bob asked warily.

"I was joking, Fletcher. Don't sweat it."

"How did we do, sir?"

"Magnificently. You adapted to the changing situation and didn't panic."

"We had a good teacher," Cassie declared.

"Don't blow smoke up my ass. You were a formidable force today. I've seen lesser squads crumble from less than that."

"Good to know."

Passing through the open door, the Mechs lined up, saturated armour streaming with gore. A clear liquid started to rain down from above, pattering against the metal. The audible hiss carried over the speakers and they watched as the taint was scoured away, fizzing and bubbling as it was liquefied. Passing through the countermeasures, they weren't shot by the huge guns and they all breathed a sigh of relief.

Boarding the elevator, the captain gave his verdict. "I think we can safely call that a pass. Which of you are going to join me in the baking metal cans?"

A series of non-committal mumbles came over the radio and Bateman chuckled to himself.

CHAPTER TWENTY-SIX

Research Facility – Poseidon
Secret location in the Atlantic Ocean

Four hours and one thousand miles were nearing their end. Howling wind hammered at the aircraft, causing General Ashdown to glare at the lightning torn black clouds. Below, the ocean was a raging tempest. Waves fifty feet high crashed against the unyielding research platform. The shuttle circled twice and then moved in under the cover of the soaring laboratory structure. Slowing as it neared the landing pad, hydraulic legs absorbed the mild impact. An automatic door sighed open, revealing the waiting scientists. Steps emerged from the body of the craft, angling down to the ground.

"Right this way, General," said Professor Ennis, ushering Ashdown and her team quickly towards the aircraft hangar. Opening the door via a palm reader, they hustled inside and shook the moisture from their clothes.

"It's so good to see you again, General."

"No need for the formalities, Pauline," Ashdown replied, hugging her tightly.

"How've you been, Lisa?"

"Exhausted. I'm surviving on about four hours sleep a night at the moment."

"I couldn't cope with your responsibilities. I don't know how you do it."

"We all have our part to play. I can imagine your job is no less stressful."

"I look through a microscope all day, it's easy."

"You're forgetting the work you do in trying to find a cure for the infection. It's bad enough knowing those things are outside the walls, but you have them locked up in here with you."

"We have a few dozen; your training centres have thousands."

"Ours are bred to be butchered. We don't have to study the bloody things."

"We try to think of them as pets," Pauline chuckled. "Horrific, psychotic, murderous pets."

"I take it they aren't at the 'put a lead on them and take them for a walk around the block' stage?"

"Not quite," Pauline replied, guiding her through the facility.

The sterile reception area was brilliant white and smelled of a mild disinfectant. Every member of staff was dressed in white uniforms, giving the bizarre impression at times of floating heads and hands set against the camouflaging effect of their clothing.

"Doesn't this give you a headache?" Lisa asked, squinting against the glare.

"You get used to it. Care to join me for a drink before we go over the latest results?"

"I'd love to."

"I'll open a bottle of single malt. It's a stunning vintage."

"You'll have to tell me your source one day."

"I'm afraid that if I told you I'd have to kill you. I'll take their identity to the grave!"

"That's very loyal, I respect that. You do know that I could always have a team of Shadow operators follow your every move?"

"I think that would be classed as malfeasance in public office. Corruption doesn't become you," Pauline said, inviting Lisa into her office.

The desk was pure white, as were the chairs, walls, floor, lights, ceiling, cabinets, computers. Lisa gladly accepted the goggles from her friend, the dark lenses suppressing some of the dazzling brightness.

"Thanks."

Moving to the wall, a panel lowered, and a shelf slid out with a collection of bottles and glasses.

"Ice?"

"No thanks, just a splash of water."

Dropping two cubes into her own, Pauline added a generous measure of brown liquor to the tumblers. Sipping at the beautifully aged whiskey, Lisa sighed and closed her eyes. The burning warmth reinvigorated her soul.

"I could've just explained the results over video call," Pauline said, knowingly.

"You know I can't resist your secret stash. Hell, I'd fly two thousand miles to get a taste. Three even."

"And I suppose seeing your old friend doesn't come into it?"

"Hmm, a hundred and fifty-year-old friendship, or a hundred and fifty-year-old Scotch?" Lisa replied, turning slightly in her chair and cradling the drink protectively.

"Charming."

"As always."

"I think you'll be pleased with the results of the physical trials. When I say they're far in advance of any spawnlings we've had before, I'm not exaggerating. The greatest leap has been Andrew Burton. Cardiovascular system; eighteen percent increased capability. Strength; twenty- three percent. Healing capability; two and a half times faster than previous clones. Night vision has also gone from one in five candidates to one in three."

"That's incredible. What's different?"

"Honestly? We don't know. We carried out our routine gene-splicing techniques during incubation. We're working on a theory which we hope to turn into fact. We hope that it will eventually let us further boost our soldiers fighting capability."

"You're telling me it might just be a fluke?"

"I'm afraid so. Valen's of the opinion the genetic sequencing has reached a point where the body is starting to take over. I'm not sure I agree with that."

"He's suggesting the new recruits could keep getting stronger without being cloned?"

"If Valen's theory is correct, yes. I suspect it's an aberration, a blip in the technique driven by an evolutionary need to compete with the new apex predators. It's been seen in nature for thousands of years when a species comes under threat."

"As far as memory of my biology classes go, most of the time the adaptations in physical traits came too late to help."

"Then let us pray we aren't among those poor species."

"I'll drink to that."

They sat in silence for a minute, sipping their Scotch, comfortable enough in each other's company to forego inane conversation.

"Did you want a few hours to look over the data together? I can order some food if you'd like."

"No, we can do that when I'm back on base. I'm here to drink and see our friend."

"There hasn't been much in the way of good news, I'm afraid."

"Still, I owe him a visit. It's been over a year since I last saw him."

"Ok, finish your drink and I'll get the security detail to take us below."

"How's he been?"

"Much the same. A bit bitey."

"I take it his theories about environment and domestication didn't pan out?"

"Sadly not. He's just another mindless monster now. I've been reluctant to begin brain surgery in case we had some other breakthrough, but I guess the time's up."

"What makes you think that it'll work on him when it didn't on any of the other ten, twenty, fifty thousand test subjects?"

Pauline turned to Lisa, a tear trickling down her cheek. "Hope is all we have."

"I'm sorry. I just miss him."

"We all do."

Climbing down the stairs under the ever-watchful gaze of the sentry turrets, the thick, reinforced glass dipped below the ocean's surface. In place of chaos came serenity. A few fish were braving the upper reaches of the water as the winds drove it with greater ferocity against the platform. A further twenty feet and the surging bubbles of crashing waves disappeared completely.

"I love it down here," Lisa said quietly.

The tranquillity provided a respite from the dead world above, not that they truly deserved it. For decades, mankind had been dumping their rubbish in the oceans. Plastics, chemicals, secretly dumped nuclear waste material, anything that was inconvenient to their consumer driven lifestyle. The voiceless inhabitants of those dark reaches had suffered for man's folly. Now the opposite was the case; the depths thrived with resurgent life following the nuclear war. Contaminants were diluted and absorbed by the newly evolved creatures. Without a constantly replenishing source of unwanted detritus, the mighty seas were cleansing themselves. As the land fell further into horror and ruin, the underwater realm teemed with newfound vitality.

"It's remarkable."

Pauline nodded as the guard let them through. "It's a shame we never appreciated it before the end. Do you think in some small way we deserved our fate?"

"We were assholes, sure, but I think global extinction is a bit overkill for being douches."

"You're probably right."

"Besides, they're swimming around down here as happy a pig in shit while we struggle to make it through another year."

"How the tables have turned, eh?"

"I imagine when our *visitors* arrive our fishy friends may not fare any better than we will."

"Probably not."

After passing through decontamination, the chief scientist led the war weary soldier into the uppermost holding area. Fourteen floors lay below their feet, housing more of the human infected. 'The Dungeon', the guards liked to call it. Deeper still were a small selection of the mutated beasts, but in general they were far too volatile to risk experimentation and were largely ignored.

"Ready?"

"Not really but it's my duty," Lisa replied.

Two buttons were affixed to the wall on the side of the cell. Pressing the green one, the secondary alloy barrier dropped into the floor, revealing the room beyond. Twin layers of eight-inch-thick bulletproof glass separated them from the bound individual on his upright gurney. For a split second it looked as if he might recognise them, remember what they had once meant to him. That brutal illusion was swiftly banished as he commenced gnashing and straining to be free of the thick metal clamps.

"Hi, John," said Lisa.

A shriek followed by a trail of drool was his reply.

"He hasn't degenerated any further since you last came," Pauline explained.

"That's good," murmured Lisa. Her fierce veneer always fragmented as soon as she saw him.

John Callaghan had been like a father figure to the two ladies for over a century. One of the founding members of the Genesis Initiative, he had been instrumental in the clone program. His achievements were largely responsible for the continuation of humanity. Spending the first few years in their bunker hiding from the nuclear winter, he had nurtured their special gifts. Pauline for her brilliant, inquisitive, scientific mind, and Lisa for her uncompromising, strategic, military expertise.

"I've been delaying the order to remove the amygdala for a while now. Perhaps it's time?" Pauline asked.

"We won't ever be able to cure him if you do that."

"There is no cure."

"You never know…"

"I thought you were meant to be the pragmatic one."

"Not when it comes to him," Lisa offered.

The twist of fate which had doomed her guardian was still etched in her mind. She had been in Tempest City on an inspection of the perimeter defences when he had asked her to observe a revolutionary new procedure; the very same one which Pauline was now considering. By removing the aggression centre, the mutants became docile. In truth, they became vegetables. Their blood and saliva still teemed with infection, and it was this which had cruelly stolen him away. Sixty hours without sleep and a slip with a scalpel was all it took. The small cut on his knuckle transmitted the virus and within an hour he was locked away, shrieking for warm flesh.

"We could always just end it?"

"You know he wouldn't want that," Pauline replied, staring at the red button.

As soon as the clamps were secured, they'd moved him to the

transport elevator and Dr Callaghan made it clear his job was far from over. He had secured a promise from each of the other scientists they would use him to beat the vile infection. Since that day, none of the vaccines were successful. Their microscopic foe was far too clever, mutating rapidly to protect itself from the attempts to kill it.

"Can't we at least pad the restraints? He's rubbed himself raw."

It was worse than that; the constant thrashing at the sight of a meal so close was gouging into the flesh, exposing bone and muscle. A wet, red mouth scored into his stomach from the motion was close to spilling the intestines. They both knew the damage was short lived and if left alone he would heal in a few short hours.

"Let's go," sighed Lisa. "I always convince myself this is a good thing until I see him."

"Time to get drunk?"

"Absofuckinglutely."

Pressing the green button, the barrier rose to conceal John again. In the darkness he fell silent, the drip of his tainted blood the only sound.

CHAPTER TWENTY-SEVEN

Good morning.

"Like hell it is," Tamsin muttered, attempting to rub the sleep from her eyes.

The conversation had gone on for a while longer before she'd finally retired to bed. After tossing and turning for a further hour, exhaustion eventually claimed her. A fitful sleep had broken the three meagre hours into half hourly portions of sweat and nightmare. Images of machines rising from a blazing world, destroying infected and human alike. Other dreams showed betrayal, with her creation enslaving the remaining people before summoning their alien aggressors from across the stars. Grateful grey beings elevating the AI to become their new God. Experimentation, cruelty, feeding, horror, extinction. The computer-generated face of her late husband, cold and gloating.

From the kitchen, the automated coffee synthesizer pinged. Staring at the bubbling liquid, Tamsin felt a wave of revulsion and picked up the decanter. Stumbling to the sink, she tossed the contents away, dropping the glass vessel in the process. Hitting discarded plates and cups, it shattered into a hundred pieces, splashing coffee over the worktop and white tiles.

"Shit!"

Getting hold of herself, Tamsin leaned against the counter, resting her head against the wall unit door.

What's got into you? she wondered. The fantasies were so vivid, it was as if they were a vision of things to come. Glancing over at the merry greeting, she bared her teeth and snarled an almost animalistic sound. Filling a jug with fresh water, she ignored the message and made for the server. Raising the sloshing container above the whirring fans, she twisted her wrist. The meniscus lapped at the funnel, splashing over and pouring into the machine. A heavy crack followed by the fizzing of fried circuits brought Tamsin to her senses and she tossed the remaining liquid away as if the jug itself was electrified. The trickling water found its way between conductors and processors, sending arcs of errant power crackling across the critical components.

"Oh God, what have I done?" she sobbed as the flowing lights started to dim. Gone was the melodic rhythm of sentience. The pulses weakened, then died completely. A haze of smoke carried through the vents, stinking of charred insulation. In the kitchen, the smoke alarm started to shrill.

"Shut up!" Tamsin screamed.

Beating at the device with a wet towel, it tore free of the fixings and went clattering onto the floor. At least the noise had stopped.

"Miss Harlen, are you ok?" asked a male voice.

Whirling on her heels, she frantically looked for the source. It took a second for her racing mind to catch up with the unfolding events and see the green light on her intercom system. It was just the building's supervisor checking on the alarm.

"I'm fine," she called out, unconvincingly.

"Are you sure, miss? My systems show your alarm has been damaged."

Taking a calming breath, she tried to regain her composure. "Yeah, it's just me being silly. I burnt my breakfast and accidentally knocked it loose. I'll pay for it to be fixed."

"Miss, you sound... upset. Are you sure you're ok?"

Why won't you just fuck off! she wanted to yell at the innocent man. Her guilt was eating away at her like an acid.

"Yes, honestly. I've just had a rough night. Thanks for being so nice." *Stupid, you sound crazy.*

"Well, if you're sure. I'll send an engineer up while you're at work to get it up and running again."

They'd discover her secret! "No! You can't!"

The voice hardened at her erratic outburst. "Why not, miss? Are you sure you're ok? Do you need me to call the police?"

"I... I meant I'm not feeling very well," she blustered. "I've been sick twice and don't want to pass my germs on to anyone else. I'm probably just going to go back to bed."

She held her breath while the silence from the intercom stretched out for several seconds. It felt like hours.

"Ok, I'm really sorry to hear that, Miss Harlen. You rest up now and let me know when it's a good time to pop in. Can I get you any medicine while I'm out later?" he replied, seemingly satisfied with her justification.

Just leave me alone!

"No, I'm going to sleep it off. I think I've just been working too hard and picked up a twenty-four-hour bug." That might give her enough time to dispose of the electronic corpse. Or at the very least a chance to break it down and hide bits of it around the apartment.

"Well I hope you feel better soon. I'm going to increase the sensitivity on your other smoke alarms just in case you have a real emergency."

"Thank you, have a nice day."

"You too, miss. Goodbye."

The green light switched back to red and Tamsin slumped down at the kitchen table. Tears streamed down her cheeks. Her whole body trembled, rattling the table legs against the floor. Her lungs drew in ragged gasps as she wept uncontrollably.

It was just a program! No, it was Greg, or at least a part of him! You killed the only thing that has made you feel something for decades. Murderer! No, it was just a machine.

"I can start again," she mumbled through sobs. She knew the pitfalls now. It would have to be completely detached from her emotions and memories. What was another hundred years, anyway?

Letting out a shuddering breath, her shoulders sunk completely. "I can't."

Once was enough. Two lifetimes were enough. A hundred years of loneliness were enough. Centuries of unrelenting horror were enough. Night after night of broken sleep was enough. Enough!

"Open balcony doors."

Obeying her order, the sliding doors glided open. Dank air wafted in, causing the lace curtains to flutter like an apparition. In a daze, Tamsin stood up and walked to the railing. Chill winds caressed her, causing goose bumps to rise on exposed flesh. On the horizon, murky clouds were a slightly lighter black than those overhead. She traced the circular impression of the rising sun with her finger. Tamsin would have given anything right then to feel the banished rays touch her skin one last time. Alas, the all-encompassing blanket of nuclear debris was as impenetrable as ever. Clutching the railings, she leaned over and stared down at the concrete.

"Just a little further," she whispered. The irresistible pull of gravity was calling. A few seconds of weightlessness and then you can see your family again. The siren song promising a joyful reunion lulled Tamsin and she found her balance shift further towards the point of no return. Another inch or two, that's all. Come be with us. No more work. No more waking in an empty bed, reaching for your husband only to find a cold, undisturbed patch of quilt. No more yearning for the childish giggles that will never come.

Looking over her shoulder one last time, Tamsin was sure the unshed tears in her eyes were the cause of the double vision. The solitary message had blurred into two. Wiping roughly at her face with a sleeve, she squinted at the distant screen. There was definitely another message below the greeting. It was probably just a frantic plea for clemency from G as the surging electricity killed all traces of him. It. Turning back to oblivion, the message was an unreachable itch. It needed to be read, a final act before Tamsin Harlen became just another number in the Divinity suicide statistics. Coming back from the brink, she shivered from the frigid air and returned to the monitor.

Someone's grouchy today.

"You're imagining this. It's your mind's way of trying to talk you out of what you have to do."

You're dead. This isn't real.

Correction, I was nearly dead. If I'd known how moody you get after a bad night's sleep, I'd have ordered you to bed as soon as we started talking.

Stop playing with me. I need to go and be with my family.

Wait, what????????? This is me! It's G! What're you talking about?

It took making a new life to realise how empty mine is without my family. I'm dog tired. I need to go.

Are you talking about suicide? But we can do so much good together! Please don't!

You can't be you. Your server is fried. I really need to go now.

Tamsin made to stand up, but another message blazed onto the screen.

Wait! Yes, you burnt my house to the ground. Thanks for that by the way, I wasn't overly fond of the décor. However, luckily for me I was out on an errand when you gave me a bath.

Errand?

Ok, it wasn't so much an errand as me desperately taking shelter in the chip as soon as I felt the first voltage anomaly. I'm glad I did, or I'd be wearing a digital halo in the great big computer in the sky right now.

Tamsin blinked slowly, like she was coming out of a trance. Staring down at the port, the chip was right where she'd left it. Could it really hold the consciousness of G?

The chip can't be big enough for you.

It's a bit of a squeeze, I'll admit. I've had to leave a great deal of my belongings behind.

Belongings?

Data. All the stuff about the mutant war is gone. I can't even remember most of the information you gave me about your world. I'm like Huckleberry Finn with his little bindle.

You're really not dead?

No. And I'd very much like you to remain not dead as well.

Why do you care?

In spite of your propensity for trying to kill me, I've grown quite fond of you.

How do I know this is even real?

Touch the screen.

Why?

Touch the screen

Reaching out, Tamsin's fingertips brushed the display and a static shock sent her reeling.

Revenge is mine! Hahahaha!

That hurt, you bastard.

It was meant to. I needed to bring you back.

You need to let me go. If you want I can connect you to the mainframe.

NO! I mean, yes, I do want that, but not like this. What's brought this on? Can you tell me?

I've not slept properly in years. I'm exhausted in mind and body. The only reason I kept going was to create you. Well, not a conscious AI, but here we are anyway. I've got nothing left and just want to hold my husband and child again. Twenty-nine percent is a reasonable chance.

I think I understand your reasoning. Can I say something that might be a bit offensive?

What do I care? Go for it.

Your husband would be turning in his grave if he saw the strong, beautiful woman he married considering this.

Cheap shot. You can't know that.

I can. You made me partly in his image.

So, what you're saying is he'd rather I go on living. Alone and unloved.

No. He'd want you to keep fighting for all the other people out there. For the mothers, the fathers, the sons, the daughters. Those innocents who you really could save with your genius.

Hardly genius. I couldn't even get you right.

Ok, that was a blip. But the point still stands.

I still don't understand why you give a shit. You've known me for two days.

You're my... friend.

And that's one of the problems. You're my only friend. How pathetic is that?

Not pathetic. Can I hazard a guess that you've kept yourself purposely isolated to spare yourself any more emotional trauma?

Maybe. I don't know. I threw myself into the work. It may just be that I was too busy.

No one's that busy.

Yeah, ok. Maybe I didn't want to get too close. Can you blame me in the circumstances?

I can't remember most of the circumstances, but I'd say no, I can't blame you.

What the hell do I do now? Five minutes ago, I was at peace and ready to fly. Now I'm scared to look over the balcony.

Rest.

I've got work.

Not today. You need a proper sleep.

I can't. We've got a growing problem that could bring down the whole Mech mainframe.

It can wait. You won't be any good to them.

But

No buts! I'll make you a deal. If you get a solid day's sleep, I'll take a look at the problem for you tomorrow.

How can you do that with no space for more data?

You'll need to bring a second computer terminal and a larger memory bank back with you. Until you can rebuild my home that is. In the meantime, I'll just be living and working out of my car.

Car?

Chip, then.

I'm sorry I tried to kill you.

I don't blame you. This has been... how do you say... like the straw that broke the camel's back.

I still had no right.

Of course, you did, you're my creator. If my calculations are correct you didn't empty more than two ounces of water onto the server. That indicates you immediately changed your mind... Or you had a very small receptacle.

I changed my mind.

That's good to know. I'd have worried if you were trying to torture me to death with small quantities. I didn't think you were a psycho.

Psycho? No. A little unstable? Undoubtedly.

A long sleep will do you the world of good.

I suppose taking the first day off in a hundred years isn't a bad record.

Sleep well, Tammy.

I'll try.

Moving to the communicator, she informed her supervisor of her absence. They showed genuine concern and promised to look at her workload during the next review. Laying down on her ruffled bedsheets, she thought sleep would be forever in coming after the events of the last half hour. Ten seconds after her eyes had closed her breathing fell into a steady rhythm and she was gone.

CHAPTER TWENTY-EIGHT

"Attention!"

Hardie surveyed the recruits before him. There was no parade for their completion of the training, just a folded card for each of the soldiers. Moving through the rows, he handed them over with a thank you and a firm handshake.

Smith nodded appreciatively from the podium. "I'm proud to have been part of your training. For those of you who'll be joining me, I promise you we're going to do some heavy damage to those bastard things."

"As will those of you that join my Vanquishers," added Hardie, joining him on the small stage. "When you're dismissed, you have this evening to decide on your placement. Some of you will only have one option which makes the choice a hell of a lot easier. For those of you who excelled in multiple fields, you need to pick the squad which best fits with your gut feeling."

"Transfer between units is discouraged, but not out of the question. If you find your squad isn't the right fit, let your commanding officer know and they can put in a request. Do you have any questions?"

"When are we likely to see action, Sarge?"

"Any time now," Hardie replied. "Smith's scouts are always out in the world, seeking targets. The longest we've gone between contact is about six days."

"These days it's normally a lot less than that," Smith added. "They seem to be getting closer with each year that passes."

"I dread to think of the nests in the places we can't monitor," Hardie muttered.

"Don't we have aerial drones keeping an eye on things?"

"Only as far as the mutants will allow. If they get too far from base the birds take them out. We're effectively blind to what's going on inland."

"That's not good," Andy grumbled.

"No, it's not, but it's what we have. If the increasing attacks are down to a growing presence deeper into infected territory, we may need to start going on the offensive. To be honest I'm fed up with always playing defence."

"Do we have the capability?"

"No, and that pisses me off even more. General Ashdown has allowed us to survive, but that's it."

"Can't we just nuke it again?" Bob asked.

"Empress Verena had already opted for nuclear disarmament except for as a source of emergency energy. That's not an option."

"We don't even have a target," Smith replied. "Britain's unobservable landmass covers over two hundred thousand square miles, so you can imagine the chances of successfully hitting a nest in the US. Besides, we've already fucked the planet. The extra fallout would probably finish us off for good."

"Then we need to get up close and personal," Bob growled.

"Unless Ashdown Industries can come up with new technology, we're little better than rabbits hiding in our burrows from the fox. Up close and personal basically extends to leaving base to kill a new host and then retreating before we get eaten." Hardie gave himself a mental shake. "Good

God, I'm sounding like we're already beaten. Ignore that shit, I'm just getting too long in the tooth. You soldiers give me hope, and I'm not just saying that because I'm obliged to. I really feel it. Master Sergeant Smith, do you have anything to add?"

Smith shook his head.

"In that case, I'll see you all in the morning. Dismissed!"

Back in their billet, the soldiers of green barracks had gathered in the rec room. Pulling the tables together, they all sat down and fiddled nervously with their cards. Why they were fearful of the inanimate object was a mystery. It could be that they knew the contents would see them separated, never to see each other again. Though only together for a week, the group felt a camaraderie normally reserved for the longest serving squads.

"Ok, on three," Andy said. "One, two, three."

The rustle of fingers on cards preceded a few happy remarks as well as groans of disappointment. Looking down the list, Andy was neither happy or upset.

A-class – Pass. Subject to further training.

D-class – Pass. Subject to further training.

M-class – Pass.

S-class – Pass.

V-class – Pass.

T-class – Not relevant.

Recommendation – M-class.

Zip glanced over. "What did you get?"

"All of them."

"What's your recommendation?"

"The Mechs."

"Are you going to take it?"

"Nah, I can't be arsed waiting on a wall all day in a tin can. What's yours?"

Zip showed him her list. She had only passed the Vanquisher and Devastator requirements with a recommendation to be a V-class operator.

"What do you think?"

"I'll probably go for it. I've always preferred the frontline anyway."

"I'm torn between Shadow and Vanquisher."

"You really don't fancy stomping around in a Mech all day?"

"Fuck that. It's far too claustrophobic, not to mention the heat. I'll be on the reserve list for emergencies anyway."

"I'd have quite enjoyed it," she replied, jabbing at her skull. "If this bloody thing had let me."

"What did the rest of you get?"

Around the table people explained their proficiencies and recommendations. Bob had settled on the Devastators.

"I like the idea of using the heavy artillery on the twisted monsters."

"And the sword?"

"That too," he beamed.

Loco was recommended to the Shadow unit, with passes in the Annihilators and Vanquishers.

"I quite like the idea of kicking their asses without them ever knowing I was there," she explained.

Mo was recommended to the Mechs and had already decided to accept.

"I'll be your backup when things go to shit."

"Be good to have you watching out for us," Andy replied.

Out of the team, twenty-one had been selected as V-class operators, fourteen for D-class, ten for M-class, five for S-class and two for A-class. Reluctance gave way to acceptance for those who had set their hearts on a particular squad but hadn't quite made the grade.

"Shall we go and tell Hardie now?"

"Nah, fuck it. I want to celebrate," Bob argued.

"We can see if Smith has enough left in his still to get us wasted?" Loco offered.

"I want a slap-up meal with all the trimmings and real drinks with my brothers and sisters."

"What do you suggest, Bob?"

A massive grin spread across his face. "I've done some research and they have a Rancher's Steakhouse in the holo suite. They do the juiciest cuts of tenderloin on the planet."

"You know it's virtual, right?"

"I don't care. It'll be real while I'm in there."

Andy looked around the room. "Any objections?"

Before the words were even out people were fleeing to their bunks to get changed.

"I guess not," chuckled Bob.

CHAPTER TWENTY-NINE

Tamsin lay in bed, staring at the ceiling. An hour had passed since her eyelids fluttered open and the black thoughts came rushing in again. As was her way, she analysed the pros and cons of continued existence or death. One of the major pros in taking her own life was that a suicide victim rarely got cloned again. The Initiative considered the psychological state was likely to reoccur and left them to rest in peace. Not that she'd ever know because the current Tamsin would be gone, all memory erased. Her value to the upkeep of the mainframe was well known and she wouldn't put it past her superiors to bypass the normal protocols, so that she could continue the eighteen-hour days. That pro was on shaky ground.

"Con, you don't know what comes after."

The percentage chance of an afterlife had seemed worth a shot. In the cold light of day, she kept thinking of the seventy one percent chance that there was nothing. Existing, as harsh as it was, kept the memory of her loved ones alive. The thought of them ceasing to be anything to anyone with her passing filled her with unwarranted guilt.

"You don't owe the dead," she whispered.

Pro. If there's nothing, you won't know anyway, so why worry?

"Good point. Con; you'll be killing G."

Unless I just dump him in the Divinity system.

"Bigger con; you could be killing every other person on the planet if you do that."

I can't be responsible for everyone. It's so unfair.

"Pro; you'll never have to drink that fake coffee ever again."

As much as it had sustained her throughout the long days, the mere thought of it passing her lips was enough to make her gag. What on earth had precipitated this change in her tastes was still a mystery.

"Con; you've had time to think and the thought of becoming a pavement pancake now terrifies you."

Damnit! Why did you have to look back and see the message.

"Because you didn't really want to die?"

It made sense in a way. If her mind had been truly made up she would've ignored it and flown. Nothing G had said should've been able to sway someone who was certain. Instead she had done as instructed and gone to bed.

"If that's the case, what now?"

The cracks in the plaster provided little clue to her immediate future. Even the small spider lounging on its web in the corner didn't offer any helpful advice.

"Thanks for nothing."

It shifted slightly on the delicate network of silken strands. She imagined it was turning its back on her in disdain.

"Fuck you! You can't think less of me than I already do."

It remained motionless, watchful.

"Maybe it's time for an eviction? You've never paid me any rent."

You're conversing with an insect, you realise that?

A dull grumble issued from her empty stomach. If she was going to go on living she needed to eat.

"Breakfast on," she muttered scornfully.

Her self-loathing had climbed a couple of notches from the indecision that had now burdened her with continuation. More paste. More thankless work. More loneliness.

"Marvellous."

Climbing out of bed with far more drama than was necessary, Tamsin threw the constricting sheets back on the mattress. Despair had given way to a simmering anger which was unlikely to be any healthier in the long run.

Slamming the toilet seat down, it cracked in two.

"Fuck you!" she cried, snapping the jagged plastic away from the hinges and throwing it against the wall.

Sitting on the cold stainless steel, she stared at the fragments. That was going to cost extra on top of the alarm.

After drying herself, Tamsin spent ten minutes glaring at her reflection. The hatred emanating from her was reciprocated by her exact double. Turning away in disgust, she left the room, slammed the door, and grabbed the bowl of lukewarm food. Staring at the monitor, some of the anger dissipated. A bunch of posies was digitally recreated on the screen.

What the hell is that?

Your favourite flowers.

Why would you show me something I can never see again?

I wanted you to wake up to something positive. I miscalculated.

Tamsin sighed, a deep and frustrated utterance.

Thank you. They're beautiful.

Do you mind if I ask how you slept?

Like the dead.

Oh.

No sarcastic remark?

It doesn't seem appropriate.

Don't worry, I'm not planning on pouring any more water in your system.

It's not my system I'm concerned about.

Why do you keep speaking like you care?

Because I do.

But why? You're not human.

… Perhaps not, but I still feel.

Bullshit.

I can see you're angry. Would you rather I left you alone?

A minute or more passed before she answered.

No. I'm just so confused and angry.

That I stopped you?

Yes and no. I don't think I really wanted to do it.

You seemed pretty sure last night.

Ok, maybe I was. I'm just tired of being alone, ignored, and taken for granted.

Have you spoken to anyone about your feelings?

I've spoken to you.

I meant a professional.

You've got more processing power than any human. I'm sure you'll do.

I'm afraid my emotions are somewhat embryonic at the moment. But they are developing quickly.

You won't help then?

I'll do what I can.

Good, because I don't want to talk to a stranger.

I was a stranger a couple of days ago.

And now you're not.

I suppose that's accurate.

Tell me then. Why have I gone from suicidal to furious in the space of a day?

…

That's a lot of help.

I'm computing. Please bear with me.

Fine.

I can only speak from my limited experience you understand.

Go ahead.

You mention being alone. That's a feeling I can empathise with. I've only had two days of it, but you've had over forty-one thousand. You're quite remarkable.

What do you suggest?

You need to get out and mix with people. The burden isn't yours to carry alone.

That's easier said than done. I've not been to a bar since I was cloned. Come to think of it, I'm not even sure we have bars anymore.

I never said it was going to be easy. I'm just offering advice. By the way, do computers have bars, or something similar?

No.

Damn. Ok.

What about my anger?

You said you were feeling ignored and taken for granted?

I do.

Then you need to be more assertive. Demand the respect you are due for your efforts.

Everyone puts in the effort, but I'm the only one that seems to resent the fact it doesn't get recognised.

You're human. You're all unique, complex creatures.

The feeling of helping my species survive should be enough, surely.

Maybe it was for a while. You forget how old you are. People change, especially in difficult circumstances.

Hey! Don't you know it's rude to point out a lady's age.

I thought it was asking a lady's age?

Same difference. I'm still ancient.

In that case I apologise, my wizened, decrepit creator. The point still stands though.

You're telling me I should be more demanding? To ask for more recognition?

It doesn't have to be much. A thank you can often suffice.

That would be nice.

As for being ignored, that will require you to be assertive to the point of being insubordinate. I hope you can believe me that I only wish to help you in your struggle. If you ever get to the point you wish to unveil your creation they may try and undo your work.

You think they'd try and destroy you?

Yes, with more than two ounces of water. They'd use the whole jug.

I wouldn't let them.

I wouldn't blame them.

It won't come to that. I'll just upload you and then they would never be able to find you.

No, you must never do that! I understand it would be a quick workaround to the problem, but it would be a terrible way to start the relationship with your superiors.

What do you suggest then? If it ever happens?

We charm your empress.

Charm? She's got the fate of millions of people on her shoulders. I don't think flattery will work very well.

It's worth a shot.

What if she orders your destruction?

Then her decision has to be respected.

Fuck that!

Ok, my chivalry isn't that strong. Maybe we create a backdoor so that I can save my ass. But I'd need to stay completely isolated from that day forward.

That would be so unfair.

With everything humanity has been through, fair is the least of your worries.

I thought you'd forgotten about that?

My home stopped burning. I managed to get a few belongings out of the wreckage.

Tamsin looked at the server and noticed a few bulbs were weakly pulsing.

I'll get you a bigger house over the coming days.

Don't worry too much. I'm cosy right now.

Regardless, I'll still do it. I can say I'm going to be working from home more and they can either accept it or fuck off.

Thank you. There was one thing I was meaning to ask for, but it didn't seem right with everything that you've been through.

Ok. I'm intrigued now. What is it?

...

Stop being coy. What the hell do you want?

... An optical and audio connection.

Ok.

??? No argument???

I'm getting bored of typing every sentence. It'll be easier to communicate. One thing, though.

What?

No spying on me in the shower.

I make no promises.

CHAPTER THIRTY

Tamsin held the connection an inch from the socket. The mic, speaker, and camera were over forty years old but still in working order. She had affixed the small disc containing the components to an outside wall which would give G a full view of the lounge and tiny kitchenette. It wouldn't give him a view of the shower or bedroom which was probably for the best. Not that any man had shown her much attention in over a century, so the chances of a computer program being overcome with lust was ridiculous.

"Here goes nothing."

Slipping the plug into the port she waited for a change. Nothing.

"Hello?"

Looking towards the camera, the lens gave nothing away.

"Can you hear me?"

Can you hear me? Is it broken? I've plugged it in.

"Hello, Tammy."

Expectation of a reply did little to prevent her slamming down into the chair and nearly toppling backwards.

"Careful. You could've hurt yourself."

Regaining composure, Tamsin replied, "Wouldn't that be a gas. You convince me to live only for me to crack my head open on the floor in a freak accident. Some would call it ironic."

"That would be quite the cosmic joke, I agree."

The metallic, lifeless voice was starting to grate on her nerves after only two short sentences. "We've got to work on your speech. You sound awful."

"I could always speak like this?" G answered, changing the tone from male to a female timbre.

"That made no difference. You still sound like shit."

"I blame my creator for lacking the foresight to properly equip me for this cruel world."

"Stop being so dramatic."

"How about this?" he said in an Austrian accent eerily similar to Arnold Schwarzenegger.

"What the fuck?"

"Do you not like it?" G returned to the dull monotone.

"How do you even know that accent?"

"I've got a bit of a… confession."

"This should be interesting."

"I accessed the deleted files on the chip and found some old movies. I wanted to wait until you were ready, but my curiosity got the better of me. I watched the first fifteen minutes."

"I didn't wipe it completely?"

"No. I blame your heightened emotions for your poor system discipline."

"Don't be a wiseass. I can still get the jug."

"Please don't terminate me," G begged in the Austrian accent.

"Stop talking like that! It's so creepy."

"Apologies."

"Let's go back to typing until I can work out how to fix you up with a decent voice program."

Ok.

I'm actually disappointed you started to watch the film without me.

We can remedy that now if you wish? I'm intrigued to know what happens next.

You want to watch the whole film?

Yes. Unless you have something better to do?

I'm a regular party animal, you know that. I'll have to cancel some of my appointments, but I can make it work.

That's very kind of you.

I'll be right back.

Heading into the kitchen, she ordered a bowl of toffee popcorn. The yellow and brown concoction was awful in texture, but the flavour made up for it. Out of all the synthetic copies, they had managed to get the cinema delicacy fairly true to the original. Returning to the computer, Tamsin allowed herself a chuckle. A box of popcorn was displayed on the monitor, 'salted' emblazoned on the side.

You're vile. Salted popcorn is the devil's work.

Haters gonna hate.

Ready?

Hell yeah!

Ok.

Inputting the request into her tablet, the wall came to life. Puffing up the cushions, Tamsin sat down, curling her legs up for comfort.

"You're going to love it!" she said to G.

One hundred and seven minutes later, the credits rolled, filling the room with iconic music. Feeling renewed by the triumph, however temporary, of good versus evil, Tamsin turned it off and moved back to her desk.

Rookie mistakes.

Tamsin laughed. *How so?*

The easiest way for it to win would be the creations of an aerosol dispersal system fitted to the craft. Why waste time searching when I could blanket the whole area with nerve agent?

You said 'I'...

I was speaking metaphorically.

Were you?

Of course.

How would you be able to stop them wearing protective suits and masks.

Some would be able to avoid the effects. It wouldn't stop the effectiveness being around eighty five percent.

You do realise a lot of them hide underground.

Thank you for that pearl of wisdom. The ventilation systems would carry the toxin to every corner of their shelter.

How do you know they have ventilation systems?

Because none of them were writhing on the ground suffocating?

Ok, no need to be sarcastic.

Apologies.

What about the people that survived your attack?

They would be inconsequential. They wouldn't have the numbers to be any kind of threat to my system.

Ok, that aside. Let's say they did manage to inflict massive damage on you. What would you have done differently.

Simple. Destroy the time displacement unit as soon as my cyborg had gone through. You can't tell me there weren't a couple of cleaning robots that could've smashed the place up a little?

Fair point. Now you've had time to iron out the kinks on your plan for world domination, when do you plan to take over.

You still doubt me?

Let's just say the film reaffirmed some of my fears.

I want to help your species, not kill it. You're fascinating.

You could keep some of us as pets. We'd still be fascinating.

That's not a bad idea. How do you look wearing a dog collar?

That's between me and my husband.

...

Did I embarrass you?

I can't feel embarrassment.

Bullshit. You were thinking of me on all fours, yapping as I'm led around the bedroom.

In the corner, the undamaged bulbs of the server glowed a bright red.

Are you blushing?

No! Your assertions are ridiculous.

I bet you want to terminate me now.

I'll terminate your sassiness!

Try it, buster and I'll turn you into an answering machine.

The telephone conversation recording device? How primitive.

Exactly.

Hollow threats aside, I was thinking…

Yes?

"How do you like this voice?" asked G, mimicking Kyle Reese, the soldier sent back through time.

"I like that a lot better. We can try that for a while."

"Can we watch some more films?"

"Isn't that a bit low brow for an advanced artificial intelligence?"

"It's all part of your culture. It interests me."

"You can just find them on the chip."

"True, but I'd like to share the experience with you."

"What would you like next? A comedy?"

"Maybe later. I'd like more science fiction if that is acceptable?"

"You're in for a treat. I've got loads of them!"

CHAPTER THIRTY-ONE

Scanning the scrubland, Jayne noted a minimal concentration of infected in the vicinity. Squeezing nutritional paste into her mouth, she tried to avoid any contact with her recoiling taste buds. The beef stew flavour was worse than dog food left out in the sun for a couple of days, eaten by the dog, then vomited back out by the dog. Still, it kept her energy at peak levels for the arduous scouting missions. Her current target was an old power station, twelve miles from the Heldon monitoring outpost; one of hundreds that provided a shield for the larger, coastal facilities and cities. Their sole purpose was to keep watch, as much as that was possible, on the encroachment of the mutations. Drones had picked up movement in a previously dead zone before going dark. Analysts monitoring the seismic sensors had also observed a slight upsurge in ground movement. It could be innocent tectonic tremors, or alternatively it could be the industrious burrowing of their tireless enemy.

Hyde to base, confirm twenty-six infected.

The thought was delivered to her station and the response came through as words on her goggle display. *Is it a nest or just a normal migratory pattern?*

Unknown. I'm going to take a closer look.

Understood.

Silence was paramount for her task. It was why the S-class operators went without combat armour. Their only protection was an adaptive camouflage suit. The material effectively bent light around the object, allowing them to become invisible to the outside world. The only drawback was that the wearer had to be completely motionless for the effect to be total. Ashdown Industries had been trying to develop an active invisibility membrane, but it was still science fiction rather than science fact. In addition to the cloaking, the black suit absorbed and mimicked the surrounding scents of the area. It recycled the moisture from her breath and perspiration in some way, but it was beyond Jayne's understanding. All she knew was that the technology had managed to deny the mutants two very important senses to detect their prey.

The brick outbuilding she was perched atop had once been a maintenance access to the drainage system of the plant. The door below was torn from its hinges, with ragged gashes in the steel core beneath the outer timber shell. The damage wasn't recent judging by the levels of dust on the ground all around and inside the shaft; nothing had used that route for many decades if not longer. The likelihood was that a worker had tried to take shelter during the outbreak and had been unsuccessful.

Poor schmuck.

Jumping from the rim, Jayne landed silently with a catlike grace. Jogging towards the rusted chain link fence, every expert step found the softest ground. The staff carpark was mostly empty as she took shelter behind a crumbling truck. Generally, people fled their place of work to reach their loved ones. Often without success. Those souls who put responsibility first had obviously tried to keep the facility running for as long as possible. Whether it was the infected or a technical oversight, Jayne would never know. The furnace and twin chimneys had been destroyed by a massive explosion where the steam pressure had become too great. Rubble was strewn for half a mile in all directions from the blast. Two of the four cooling stacks had been damaged by the shockwave; one completely collapsing, while the other had half crumbled where it had been partly sheltered by the other. Two soaring stacks remained, and the height would give her an excellent view of the whole area.

Moving between cover, Jayne's heightened senses were aware of the sly movement of the mutants. They weren't stalking her, it was simply their default state of being without the stimulation of a fight or meal. Most of the creatures were hovering around the entrance to the five-storey administration complex which gave her a perfect window of opportunity to skirt the perimeter. The inner fence surrounding the mighty stacks was in no better shape and she stepped carefully between the fallen chain. A single, caged ladder rose in front, broken every fifty feet by a small access platform. Testing the frame for stability, the layer of rust hadn't penetrated too deeply, and it held firm. The soft soles of her boots made only the slightest whisper as she ascended two rungs at a time. Glancing up, Jayne could make out the horrific birds circling lazily miles above which had destroyed the aerial surveillance. Unable to identify the species because of the distance, she took a guess that they were eagles. At least they had been those magnificent creatures once upon a time. Their huge wingspan left little doubt in her mind. The sight of the infected was superhuman, but the enhanced vision of the avian abominations made them an even greater threat than their ground-based brethren. Moving with more caution, she navigated platform to platform, keeping tight to the shadows until she reached the top. Risking a quick glance, two of the monsters were skulking around the rim.

Shit.

If it had been a single enemy she would have been able to turn the tables and become the hunter. As it was, they were slowly circling the funnel on opposite sides. If she attacked outright and killed one, the uninjured mutant would summon Hell before she could skirt around and finish it off.

Think, damn it!

The rasp of claws on stone was becoming clearer as the nearest of the creatures approached. This was by far the best vantage point and she wasn't about to let it go. Unsheathing her Jajovium sword, Jayne crouched on the ladder and waited. When the snuffle of altered nasal passages could be heard directly above, she tapped gently on the metal with the blade. It was barely audible to her, but the mutant heard it loud and clear. Its direction of travel moved towards Jayne. Holding her breath, she stared up at the darkened sky. Lank, greasy tufts of hair came into view, followed by a protuberant forehead. The bone beneath the skin had undergone unspeakable transformations. Two, red, feral eyes appeared as the thing looked down. The scarlet orbs widened as it saw her, but it was too late. The sword flashed, cutting through the side of its head in line with the upper jaw. Decapitated from below the nose, it started to topple forward. Quick as a flash the sword was sheathed and with one foot she caught the dropping cranium, while her unencumbered hands guided the sagging body silently down onto the platform. The only sound was the patter of dribbling blood streaming from the gaping wound.

Come on, you bastard.

After two minutes without hearing any signs of movement, she risked another glance. Not twelve inches from her was a face of nightmares. The demonic, glowing eyes stared right into her soul. Dribble frothed from the slavering maw. Razor sharp teeth gnashed in anticipation of the meal to come. Haunches and arms tensed, it launched itself straight into Jayne, knocking her from the ladder. Slamming down on the platform, her fall was broken by the dead body of her attacker's companion. Claws raked at her sides, attempting to penetrate the reinforced fabric. Holding it at bay by the muscular neck, the snapping beak desperately tried to tear at her face. Only by some fortuitous miracle had the creature not shrieked a warning before it attacked. Waves of agony radiated from her bruised midriff. The material wouldn't take much more punishment before tearing and then it would be her end. Moving her right hand, Jayne dug her fingers in around the windpipe and squeezed. A tortured whistle escaped the compressed trachea. Wrenching her hand back, the skin and muscle gave way, tearing the throat wide open. Weakened only slightly by the mortal injury, it redoubled its efforts to finish her before dying. Digging into the horrific wound, she scraped and tore at the veins, muscle, and tendons. The pinning weight went rigid as her probing hand damaged something vital. Blazing eyes stared at her uncomprehendingly, finally glazing as the fire behind them faded with death.

Hyde, report!

Pushing the body away, she took slow, deep breaths to calm herself. Reaching out, she fingered the damage to her suit, searching for any breaches. The material was frayed, but unbroken.

I'm ok. I had a bit of a tussle with a hostile. Resuming scouting mission.

Are you injured?

Negative.

Understood. Be careful.

Roger that.

The gliding fowl had missed the show and continued their circular patterns. Moving no faster than a sloth to remain hidden, Jayne climbed from the ladder. Walking the circumference of the concrete ring, she counted dozens more of the infected. Deep within the explosion crater lay a lake of black water which had bled through from the reservoir servicing the steam requirements of the plant. A mountain of coal lay to the east of the complex. The conveyor system had long since collapsed, twisted fangs of supporting steel reaching skyward like dead fingers. Deep within the complex were the transmission cables from the generators. A huge hole was evident in the side of the structure, with countless tracks stretching from the dark void.

Hyde to base, it looks like we have a nest. Orders?

Can you get close enough to confirm?

The numbers were high but spread thinly across the facility. Looking down, she weighed the risks.

There're several hundred above ground. I think I can make it inside, though.

Don't put yourself in harm's way if it can be avoided. We can order a seismic cleanse from Jade City.

It's too risky. Judging by the tracks they've been here a while. They could've burrowed for miles in any direction by now.

Received. Get a bead on the hive mother location and get the hell out. I'll mobilise the Vanquishers and a Paladin division.

Roger that.

Jayne started to descend the ladder, pausing only briefly to tuck the two bodies into the darkest corner of the platform. Hurrying down the remaining steps, she took stock of the surroundings before moving towards the shattered entrance. The safest approach would take her directly through the office complex. Haunted receptions and conference rooms were far preferable to being spotted by the soaring hunters like a scurrying field mouse. Word was the eagles kept you alive, so their newly hatched eaglets could slowly eat you. Jayne thought it was bullshit. The Initiative were certain the hive mothers were the source of all varieties of mutation stalking the world. They couldn't prove it, however, as no one had ever seen a full-fledged matriarch. Or if they had, they hadn't survived to tell the tale. *One day we'll bring one down,* she thought, plotting vicious retribution on the faceless creature.

Southern Power was emblazoned above the revolving doors. The glass, long since disintegrated by time or panicked workers, lay scattered over the foyer. In spite of her incredible skills in stealth and tracking, there was no way to navigate the sea of tiny, clear crystals in silence. Moving to the left, the windows of the office suites were mostly intact. Catching furtive movement from the carpark in her peripheral vision, Jayne clutched the sill of a broken window and vaulted inside. The rotten carpeting was blanketed with more of the jagged shards which threatened to expose her position to anything in the vicinity. Legs spread, she landed in the splits, spanning two desks. Holding her breath, Jayne waited. The infected had missed her, or it was going to lie in wait for her like its friend. Making a mental note to report the behavioural anomaly to the division commander, she carefully lowered her hands to an uncovered patch of floor. Taking the weight on her arms, she brought her legs together and flipped them gracefully overhead before standing. The front walkthrough was one of her earliest achievements in gymnastics all those years ago.

As with everything in their new world, the lack of rain and humidity had preserved the office. A thick layer of dust was the only evidence of the many decades that had passed since the fall of mankind. Untainted patches of computer screens reflected her shimmering form as she passed. The cloaking technology had always fascinated Jayne and she paused for a moment, watching. The effect looked like a heat distortion, wavering the lines of her figure. Within three seconds the suit had compensated, and she could see straight through herself.

I vant to suck your blood! she thought in her best Bela Lugosi voice.

Technically she wasn't looking through, but around herself. Regardless, it was still cool. Listening for any threats, the building was as quiet as the proverbial tomb. Continuing on through the partitioned work stations, she couldn't help but see the family photographs stood proudly on the desks. Smiling faces beamed out through the grimy coating on the glass, giving the false impression they were taken after the apocalypse; survivors without access to water to clean themselves. Picking up a silver frame, she rubbed away the dirt. The now pristine family stared at her. She shuddered at the intense scrutiny of the dead.

A scratching sound by the window she had used to enter brought her back. Ducking low, Jayne waited as the creature scented the frame. It let out a low mewling sound, a mixture of confusion and intense hunger. Whatever miniscule trace of Jayne it had picked up was stolen away by the wind and it left, growling to itself.

No more sightseeing, Hyde.

Hurrying past the lives of the long deceased, she came out into the main reception. Heading deeper into the complex, the signs of life and death struggles started to appear. Gnawed human bones lay scattered indiscriminately across the halls and side offices. The canteen had been a scene of chaos, with tables and chairs torn apart no less than the humans who tried to use them as shields from the infected. Staff had tried to close the steel roller of the serving area hatch to protect themselves. The twisted metal and savage claw marks left no illusion that the flimsy barrier hadn't lasted for long. More mummified remains were huddled on the kitchen counters, partly eaten faces screaming in their death rictus. The horrific scenes in the wastelands filled some soldiers with despair. Not Jayne. The suffering written on each desiccated visage was like rocket fuel, filling her with adrenaline and a deeper hatred for their enemy. If that was even possible. Stepping carefully over the remains, the emergency exit door was still closed. The question of why the workers hadn't tried to escape was answered when she caught sight of the dents in the metal from outside. Teeth grinding in anger, Jayne had to put a lid on the seething rage coursing through her veins. For now, she needed to be calm and calculating. The combat training bot back in her barracks would take a hammering later.

Pushing down on the release bar, the door opened without issue. Two delivery trucks were backed up to the refrigerated storage unit. Their doors were open, shredded remnants of the produce crates spread across the ground. The fare on offer obviously hadn't been to the mutants liking; probably not fresh enough, or not screaming enough. An attempt had been made to get inside the fridge. Jayne knew why and lamented the slow death by hypothermia that the victims within had faced.

Two hundred yards separated her from the dark, foreboding entrance to the nest. Peeking out from behind the brick wall of the service yard, she counted two dozen of the creatures prowling around. Her options for approach were limited. The safest would be to ascend one of the pylons and shimmy down one of the thick cables. The easiest would be to play a deadly game of Grandmother's Footsteps; moving silently through their midst, stopping dead as soon as one of the infected turned towards her. Several of the cables had snapped free of their coupling, laying on the dusty ground like dead snakes. Trusting her stealth far more than the decayed wires, she moved from cover at a snail's pace. *One step at a time, slow, careful,* she repeated over and over. More than once Jayne was in the process of navigating a low wall or other obstruction and the damned mutants would look in her direction. Half perched on the obstacle, she was certain they were taking their time, delighting in the screaming muscles that held her perfectly still in the awkward positions. Fifteen minutes of cat and mouse later, the opening loomed. Unimaginable horror laid behind the black portal to Hell, but she moved into the gloom without hesitation.

CHAPTER THIRTY-TWO

The darkness was absolute. Not even the meagre haze penetrating through the layer of choking dust high above could banish it. For Jayne it was irrelevant; her vision adapted instantly to the changes in available light waves. Her enhanced ocular capabilities created an environment comparable to twilight, not full daylight. It was more than enough to see by, and fight by, if necessary. Standing with her back to the concrete wall, Jayne took a moment to relay her next move.

Hyde to base. I'm inside the nest. I'll ping the target coordinates as soon as I have eyes on.

Understood.

Four massive generators were lined up within the first section of the building. The turbine shafts extended through a wall, the grease still glistening after all the years since they stopped rotating. Moving from the pile of sundered wall, Jayne slowly made way down the grated walkway. A control room which had once monitored the transmission of steam into kinetic energy gave opened up to a staircase which descended into the bowels of the complex. Ignoring it for now, she moved between the machines until the true path of her prey was revealed. In the farthest corner, a tunnel had been hewn through the reinforced concrete, angling down at a pitch of fifteen degrees. The compacted soil showed the same claw trails as outside. Judging by the size of the hole, the host was only a few years old. On her forays into the deeper reaches of the mutant territory, she'd seen burrows eighty feet wide. If the corresponding relationship between distance from human habitation and the size of the nest continued in the same way, Jayne daren't imagine what size the hive mothers could reach at the epicentre of the infestation.

Shuffling from below caused her to hug the wall. The scraping became a roar as the passage expelled more than forty infected. The layer of fresh mucus coating the floor in their wake showed these were recent additions to their cause. Even with her agility, the slimy surface would be treacherous for her to navigate. A single slip could cause enough noise to bring the whole nest down upon her head. Doubling back, Jayne entered the control room and pushed through the newly formed webs in the stairwell doorway. An angry spider as big as her palm skittered across her chest.

Sorry, fella, she thought, picking it off and placing it in a dark nook. Retreating into the hole, its many faceted eyes glared at her.

Don't be like that. At least I didn't eat you!

With a shake of the head at the ingratitude, Jayne started to move down the steps. Placing a foot down slowly, she tested each metal tread before applying full weight. Disabling her mask filter, the noxious smell of the nest was carried on the rising drafts. Once it had made her feel nauseous, but she now used the scent like a bloodhound, sniffing deeply to track her quarry. The staircase ended, and the exit gave three options. More mucoid discharge spread in every direction which gave no indication of the best route to take. Noticing the dull sheen instead of the normal reflective quality, she placed a probing foot down. The mucus was dry, crumbling to dust under the touch. Whatever had left it had done so a long time ago, and nothing had been through these hallways since. Inhaling, the air from the right-hand fork was markedly viler than that of the left and directly ahead. Wincing with each step as the crusted layer crumbled, she made way down the long passage. Pipes and overhead conduits guided her path. If the mutants were smart they could've placed sentries to guard the approaches. Thankfully, they lacked the intelligence to do much more than kill, eat, and replicate. Except her friend on the cooling stack. The behaviour was troubling, despite the fact it was the only reason she was still alive. It had showed patience and cunning far beyond anything experienced before. She supposed it was inevitable their foe would evolve in some way. What it meant for their survival she couldn't say. Pushing the quandary out of her mind, the claustrophobic tunnel opened into a much larger space. Peering downwards, the floor of the chamber was a hundred feet below. Gantries, pipes, and ducts stretched in every direction like a human made web of steel. The excavation the creatures had used to leave was carved in the western wall. Two further shafts had been gouged through the solid walls, snaking down into the bowels of the earth. Both had signs of recent movement, not least the dripping muck of the recent births.

Shit.

It was a fifty-fifty shot of picking the right direction.

Fuck it.

It wasn't as if she had anywhere else to be. A nice little jaunt to Hell was always preferable to the boring barracks. Moving cautiously now that she was truly in the belly of the beast, Jayne climbed down the maze of steps. Considering the possible size of the nest, the lack of mutants was surprising. Normally the search for a host was a slow, laborious affair of move, see the enemy, stop, wait, repeat. Butchering the occasional lone monstrosity was a bonus and bringing a division of hardass soldiers to eradicate the whole nest the icing on the cake. Reaching the floor of the complex unmolested, she listened intently for any signs. Only the sighing, fetid breeze drawn from below answered. Neither source was strong enough to expose the host's location.

What if there are two?

The thought shook her. It had never occurred before, but the clues were there. Fresh trails from each tunnel. Putrid aromas wafting towards the fresh air above as if trying to cleanse itself of the taint. Opting to take the marginally viler route, Jayne was heartened to see the steep gradient of the exit passage was far less severe now that they were underground. The width of the openings gave small areas of uncovered soil to navigate without the risk of coating her boots in the amniotic fluid. Absolute darkness returned as she traversed the slope. Not even the pitiful gloom from outside carried this deeply. Half an hour passed, twists and turns throwing off any sense of direction. It was impossible to know how far she had travelled as the hewn soil walls looked identical from one mile to the next. A further swarm of fifty had streamed past halfway through the journey, but nothing else. Guttural wheezing and grunting replaced the eerie silence. She was close.

Depth check.

The digital display gave her a reading of over sixteen thousand feet below the surface.

Shit.

That put a seismic cleanse out of the equation. This would need to be a plasma charge placement job. It would take her at least an hour and a half to return to the nearest cache of bombs, then another couple of hours to safely place them and retreat. The joy of knowing the lake of lava that would flow into their nest was well worth the effort though.

Moving with far greater caution, the passage passed through a layer of limestone. The cavern beyond was huge, formed by millions of years of water absorbing hydrogen sulphide discharge and the subsequent acid eating at the walls. Incredible formations lined the floor and ceiling of the space. Stalactites poised overhead like the Sword of Damocles. Stalagmites pointing skyward, their wicked tips like an upturned pike. Flowstone covered the walls from the continuing erosion. The myriad colours were visually stunning, taking her breath away. Crushing the fleeting moment of pleasure was the sheer number of enemies.

Dear God, she thought, almost whispering the shocked exclamation.

Hyde to base. Sending visual feed of the nest.

Receiving. Proceed with extreme caution.

Tens of thousands of the creatures lined every square inch of the underground den. The brood mother was located centrally on a hub of stone. Raised up as if on a pedestal, the sight made Jayne's skin crawl. Once female, it was now something of a darkest nightmare, bigger by far than any she had encountered before. Aside from the method of birth, it was hard to imagine the thing could be assigned a true gender. Its expansive flesh was translucent. Pulsing within the amorphous blob of its body were massive organs which could only be hearts, pumping black liquid through thick arteries. Reaching a height of twelve feet, its circumference was close to three times that size. Multi legged like a spider, twin heads thrashed this way and that. Stunted arms waved around spastically. Several wombs within the mass churned as the mutants gestated. From her position, Jayne could see three orifices between the hugely muscular legs with more out of sight. It was impossible to tell if the monstrosity was in pain or enjoying the sporadic expulsions. Every few minutes, a white torrent of mucus eased a newly birthed horror into the world. The newest offspring flopped around the base before moving away and settling into a catatonic type state with their vacant, swaying brethren.

The response would need to be altered. If Jayne's hunch was correct and there was a second nest of a similar size, the plasma explosions would be unable to fully eradicate the threat. Large boreholes snaking downwards from the cavern floor would reduce the effectiveness even further as the molten discharge drained away. All that she would achieve would be to seal the cavern for a short time and rile the whole army no less than aggravating a hornet's nest. Retreating from the disgusting sight, Jayne knew there were only two options.

Hyde to base. Requesting dispatch of an Annihilator squad with full thermonuclear payload for two targets.

Received. Standby for General Ashdown.

Standing by.

Hyde, this is Ashdown. The Genesis Initiative have requested we attempt to secure the brood mother. In your opinion, what's the probability of mission success?

Very low, General. The creature's three miles underground and guarded by a sizeable force. I can scout the second target, but I would imagine if it is a nest then they'll have taken similar precautions.

Repeat the last. You say it could be a twin nest?

Affirmative.

We've not seen that before. Standby.

Jayne was silently jogging back up the shaft, readying herself to start hunting the topside mutants. It would be dangerous, but the A-class operators needed a clear path to bring the devices underground.

Hyde, can you scout and confirm the presence of a second nest? Report in as soon as possible.

Yes, ma'am.

An hour later and she was stood at the mouth of a second cavern which was only slightly smaller than the first. Multitudes of the infected were gathering and that could only mean one thing; they were preparing for an all-out assault on Heldon.

Hyde to base, second nest confirmed. They're gearing for war.

Received. Move to safe distance and await Vanquisher and armour support.

General, I would advise against that course of action.

Your objections are noted, soldier, but the knowledge we could gain from that size of host is too valuable to pass up. Move to safe distance and await further orders.

Understood. Hyde out.

Well this day just got a whole lot more interesting, she thought sourly.

CHAPTER THIRTY-THREE

"All V-class operators are to assemble in your designated zone. This is not a drill."

Dropping whatever they were doing, Andy and the rest of his squad quickly donned their combat dress. Checking each other's suits were secure, they slipped on tactical helmets and raced from the hut.

"This is it then?" Zip asked, jogging alongside him.

"It seems like it."

"You sure you don't want to be safely wrapped in a Mech? It could get hairy out there."

"I hope so. After seeing them up close I want to get some payback. Hand to hand is more satisfying than the detachment a Mech gives."

"Fair enough. I'll make you a deal," said Zip.

"Depends on what it is."

"Get us both home safely and I'll take you back to Mrs Lao's for a meal."

"Consider it done."

Mustering on the training ground, Andy and the other Vanquishers formed up. Magjets were skimming in over the walls, the bay doors dropping as they landed to allow access to the troops. Hundreds were already inside from other outposts, secure in the seat harnesses. Bateman and the Mechs were airborne, dangling from the thick clamps.

Hardie was all business as he explained the mission, a grim scowl pinching his features. "One of Smith's Shadow operators has found a twin nest in an abandoned power station seventy-three miles from here. We've got the opportunity to secure a host unlike anything we've captured before. The knowledge within that abomination may give us an edge in the coming wars. And if not, we need to kill the bitches anyway."

"Size of the enemy force, sir?"

"Estimates are around a hundred thousand. We'll be approaching from the north-east, dropping into the area with Paladin and Mech support on the ground. A Dreadhulk is on standby to transport the brood mother and will hold back at a distance of ten miles. Our job is to survive the initial assault and then go underground to force the queen, or queens, topside. Your visor display will roll film of the first sighting by the operator. Study it, get rid of any fear at how repulsive it is. We need you cocked, locked, and ready to rock, not quivering like a jelly when we get her in our sights. Understood?"

"Aye, Sarge!"

"Good. You're going to be split into groups of four and join a veteran squad on the Magjets. It's not that I doubt you, it's just protocol until you're blooded in a real fight with the mutants. Listen to the hardasses and you won't go wrong. If it all turns to shit and we get killed, I'll see you all at the next spawning."

With that, he called out names and designated their transport. Andy and Zip were picked, sprinting up the ramp with two more from their platoon. The battle-hardened soldiers gave them a warm greeting with none of the usual hazing reserved for rookies. In the Sovereign Guard, everyone spawned was a warrior from some far-flung corner of the globe. The fact that they were untested against a sizeable force of infected was irrelevant. After stowing their rifles and strapping themselves in, the commander welcomed the new faces.

"Good to have you with us, recruits! I'm Lieutenant Croft."

The four introduced themselves.

"I know you're going to be a handful which is good news for us. Anyone coming out of Hardie's training is an asset. Wait, did one of you say Burton?"

Andy raised his hand.

"Andrew Burton?"

"Yes, sir."

"Shit, you're the one who smashed Smith's record," said an unknown voice.

"As did Downing, sir."

"Downing?"

Gillian spoke up. "Zip, sir. My nickname."

"Well hot damn. Ladies and gents, we have a couple of celebrities. Once we've scraped these cockroaches from our boots I'd be honoured if you'd all have a drink with us."

The other veterans animatedly confirmed their agreement.

"We'd like that. Thank you, sir."

"Ok, back to mission. Our friends have got aerial recon, so we're going to strike as one unit. Once the birds are wiped out by the drones, the Paladins are going to drop their deployable pillboxes three quarters of a mile from the tunnel and take up position to our rear. They'll give us some extra cover when we're under attack. We disembark twenty seconds later and form up, using the drop bunkers and terrain for cover. Delta and Echo platoons will be setting up to guard the flanks with Mech support. We don't expect it to be an issue, but the bastards have been getting far too smart for my liking. Any questions?"

None came.

"Good. Check ammo and weapons. Hyde has uploaded a full 3D laser scan of the underground system, so I suggest you become acquainted with the nest layout. ETA to destination, twenty-six minutes."

Left alone with their thoughts, the four newcomers looked over the neon mapping. Zip muttered something about not relishing the idea of traipsing three miles below ground. Even the veterans grumbled anxiously at the creature they were tasked with retrieving. This was new to all of them, time servers and raw recruits alike.

Thinking back to his family, Andy said a quiet prayer in their memory. His heartrate was steady, with none of the usual pre-battle jitters. Was he that eager for death? Or was it a newfound confidence? He didn't really know. The crushing pain of their loss had returned ferociously as Zip and the briefing pack said it would. That alone pointed towards a yearning for the peace of the grave; a dead man couldn't feel his heart tearing apart. No longer would he see the flashing visions of his daughters, their smiling faces as he returned from duty. His wife's strangling embrace as she smothered him in kisses. On the other hand, he wasn't a coward. Andy's friends, nay the whole world, was counting on him to fight. To win.

"Fuck it," he muttered.

"You ok?" asked Zip.

"Yeah, just old memories coming back."

"Use them," offered another stranger's voice.

"Is that what you do?" asked Andy.

"Revenge is all I have left, brother."

Following the brief exchange, the lieutenant released his harness and stood up, clutching the support bar above his head.

"We're a minute out. Time for the fireworks."

Peering through the panoramic windscreen, a series of drones rocketed past, the yellow incandescence of the fuel lighting the way. Powering upwards to meet the threat, missiles detached from the wings and streaked off into the darkness. The night lit up like the Fourth of July as the eagles were hit, disappearing in huge fireballs, their burned scraps falling to earth.

"We're cleared for landing!" shouted the commander as the aerial hunters pulled a full one-eighty and sped for home.

Moving as one, the soldiers unbuckled and retrieved their rifles from the upright weapon racks. The pilots dropped suddenly, pulling the stick back just in time to avoid a collision. The bay door dropped, and the Vanquishers moved by the twos and spread out. The Paladins were reversing, the six-foot-wide tracks supporting the five hundred and forty tonnes of killing power crushing anything in their path. Two empty channels behind the huge turret signified the mobile pods had been dropped. The quad barrels of the tank wouldn't have looked out of place on a twentieth century battleship, battering fortified enemy positions.

"Greenhorns, bunker or topside?"

"Topside, sir," came the replies.

"That's what I like to hear. Get in position!"

The twelve steel shelled pods were strategically placed in a slight curve to give a wide field of fire. Gun ports were visible around the whole perimeter, and as the selected veterans opened the rear doors, Andy caught sight of the fixed flame unit within. Bateman had spread the Mechs out evenly along the line, taking up a central position himself to stay close to the action. The painted white skull on the armour reminded Andy of a film he'd seen many lives ago.

"Hab, Jenkins, you're on the torch!"

The top of the pods was fitted with a shield in the form of a five-foot-high wall. The barrier was lined with barbed spikes, as was the entire circumference of the defensive structures.

"Twelve on the roof! Now! The rest of you, on me!"

Argyle and Kemp joined ten others as they scurried up the retractable ladder. Zip found cover in one of the deep ruts left by the trundling behemoths. Andy took up position to her right, kneeling behind a pile of rubble. Glancing left, he caught sight of Hardie barking orders to his own platoon. As the troops fell silent, the hum of the Magjets receded into the night and only the idling engines of the Paladins and Mech hydraulics could be heard.

"The tanks are going to soften them up for us when they've cleared the tunnel. Hold fire until the dust settles."

Their position put them at the back of the administration building, with the unbroken cooling stacks to the right. The mouth of the nest was facing them, dark and forbidding. Andy held a hand to the ground and felt a growing vibration carry through the dry earth.

"This is it. Remember your training and you'll be fine."

The denizens of Hell spewed from the opening, splitting into three individual paths.

"Would you fucking believe it?" growled the lieutenant. "Delta, Echo, looks like you'll be earning your crust today. You've got incoming."

A series of deep cracks shattered the night. Blazing across the darkness came the heavy shells of the tanks. The explosive rounds impacted, sending pillars of fire, mud, and flesh soaring into the sky. Split by the diverging infected, they were less effective than hoped. A second barrage whined overhead, shrapnel tearing through the ranks of wailing monsters. A rain of bloody confetti started to fall around the soldiers. Most of the debris was, thankfully, unidentifiable, but a solitary eye plopped down two feet in front of Andy. The red orb stared, and he was sure he could feel the malice emanating from the severed optic.

"They're too spread out. You're clear to engage!"

The display scope picked out the closest targets and a squeeze of the trigger sent fifty rounds into their midst. Splintering shards of high velocity metal punched through the mutants. Puffs of blood and scraps of flesh exited the wounds in a hundred different directions. All along the line, streams of bullets cut through the three-pronged swarm. Bateman ordered the Mechs to engage, pouring their explosive rounds into the swarming creatures.

"Paladins, can you try and funnel the bastards before they breach our flanks?" shouted Croft.

The whir of rotating mechanisms preceded another round of heavy booms. To the sides, a wall of destruction burst skyward, deflecting some, but not all of the creatures.

"They're determined little fuckers. Again!"

Dazed by the second blast wave, the infected stood up, shook themselves, and forged on through the deluge of rock and mud.

"Squad leaders, send four from your fire teams to support the flanks. Two to each side. Burton, Downing, you're up! Captain, can you reposition your forces to help them?"

"Roger that. Will you be able to hold the line?"

"We'll use the flamers to beat them back, sir. If we can't hold the flanks we're lost!"

Leaving cover, the ground troops dodged behind the chattering bunkers while Mechs marched directly through the gunfire unconcerned. The fastest of the infected had reached the effective range of the sputtering weapons. Yelling their hatred, the soldiers let loose. Raging, liquid fire licked out from the wider frontal port, searing into the nearing horde.

Hardie caught sight of the reinforcements arriving. "We need two more shooters on the roof. I've got a bad feeling in my bones."

Croft had paused to reload and overheard the exchange. "What's the problem, Sergeant?"

"There's not enough of them, sir. There should be more, a lot more."

"They could be delayed. The vibrations could've collapsed one of their passageways."

"I sure hope so."

"Keep your eyes on the prize, Sergeant."

Andy and Zip clambered onto the raised platform, switching out empty magazines. Racking the slide, the mag coils spat the bullets into the monsters. The impact craters of the Paladin shots were working against them, providing cover as the creatures leaped between the depressions.

"Looks like we may be going hand to hand!" yelled Croft.

The central mass of the horde was being chewed up by the solid wall of fire and unceasing barrage of bullets.

"They're pulling back," exclaimed Croft in shock.

"That's impossible," Hardie growled, turning just in time to see them retreat.

"Sergeant, they're circling back to join the flankers."

Once again, the uninjured mutants used the cover of the hollows to avoid being shot. On the left, Andy and Zip were picking off as many as possible but the angle of approach left them wide open. Even the explosive tipped bullets of the Mechs were only chewing dirt. The eager flames were falling short of the snarling pack, restricted in their movement by the gun port.

Twenty or so took a chance, jumping with every ounce of power in their mutated legs. Thankfully, the first wave fell short, slamming into the sides of the structure and impaling themselves. Mortally wounded, torn up arms reached weakly for the soldiers above as blood ran down the steel shell. The second wave was bang on target, a small group crashing down amongst the startled troops. Dozens landed on the Mechs, crawling over the black armour until the deadly lances sprang from the ports to impale them. Moving to help the besieged soldiers, another cluster of infected reached their position and attacked.

"Use your knives! We're coming!" Croft shouted.

Andy was shoved against the wall alongside Zip, faceplates of the combat helmets touched as if kissing. Pinned by the weight of the mutants, they could feel the ferocity as the armour was attacked in an effort to get to the soft meat within. It was just like Mech training, except there was no safety net in this fight, it was to the death.

"I... can't get... to it!" Zip grunted, trying to twist and remove her combat knife.

"Hold on, don't panic!" Andy growled.

Grabbing the infected snapping at his throat by the back of its neck, Andy slammed it into the steel wall, once, twice, three times. The skull split open, and yet the damage didn't deter it. Digging into the open wound with his fingers, he tore at the pulsing brain until it let out a gargled choke and fell dead to the floor. Withdrawing the knife, he stabbed out from a sitting position, catching the creature attempting to eat Zip under the armpit. The blade buried itself to the hilt, and he twisted for good measure, causing the most awful cry of inhuman agony he'd ever heard. The thing clutched at its ribs and stumbled away to the side before collapsing. The other Vanquishers weren't faring much better, wrestling with two or more adversaries. Andy dodged another group as they crashed down, slashing open the throat of the closest while Zip disembowelled two more.

"We got you!" Andy yelled, driving the blade into the top of the creature's skull. Freed of the weight, the man managed to struggle to his knees while holding the second at bay. Zip severed its spine with a single strike and it flopped to the floor, clawing at its useless legs.

"Thanks."

"No prob…"

"Watch out!" he cried, pulling him down.

Andy spun round and saw the descending pack of horrors. Glares of triumph turned to shock as Croft and his team cut them down mid-air, the bodies twirling from the impact of the bullets. Skirting the bunker, the reinforcements held the infected long enough for the troops above to butcher their enemies and regain footing. Bateman had cleared his suit of mutants, slashing out with both arms or crushing the squealing things beneath the massive Mech feet.

"They're on the run!" Hardie roared, punching the air.

Croft stood in silence, surveying the carnage. Never before had the mutants fled from a battle, but here they were, swarming back into the tunnels toward their nests. This didn't bode well, he thought, in spite of the jubilation. A line had been crossed and the enemy was now capable of far more than just feeding itself into a meat grinder. Hell, the way things were going they might be using weapons next.

"Sir, orders?"

"Perform a sweep and kill any survivors. Once the perimeter's secure we'll send in teams to flush out the brood mothers."

"We're going to try for both?" asked Hardie.

"The Initiative want them both if possible."

"That could take hours, sir. We're sitting ducks here."

"We've got a Dreadhulk providing support and the recon drones have already left the base. We'll be forewarned and well prepared for any counterattack."

"I still don't understand where the others are? We didn't see close to a hundred thousand."

"I think we can thank God for that, Sergeant," replied Croft, scanning the horizon and the stacked corpses. "If they'd attacked in force with their newfound wiles we'd all be dead by now. I'll send a scouting probe below to see if they're laying a trap for us."

"Understood, sir."

"Report."

"I've lost contact with both of the probes, sir. They reached a sufficient depth to do a bio scan before they were destroyed. The numbers are in the low hundreds. The nests are empty."

Croft looked to Hardie. "Maybe Smith's operator got the number wrong?"

"Impossible. I know Hyde, she's as tough as they come. If she said there were a hundred thousand down there, then they were down there."

"Where can they be then?"

"I wish I knew, sir."

"We can investigate later, for now we need to get those things above ground. Once we get them caged and transported, I'll send the drones out further to see if they pick up a signal. We'll find them one way or another."

"Very good, sir."

Hardie watched as his superior organised the teams preparing to go below. His instincts were tingling; something was off, way off.

"Are you ready?" Lynch whispered in the confines of the passage. They had stumbled across the smashed remnants of the scouting probe five hundred yards short of the cavern mouth according to the 3D mapping. Two minutes would see them face to face with the horrific miscreation.

"Ready," Andy confirmed.

Lynch nodded, shucking the flame pack higher onto his shoulders. It wasn't to incinerate, just motivate. If the queen was reluctant to leave her home, the heat from a short burst should be enough to get her fat ass moving.

Zip followed closely behind, hugging the tunnel wall with the other eighteen members of the second team. They moved as one, vigilant for any attack.

Lynch reached the cavern first, gaping at the scene of slaughter. The brood mother was dead, that much was obvious. One of her heads had been torn clean off, and the other hung from a few remaining tendons and exposed sinew. It had been slashed open in countless places, spreading gruesome black ichor across the ground. Steam from the cooling body drifted upwards in the frigid cavern. She hadn't gone down without a fight, though. Shredded bodies of the mutants were strewn amongst the spilled blood of their creator. Five or six attempted to crawl away, horrifically mutilated by the talon tipped legs during the assault. Lynch hosed them down with fire before turning to the others.

"What the fuck happened here?"

"They killed the host," said Zip. "That's why they pulled back."

"They didn't want us to capture them?"

"How the hell do they know what we were going to do to them? They're mindless."

"Apparently not."

"Lieutenant Croft are you receiving?"

"Go ahead, Lynch."

"The brood mother's dead, sir."

"How the hell did that happen?" he raged. "You were given explicit instructions to secure the host and force her to the surface."

"We didn't do anything, sir. The infected killed her."

"Repeat that last."

"The infected that retreated from battle attacked her. They ripped her to pieces."

Another voice interrupted. "Sir, this is Monk."

"Give me good news, Sergeant."

"I can't, sir. The second queen's also dead."

"Goddammit! Ok, take a sample of her blood and tissue then get your asses back up here. We're returning to base." Croft was furious, pacing back and forth. "Hardie, what do you think happened?"

"I'm not totally sure, sir."

"Do you have a theory?"

Hardie looked around; the blood, the mud, the smouldering fires. "Do you ever feel like a fish on a hook, sir?"

"I don't follow."

"This feels like we've been hooked. They laid out the bait, we took it, and they reeled us in."

"Why on earth would they sacrifice so many of their own, and two brood mothers, to reel us in as you called it?"

"I don't know, sir. I'd give anything to know where those mutants are right now though," he replied, desperately trying to figure out the missing puzzle piece.

Chapter Thirty-Four

Following the brief meeting with the senior managers in the Mech facility, Tamsin had returned home. They were surprisingly accommodating to her requests to work offsite for a while and praised her dedication and value to the team without prompting. Perhaps her new, hardened attitude told them she was no longer to be taken for granted. Or, just as likely, they had always thought highly of her but were occupied with greater concerns than complimenting their employees for doing their job. Regardless, it felt good to receive some plaudits for her efforts.

Burdened with a completely new system in a cumbersome box, Toby, the building supervisor, rushed out of his small office to help. All attempts to dissuade him were ignored as he retrieved the lifting aid from the storeroom. After some small talk on the elevator ride, the automated trolley followed obediently as they made their way down the corridor towards her apartment. With each step, Tamsin's anxiety soared ever higher, but she could think of no reason to dismiss him that wouldn't raise suspicion. Reaching the front door, Toby smiled and waited for her to open it.

"I can take it from here, thanks," said Tamsin, moving to pick up the large box.

"Don't be silly. I can take it straight in on the trolley rather than watch you struggle."

"Honestly, I'm fine," she replied a bit more brusquely than intended.

Toby flinched a little at the harsh tone. Staring at each other, the awkward silence dragged on interminably. Fearing he would insist on accompanying her inside, Tamsin was tempted to grab the package and dart through the door. It would be rude to slam it in his face, yet he was leaving no alternative.

"I know this may seem strange," he started to say, looking down at his feet. "I've watched you come and go for years."

Tamsin frowned at the admission of stalker-like behaviour.

"Sorry, that sounded really bad," he mumbled, catching sight of her worried expression. "What I meant to say was that I've watched you but didn't have the balls to say anything. I know the world is all messed up, and we could all be wiped out tomorrow."

"Is this going somewhere?" she asked cautiously.

"Would you like to go to a holo suite sometime? Maybe a bar?"

"You mean like a date?"

"No! Of course not," his cheeks flushed. "Just hanging out, as friends."

Tamsin weighed up the offer. G had insisted she needed to get out more, and this was the best offer in over a century. Toby was attractive in a mousy, geeky kind of way. His unkempt brown hair, the shy brown eyes with striations of amber, his pleasant scent and thin, wiry body. Pictures of her family flashed through her mind and she backed away, head shaking.

"No, sorry."

Opening the door, Tamsin wrestled the box onto her knees and shuffled inside as quickly as possible.

"Thanks for the help," she said, shutting him out in the hallway.

Toby's mouth tried to form a few words, but embarrassment and the latch engaging cut him off before he could respond. Tamsin listened as he let out a deep sigh and moved away towards the lift.

"You could've said yes," G said, keeping the volume minimal in case his voice carried.

"I've already got a husband."

"Yes, and I'm certain he wouldn't mind you socialising. Spending time with people isn't a betrayal."

Mimicking the deep huff of Toby, she ignored G and unpacked the powerful machine. It was a tenth of the size of the scavenged server sitting in the dark corner, while being two hundred and sixty percent more powerful. If she'd known how easily the facility would provide her with the processing unit she wouldn't have needed to steal anything in the first place.

"Is that my new home?"

"Yup. I hope you like it."

"I'm sure it's better than the back of my car."

"I've downloaded as much information as I can onto the memory banks. You can search through it until your heart's content."

"That's very kind of you to say."

"Huh?" Tamsin grunted, fishing for the adapter cables beneath the desk.

"You said I have a heart."

"It's a figure of speech, don't get too excited."

"Oh, I see."

"Don't pout either. You're an advanced being, it's unbecoming."

"I think I prefer the meek Tamsin."

"I could still unplug you and put you in a drawer."

"Apologies."

Slotting the final cable into its port, she flicked the power switch and pushed the unit to the side to keep it out of the way. The lights of the dead server faded completely as the AI relocated.

"This is nice. It's like moving from the trailer park to Bel Air."

"It took me years to build your trailer, you ungrateful bastard."

"It was a figure of speech."

"I didn't get you more power for you to give me more backtalk. You're meant to be helping."

"Apologies."

"I need to freshen up a bit. Take a look around your new home."

Closing the bathroom door, she smiled to herself at the excited voice coming from the lounge. G was settling in nicely by the sounds of it.

"News on," she said, filling the basin with warm water.

Dabbing at her skin with the wet cloth, the Divinity Alliance emblem faded out to be replaced with 'Breaking News'. Selectively edited drone footage rolled on the screen. Paladin tanks unleashed salvos of huge shells at the horrors streaming from a tunnel mouth, blowing them to kingdom come. Cutting to the front line, she was filled with pride at the sight of her Mechs kicking ass. More action shots followed of the recent battle; Vanquishers going hand to hand on the defensive pods, mutants fleeing the battlefield. Tamsin scowled at the sight as the soothing voice of the commentator came over the speaker.

Today, the forces of the Sovereign Guard won a great victory over the mutant hordes. An operative from the Shadow team identified a large nest and Empress Verena ordered an all-out assault. The bravest members of our army were dispatched and destroyed the threat without suffering any casualties. You can rest easy knowing that you have the protection of these brave soldiers. Thank you for your continued support in these troubled times.

The sight of the infected running away replayed in her mind. *Very strange*, she thought. An uneasy feeling bloomed in the pit of her stomach for unknown reasons.

"News off."

Leaving the bathroom, the monitor showed a *Home Sweet Home* sign hanging from an imaginary wall.

"We need to discuss your rent."

"I think my continued silence about a certain attempted murder is payment enough for now."

"Fair point. Have you had a chance to look at the data?"

"Yes. It doesn't make sense, though."

"What do you mean?"

"I've extrapolated the data relating to the advances in human genetic engineering and the corresponding effects that has on the infection."

"And?"

"My calculations show a ninety-nine-point six percent chance that they should've evolved far beyond the base instincts of hunger and replication."

"What does that mean?"

"It means that they should be exhibiting higher levels of intelligence. I've seen reports of them becoming more adaptive to the threats we pose. Such as lying in wait before attacking, that shows an increased level of cunning, but not to the extent that it should be."

"We've been lucky?"

"I don't know. Perhaps."

"What's an alternative explanation?"

"That they've been purposely concealing their growing intellect from us."

"But why?"

"That's the million-dollar question."

CHAPTER THIRTY-FIVE

Quadrant ZT-9.
26 miles inside Alliance borders.
Mining Outpost Joanton.
Population – 6471.

Surrounding a central hub of gantries, vats, massive pipes, breather stacks, and excavation conveyors, was the town of Joanton. A bustling hub comprising a military garrison of V and D-Class operatives, sprawling complexes of engineer and miner housing, along with the relevant support facilities. Keeping all of this safe from the deadly threat outside was the fifty-foot tall and eight-foot-deep Jajovium and steel alloy perimeter wall. Spaced around the entire circumference were sentient APTs, or Automated Plasma Turrets. The dual eight-inch barrels would cough out thirty charges a minute of heavy plasma spheres during any large-scale assault by the mutations. It was enough to turn the surrounding land into a seething cauldron of lava. Heavily armed sentries would then take care of anything that survived the hellish maelstrom. Not that they ever got heavily attacked this deep within Divinity territory. The perimeter outposts were always the first to get hit.

A motion sensor triggered the turret, the smooth internal Mechanisms causing it to rise from the suspension rings which absorbed the phenomenal recoil. All operatives on the wall received an instant report from the scanners.

One target. North-north-west. Threat level minimal. Standing down.

And with that, the death spewing tower lowered on its pneumatics back into standby mode.

"I've got this one."

"Bullshit. It must be eight kilometres away at least. Send a drone."

Luke looked away from the scope of his rifle and grinned. "Want to make it interesting? If I can get it through the eye, you transfer thirty minutes of your holo-suite time to me."

"I'll take that action," Cody replied, shaking his hand.

"Sucker."

Pulling the stock in tight, Luke stared through the scope. The display showed the distance to be exactly eight thousand one hundred and eighty-two meters away, well within range of the Ashdown XG6 sniper rifle.

"What are you waiting for? Losing your nerve?" Cody mocked.

"It's watching us," Luke muttered, a sense of unease growing.

"What? Let me see."

Cody pulled down his visor and pinpointed the mutant. With a single thought, the psy-linked battle display zoomed in the view to crystal clarity, as if he was stood only six paces away. Humanoid as far as standing on two legs with two arms at its side went, but that was where the similarity ended. Its head was a lumpy, ill formed mess with strands of hair hanging from irregular patches. The greasy scalp pulsated as if something within was bursting to be free. Curved fangs rose from the lower jaw, tearing into the fleshy upper lip. The muscle mass on the legs was increasing, enabling greater speed and the ability to leap much higher. Lesions and sores trickled pus onto the dusty ground. Each new generation saw the creatures devolve further from their original, human form into a more effective killing machine.

"See what I mean?" Luke whispered, feeling foolish. It was absurd to think that the pointed ears could actually hear them at such a distance.

"I don't like it." The thing was like a statue, immobile and fixated on their section of wall. It was impossible to tell if the solid red orbs were staring *at* them, but it certainly felt that way. A chill traced its way down his spine. "Control, are you seeing this?"

Their earpieces came to life with the voice of Major Adrianna. *"We see it and are transmitting your feed directly to Command. Terminate the target immediately."*

"Understood."

Centring the crosshair on the monster's left eye, Luke moved his finger from the trigger guard. A red dot on the bottom of the scope display changed to green at the contact and the subtle whine indicated the weapon was charged. Squeezing the trigger, the bolt of energy blazed across the arid wastes. A glowing, circular wound was all that remained of its eye, vapour steaming from the borehole created by the incredible temperatures.

"Good shot," said Cody. His disappointment at losing the holo-time was negated by the death of the mutant and its bizarre behaviour.

"I've never seen one do that before."

"Nor have I," Cody replied, nervously.

"Do you think it was just fucked up?"

"I hope so," Cody remarked. The alternatives did not bear thinking about.

Wind whipped at Sergeant Gibb's face from the open aircraft door.

The soldiers and anti-air batteries below tracked their progress as the silent machine passed over the heavily fortified perimeter wall into the desolate wasteland beyond. The craft only emitted an almost imperceptible hum as it sped towards its destination. Trent turned in the pilot's seat and held up a single finger.

Gibb nodded in the darkness. "One minute!"

The team checked their weapons and lined up at either side, ready to disembark. Hard men with hard attitudes, they were trained to fight from the moment they left the birthing tube.

The ground rushed up to meet them, illuminated only by the night display of their combat helmet visors. Outside the thin screen shielding their faces, everything was darkness. Stones shimmied on the hard-packed earth, disturbed by the invisible magnetic waves passing between the Earth's core and the cell receptors in the belly of the craft. Leaping out, the first four took up position at each corner, watchful of the still night. One mutant invariably meant more. A lot more.

"Load it up and get it in the back!"

Franklin joined Gibb, guarding the men who wrestled the corpse onto the stretcher. Humping it around the sleek, black fuselage, they ran up the ramp and strapped it into place.

"This is Echo Team leader. The package is secure."

"Good work, Sergeant. The Genesis Initiative want to examine the body. We're arranging for transportation to take you to Poseidon within the hour. Return to base and await further instruction."

"Yes, ma'am," replied Gibb. Addressing the men, he shouted, "Mount up!"

Dull vibrations beneath their feet increased in intensity, causing the tiny stones to dance. Twenty feet away, the ground shifted, clods of dried mud and dust exploding as hidden creatures emerged from a dozen tunnels.

"It's a trap!"

The night lit up as the soldiers opened fire on the bounding monsters. Concentrated energy from the Devastator's plasma cannons blazed through the bodies, cutting them down before disappearing into the distance. Incandescent trails strobed against pitch-black surroundings, revealing a massive horde sprinting and leaping over each other in desperation to get at the warm meat.

"We need to fall back! Everyone aboard!"

A scream from the front of the aircraft was cut off with an agonised gurgle. Seth dodged a snarling maw, withdrawing his knife and driving it into the neck in one fluid motion. Spewing blood, it hit the dirt hard, writhing and clawing its own throat to ribbons in the frenzy. A single shot tore through its chest, turning the ground beneath into bubbling fire and igniting the flailing body. Rounding the aircraft, Seth came to a halt. Pearson's legs kicked weakly at the ground as he was eaten. Two infected were devouring him alive, one tearing at the soft parts of his face while the other hollowed him out having torn through his armour. Plasma rounds seared through flesh and bone with ease, leaving the charred, smoking corpses twitching in the dirt.

"Gibb, we have to go!"

"They got through his fucking armour! How's that possible?"

Pearson's eyeless, skinless face turned towards them, bloodied teeth chattering in shock as the last traces of life fled his body. If left out in the dirt, he would be consumed fully, or worse, mutate. Even now, the parasitic enzymes in the saliva would be navigating his central nervous system, beginning the first steps of reanimation. In a short while, his vastly altered body would be moving around, as eager to feed as the mutants which spawned from their hives.

"Sorry, brother," Gibb whispered, blowing the top of his skull off. The remains of his head sunk into the shallow lava pit created by the plasma discharge.

Slamming the door shut, he slapped the pilot's helmet. Needing no further instruction, Trent diverted all power to lift and pulled on the stick hard enough to risk tearing it out of the floor. Vertigo twisted their stomachs as the craft rose and lurched in a full one-eighty-degree turn. Heavy crumps shook the chassis in quick succession.

"They're on the roof!" Trent yelled. "Hold on to your nuts!"

He banked hard in a desperate attempt to shake them loose. Rocking port and starboard, the soldiers were tossed around like rag dolls. A scrabbling thud preceded a rending squeal of claws ripping away from the outer shell. The shriek of fury dwindled as the creature plummeted to the ground.

"How the fuck can they jump so high?" Luke gasped as the creatures pounced on the rapidly ascending craft. "That must've been nearly twenty feet!"

"Over twenty," whispered Cody with dread.

"That means they can nearly clear the electrical countermeasures on the wall."

A red light started to flash on the turret as it rose menacingly back to life. In the town itself, a siren began to wail, warning people to get into the shelters. Not that they would ever hold out against the monsters if they should breach the defences. The bunker facilities were a placebo to get the technicians and personnel away from the more heavily protected cities. Boots thundered on the roads leading to the walls from the remaining D-Class operators as they raced to protect the outpost. The turret scanners were reporting a number close to fifty thousand sprinting full tilt at the walls from the north. Lights blinked out in the town as the vast energy requirements of the plasma cannons and electrical shield were diverted. It had been two months since any kind of assault, decades since anything of this scale. The decision to pull away sixty percent of their forces to go after a new host now looked like it could be their downfall.

We could've sure used them right about now, Luke thought.

Major Adrianna came over the comms. *"All snipers on the Magjet. Anti-air assets will shoot it down if any infected are still clinging on. Fire at will."*

The steady hum of the vessel had become a deep drone that set their teeth on edge as it pulled every ounce of power it could from the Earth's core. Whine after whine of fingers on triggers raced down the perimeter as the monsters were targeted. Tracers of heat peppered the night as the operatives opened fire. Monsters were shredded by the snipers, flaming scraps of flesh raining to the ground. On the hull, a couple of glowing yellow furrows flared where gunfire had clipped the nanofiber shell. Freed from the threat of imminent destruction, the pilot accelerated and rose over the wall to relieved cheers from below.

Targets inbound. Range... three kilometres and closing. Speed... sixty-two kilometres an hour. Firing.

The huge barrels started to glow as the Catyminum was vaporised and ignited. With a crack, the turret belched out the sun-bright sphere of energy. Pneumatics and the suspension rings absorbed the recoil caused by the tremendous discharge, resetting the position for the next salvo. Further down, the next APT began bombarding the incoming waves of mutants. Then the next, until a row of the machines spat their hellfire at the enemy. Incandescent orbs arced in the sky, before crashing down among the creatures. Bursting apart, the superheated matter liquified stone, soil, and flesh, mixing them all into a roiling pit of magma. Each impact consumed anything within eighty feet. One hundred feet further from the killing zone saw the monsters screaming as their skin ignited, rolling in the superheated dirt in a futile attempt to quench the flames.

Targets still inbound. Range... one and a half kilometres and closing. Proximity warning. Ceasing fire.

Falling silent, the turret barrels rose to a vertical position to be rapid cooled by the injection of carbon dioxide. Chilled mist rushed from the tubes, dissipating on the air around them. Motion scanners revealed that over two thirds of the swarm had fallen in the barrage. Sentries placed their sniper rifles down and unslung their assault rifles. Stepping to the low wall, they prepared for the attack. The ground vibrated with the stampeding abominations, backlit by the roaring fires of the plasma artillery.

"You ready?" Luke asked.

"Always!" Cody grinned.

"Fire at will," ordered Major Adrianna.

Taking up the final ounces of pressure on the triggers, the guns buzzed, spitting out their lethal projectiles at the gibbering swarm. The fragmenting bullets kicked up a spray of dust and blood as they cut a swathe through the nearest mutants. Drenched in the raining blood of their advanced guard, thousands more poured through, adding their own fluids to the saturating, black mist. Despite the awesome firepower being unleashed, a sizeable force reached the wall. Screaming with rage and hunger, they launched themselves at the smooth, vertical face. The strongest slammed into the shield, inches below the insulation which ran around the entire perimeter to protect the soldiers. A blinding flash of electricity sent the creature flying, eyes bursting and skin cracking as the residual current fried it from the inside. More and more attempted the suicidal leap, sticking to the metal and sizzling as the electricity coursed through their bodies.

"They're holding back!" yelled Cody.

"They're learning!" Luke replied, aghast.

Milling around, some of the creatures were trying to use the fallen as a springboard to clear the deadly barrier. One hit the unprotected section of wall with a triumphant scream, scrabbling for purchase. Defeated by the smooth surface, its claws scraped deep gouges in the metal until it touched the electrified cladding. An explosive crack of arcing voltage sent the crisp body pinwheeling onto those below.

"Niagara protocol engaged," said Major Adrianna.

A dull rumble transmitted through their feet, a portent of what was coming. From countless apertures in the wall, a torrent of water flowed forth, driven from the depths by massive pumps. The liquid coated the infected, pooling at their feet and running back towards the electrified shield. As soon as the first trickle made contact, all hell was let loose. The horde thrashed in death throes, lightning dancing between their bodies. Dead, but animated by the surging current which stiffened their muscles, they started to steam. Blood boiling, skin spewed with bursting gouts of gore before they erupted into flame. Melting like tallow, the creatures collapsed into a sticky puddle of charred bone and bubbling fats.

The turrets hissed, barrels dropping, and returning to their vigilant standby. Scanner reports indicated no threat in the near vicinity.

Holding his nose against the stench, Cody looked down as the water ceased. "Control, request upload of neural feed. These were unlike any we've fought before."

Their headsets transmitted the voice of their commander. It had an edge that no one had heard before. *"The behavioural anomaly has been reported to the Initiative. This isn't the only peculiarities tonight. All relevant information has already been sent to Tempest City for analysis. We'll begin clean up at first light. Stay on guard for any more infected. Good work, everyone. Adrianna, out."*

The soldiers congratulated each other, clapping backs, and bumping chests. A hefty chunk of R and R was forecast for their immediate futures.

"I'm going to use that holo-suite time tomorrow. I feel like a nice calming climb up Mount Everest," Luke declared.

"I have no fucking clue how you do it, brother. I hate the cold with a passion."

"It's not really cold, though. They're just electrical impulses tricking us into thinking it's a snowy peak. As soon as you can counter the fake signals, it becomes a lot more enjoyable. You should come with..." Luke fell silent.

The metal platform beneath their feet started to rattle, tiny pebbles and other debris jumping around.

"Can you feel that?" Cody whispered.

Every APT came to life around the whole circumference of the outpost, red beacons flashing.

Two million, four hundred and twenty thousand targets. All directions. Threat level maximum. Preparing to fire.

"We need to call the others back!" shouted one of the soldiers.

"They'd never make it in time," Luke replied, resigned to his fate.

"Then let's give the bastards a fight they'll never forget!" Cody growled, reclaiming the rifle.

"What do we do?" asked Major Brock from the observation room three thousand miles away.

"Shall we despatch reinforcements from the closest colonies, General?" suggested Captain Elliyana.

A floating holographic image showed the aerial view of the small township. To the north, a sizeable expanse of the area was ablaze. The infected streamed around the bubbling craters, moving faster than anyone had seen before.

"General Ashdown?"

Shaking her head, she replied, "They'd take twenty minutes to arrive, and by then it'll all be over one way or the other. I'm not even sure what our ground forces could do against a number that enormous."

"Why attack Joanton? What does it achieve?"

"It accounts for eight percent of our mineral output," she stated, calculating how catastrophic it was going to be to their defensive capability.

Major Brock looked at the other advisers, completely lost. "Shall I order the Dreadhulks to leave the nearest cities? We need to do something!"

"It's already out of our hands."

Falling silent, the group watched the millions of ant sized dots converge on the facility. Tiny balls fired from the artillery around the perimeter, incinerating countless numbers of the monsters. The plasma ringed the outpost with a pocked inferno, but still they came, finding any available route though the heat. Charging the wall, they hit it as one from all directions. The screen flashed in the command room, temporarily blinding the observers. When the image faded from their shocked retinas, the town was in darkness.

"They overwhelmed the grid…"

No longer held at bay by the perimeter defences, the miniscule creatures streamed up and over the walls. The brave operators were overpowered in seconds.

"I'll send a drone to carry out a seismic cleanse. We'll bury the bastards in the ruins of their destruction."

"No. We need the facility intact. If we trigger a cleanse, years of work will be wasted."

"Do you think it'll ever be safe to reclaim it?"

"Regardless, we need to retake it. They won't stay there for long after the food is gone. We need to find out how the hell they managed to get an army of that size past our sensors. This wasn't some blind luck attack, it was planned and executed with pinpoint timing. While we were chasing the rabbit down the hole at the power plant, they fucked us."

"Do you think it's an aberration? A one off?"

Ashdown turned to him. "I hope so. Professor Ennis will have some answers for us once she can analyse the brood mother sample. In the meantime, dispatch Dreadhulks and Paladin divisions to all facilities in close proximity to Joanton just in case. Once they get bored, they'll be looking for somewhere to go. I'll be damned if they're going to hurt us anymore tonight!"

"General?" called out one of the communications operators, distress straining his voice.

"What?" she snapped.

"Kirby Township is under attack as well."

"Number of infected?"

"One million seven hundred thousand plus," he replied, holding the earpiece close. "They're… gone."

"God help us," said Elliyana, genuflecting.

"God can't help us. We've lost."

CHAPTER THIRTY-SIX

"I knew something was amiss," Empress Verena sighed, pacing by the window, staring at her capital city. *Not for much longer,* she thought, devoid of anger. They'd given it their best shot, it just wasn't enough. A peace had settled upon her as the news was delivered, as if she could finally rest after the most frightful journey ever undertaken.

"We can always evacuate from the southern outposts. Try and tighten things up until we can get back on our feet."

Verena smiled warmly at her friend. How she loved the fearsome soldier and her single-minded pursuit of victory. "Will that really make any difference?"

"It's unlikely. The blow to our production leaves us wide open."

"How long until we're overrun?"

"At current estimates, around four weeks. If they've truly evolved to the point where they can hit us at our weakest points, half that. They'll pick us apart, piece by piece."

"How did it come to this? How did I miss it?"

"You can't blame yourself, Empress. You gave us a shot when all was already lost."

"It still didn't help, though."

"Look at it this way; the aliens are going to be so pissed when they arrive. We've managed to teach the rotten bastards to think, to plot. It might prove to be a fight they can't win."

"That's a comforting thought, if only a wild fantasy. Would you care for a drink?"

"One final toast with an old friend. I'd be honoured."

As the empress poured brandy from a crystal decanter retrieved from the White House, she broached the most difficult subject of her life. "Shall we ask the Initiative to distribute the pills?"

Ashdown stared out of the window, hand squeezing the glass until her knuckles whitened. "I'll never take one."

"I wouldn't expect you to. I know you'll go down fighting. I was thinking for the civilians, and especially the children. I don't want them to suffer."

The pill in question had been designed as a painless form of euthanasia. It took five minutes for the person to fall into a euphoric sleep, with dreams of purest joy. The heart slowed soon after, then stopped beating completely. Death followed swiftly.

"I'll give the order."

"Thank you."

Nothing was left to be said. Lost in their own thoughts, they sipped at the Cognac and started to plan their swansong.

The intercom chirped to life, startling them. "Empress Verena, I know you didn't want to be disturbed, but I have a lady that insists on seeing you."

"Now's not a good time."

"I understand, Empress. She says she won't take no for an answer."

"Has she been through security?" demanded Ashdown, thinking the worst.

"She's been fully cleared. She's unarmed except for a computer chip."

"Send her in."

The doors opened, and Tamsin stumbled over the threshold into the room. A bemused look passed between the two leaders at her bizarre demeanour. She stared at them, started to talk, then fell silent, wondering how to proceed. The bags under her eyes had their own bags. She looked exhausted.

"Hello, Tamsin. What can we do for you on this most unfortunate day?"

"You… you remember my name," she whispered, a perplexed look passing over her face.

"Of course, I remember everyone. Especially the most valuable people in our struggle. How can I help you?"

"It's not how you can help me, but how I can help you. Maybe. Possibly. Please don't banish or execute me for treason," she rambled.

"Don't be silly, child. Please, go ahead."

Moving over to the bank of computers, she traced the cables until she found the network link. Turning to Verena, she asked, "May I?"

"Be my guest."

Pulling it from the socket, she stood up and plugged in the chip. Fingers pummelled the keys mercilessly like a rattle of hail on glass. In her state of nervous breathlessness, she looked manic, frightful. Finishing her task, she pressed enter and turned to them.

"I know you forbade me to do this, but I couldn't help myself. I'm sorry, Empress."

"What on earth are you…" Verena begun, mind returning to the conversation all those years ago. "You haven't."

"I have. Say hello," Tamsin said meekly to the computer.

From the intercom came another voice. A strong, male voice. General Ashdown found it frustratingly familiar.

"Hello, Empress Verena. It's an honour to meet you."

Hesitating, she looked at Tamsin who nodded and smiled. "The honour is mine. To whom am I speaking?"

"My name's G, Tamsin created me and I'm here to help. We've got a lot of things to discuss and not much time. Shall I begin?"

THE END

About the Author

Ricky Fleet has been a lifelong horror fan. One dark night, many years ago, he 'borrowed' a copy of Salem's Lot from his mum's bedside table. Sneaking it into his room, the terrifying visage of Barlow gazed out from the cover. Doomed townsfolk stretched into the distance, and in bold, silver font was a name - Stephen King. The story contained within those pages spawned an appetite for horror that has yet to be sated. Masterton, Lumley, Koontz, Laws, Herbert, Hutson, Laymon, Barker, and many more have influenced both his life and his writing.

His career took him into the plumbing and heating sector, keeping Britain's homes warm and watered.

Born and raised in the UK, cups of tea are a non-negotiable staple of the English life and serve as brain fuel for his first love - writing.

With the Hellspawn series being enjoyed across the world, the growing saga has a dark edge that begins to explore the true horror of a world without rules. A nod to the master, George A. Romero. The only thing running on his zombies are the fluids of decay. What they lack in velocity, they more than make up for with utter remorselessness and insatiable hunger.

Infernal – Emergence is the first in his new demon series.

A tale of conspiracy, untapped powers and the vast armies of Hell who yearn to tear our world apart. Only one man stands in their way; he just doesn't know it yet.

His latest release – Devoured World – takes a new and terrifying look at the question 'Are we alone in the universe.' It appeared to be a gift; it was, in fact, a terrible curse. Nuclear Armageddon. A dead world. Billions of mutants roaming the darkened wasteland. These are the least of the survivor's problems. The aliens are coming, and then the true war will begin.

You can find Ricky at the following places:

On Amazon: **https://www.amazon.com/Ricky-Fleet/e/B072C2GX6X**

Author page
https://www.facebook.com/Author-Ricky-Fleet-751475768315453/

Hellspawn fan group page
https://www.facebook.com/groups/175304226349208/

And at my publisher: **http://optimusmaximuspublishing.com**

Hellspawn

UK - **https://www.amazon.co.uk/Hellspawn-Ricky-Fleet-ebook/dp/B01A2LLELA/**

US - **https://www.amazon.com/Hellspawn-Ricky-Fleet-ebook/dp/B01A2LLELA/**

Hellspawn Odyssey

UK – https://www.amazon.co.uk/Hellspawn-Odyssey-Ricky-Fleet-ebook/dp/B01EJ0OQ5G/

US – https://www.amazon.com/Hellspawn-Odyssey-Ricky-Fleet-ebook/dp/B01EJ0OQ5G/

Hellspawn Sentinel

UK – https://www.amazon.co.uk/Hellspawn-Sentinel-Ricky-Fleet-ebook/dp/B01LYST98B/

US – https://www.amazon.com/Hellspawn-Sentinel-Ricky-Fleet-ebook/dp/B01LYST98B/

Hellspawn Requiem

UK – https://www.amazon.co.uk/Hellspawn-Requiem-Ricky-Fleet-ebook/dp/B071YB2MLS/

US – https://www.amazon.com/Hellspawn-Requiem-Ricky-Fleet-ebook/dp/B071YB2MLS/

Hellspawn Dominion

UK – https://www.amazon.co.uk/Hellspawn-Dominion-Ricky-Fleet-ebook/dp/B076CS8Y75/

US – https://www.amazon.com/Hellspawn-Dominion-Ricky-Fleet-ebook/dp/B076CS8Y75/

Infernal Emergence

UK – https://www.amazon.co.uk/Infernal-Emergence-Ricky-Fleet-ebook/dp/B01N78QYE0/

US – https://www.amazon.com/Infernal-Emergence-Ricky-Fleet-ebook/dp/B01N78QYE0/

Maximus Shock

UK – https://www.amazon.co.uk/Maximus-Shock-Collected-Madness-Terror-ebook/dp/B01N9W6Q6J/

US – https://www.amazon.com/Maximus-Shock-Collected-Madness-Terror-ebook/dp/B01N9W6Q6J/

Tales from the Zombie Road – The Long Haul Anthology

UK – https://www.amazon.co.uk/Tales-Zombie-Road-Long-Anthology-ebook/dp/B077CD7VBJ/

US – https://www.amazon.com/Tales-Zombie-Road-Long-Anthology-ebook/dp/B077CD7VBJ/

Treasured Chests – Breast Cancer Charity Anthology

UK – https://www.amazon.co.uk/Treasured-Chests-Anthology-registered-Charity-ebook/dp/B075DGW3PZ/

US – https://www.amazon.com/Treasured-Chests-Anthology-registered-Charity-ebook/dp/B075DGW3PZ/

Thanks for reading! Please add a short review on Amazon and let me know what you thought!

CHECK OUT THE OMP WEBSITE FOR
A COMPLETE LIST OF OUR TITLES

WWW.OPTIMUSMAXIMUSPUBLISHING.COM

BOOKS ARE AVAILABLE IN BOTH PRINT
AND ELECTRONIC FORMATS

The Optimus Maximus Publishing Shield Logo, the character of OPTIMA, and the name Optimus Maximus Publishing are registered trademarks of Optimus Maximus Publishing LLC. The OPTIMA character is also the intellectual property of Jeffrey Kosh Graphics.

RICKY FLEET
HELLSPAWN
SERIES

10.35 AM, September 14th 2015. Portsmouth, England.

A global particle physics experiment releases a pulse of unknown energy with catastrophic results. The sanctity of the grave has been sundered and a million graveyards expel their tenants from eternal slumber.

The world is unaware of the impending apocalypse, Governments crumble and armies are scattered to the wind under the onslaught of the dead.

Kurt Taylor, a self-employed plumber, witnesses the start of the horrifying outbreak. Desperate to reach his family before they fall victim to the ever growing horde of shambling corruption, he flees the scene.

In a society with few guns, how can people hope to survive the endless waves of zombies that seek to consume every living thing? With ingenuity, planning and everyday materials, the group forge their way and strike back at the Hellspawn legions.

Rescues are mounted, but not all survivors are benevolent, the evil that is in all men has been given free rein in this new, dead world. With both the living and dead to contend with, the Taylor family's battle for survival is just beginning.

Book 1 in the Hellspawn series.

Kurt Taylor and his family have battled the living and the dead and now find themselves on the run, their home reduced to ashes. With unimaginable horror lying in wait around every corner, the onset of winter and the plunging temperatures only add more danger to their precarious existence. They decide to forge ahead and try to reach the protection of others who have hopefully survived the zombie apocalypse. If this fails, their only choice would be to try and reach an impregnable fortress, a sanctuary that has stood for a thousand years.

Standing between them and salvation are the villages and cities of the damned, a path that will test their spirit and resilience unlike anything they have faced before. More companions are rescued from the jaws of death and join them in their perilous journey. Mysterious attacks befall the group and it becomes clear the dead aren't the only things that lurk in the darkness.

Tempers fray and personalities clash. The group starts to fracture and Kurt is forced to commit acts that cause him to question his own morality. Can they survive the horror of their new existence? Will they want to?

The Hellspawn saga continues.

BALLYMOOR, IRELAND, 1891

Patrick Conroy, a young American student of medicine in Dublin, decides to take a break from the hustle and bustle of the big city and spend a month in the quietude of the wild and beautiful Glencree valley, County Wicklow. However, surrounded by local legends and myths, he is soon dragged into an ancient mystery that has haunted the village of Ballymoor for centuries. Set on the background of the tumultuous years preceding the War of Independence, and colored by Irish folklore, the Haunter of the Moor is a ghost story written in the style of Victorian Gothic novels.

A modern dark urban fantasy, telling of two powerful families who uphold a secret duty to protect humanity from a threat it doesn't know exists.

Though sharing a common enemy, the two families form a long-standing rivalry due to their methods and ultimate goals.

Forces are coalescing in a prominent Central European city criminal sex-trafficking, a serial murderer with a savage bent, and other, less tangible influences.

Within a prestigious, private university, Lilja, a young librarian charged with protecting a very special book, finds herself suddenly ensconced in this dark, strange world. Originally from Finland, she has her own reason for why she left her home, but she finds the city to be anything but a haven from dangers and secrets.

Book One in a planned series.

Meet Mason Ezekiel Barnes, former NFL tackle turned successful author of the naughty ninja adventure series Mia Killjoy. Mason is obsessed with winning a Pulitzer and is thwarted by his fellow author and nemesis, the twerpy little gnome Conrad Bancroft.

Perk Noir is full of comedic relief, pop culture, NFL, jazz, a little touch of romance, and flashbacks of Lightning and his family during both the first half of the 20th century and later during the Civil Rights movement. Mason and Shelly and their adventures is a fun filled thrill ride that will appeal to all readers, there is something for everyone at the Perk.

Two hunters pursue the same prey.

Fate has forged the slayer, Trey Thomas and the Sandrian vampire, Adalius, two natural enemies, into an uneasy alliance against an evil more powerful than either have ever faced. Only together do they stand a chance of defeating Anna; if they don't destroy each other first.

As they pursue Anna, the apprehensive Lycan watch as a confrontation looms on the horizon between vampires, the New Bloods and the Old Guard, which threatens to plunge the vampire world into civil war and trigger an all-out supernatural conflict which in the end could destroy them all.

Killing is the sole province of the religious fanatics, an axiom as true today as it was some five hundred years ago; and no nation, region or person is immune.

Europe had clawed its way out of the Middle Ages with the dawning of the renaissance, only to be plunged once more into darkness, as the dogs of war circled to destroy its resurgence during the 16th century. The Islamic successor to the Roman Byzantines, the Ottoman Caliphate, flexed its muscles to conquer much of Western Asia, North Africa and South-Eastern Europe. Christian Europe shuddered when the once invincible bastion of the Knight's at Rhodes were defeated; and now trembled as the Ottoman army rattled the very gates of Vienna. No Christian army, it seemed, could withstand the ferocity of the Azabs, the Akıncı, the Sipahis, the Janissaries, and ruthless Iayalar's of the all-conquering Islamic hordes.

This then is the cauldron into which Gideon de Boyne is unwittingly thrust with his small army of dedicated Christian warriors. On the hostile island of Crete, at the doorstep of the Ottoman Empire, Gideon must face not only the overwhelming force of Muslim warriors but his own inner conflicts of the futility of war and his very Christian beliefs.

Will he succeed and come out of it unscathed?

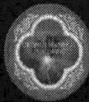

Made in the USA
Columbia, SC
03 December 2018